Anthony Gilbert and The Murder Room

>>> This title is part of The Murder Room, our series dedicated to making available out-of-print or hard-to-find titles by classic crime writers.

Crime fiction has always held up a mirror to society. The Victorians were fascinated by sensational murder and the emerging science of detection; now we are obsessed with the forensic detail of violent death. And no other genre has so captivated and enthralled readers.

Vast troves of classic crime writing have for a long time been unavailable to all but the most dedicated frequenters of second-hand bookshops. The advent of digital publishing means that we are now able to bring you the backlists of a huge range of titles by classic and contemporary crime writers, some of which have been out of print for decades.

From the genteel amateur private eyes of the Golden Age and the femmes fatales of pulp fiction, to the morally ambiguous hard-boiled detectives of mid twentieth-century America and their descendants who walk our twenty-first century streets, The Murder Room has it all. **>>>**

The Murder Room
Where Criminal Minds Meet

themurderroom.com

T0352210

Anthony Gilbert (1899–1973)

Anthony Gilbert was the pen name of Lucy Beatrice Malleson. Born in London, she spent all her life there, and her affection for the city is clear from the strong sense of character and place in evidence in her work. She published 69 crime novels, 51 of which featured her best known character, Arthur Crook, a vulgar London lawyer totally (and deliberately) unlike the aristocratic detectives, such as Lord Peter Wimsey, who dominated the mystery field at the time. She also wrote more than 25 radio plays, which were broadcast in Great Britain and overseas. Her thriller *The Woman in Red* (1941) was broadcast in the United States by CBS and made into a film in 1945 under the title *My Name is Julia Ross*. She was an early member of the British Detection Club, which, along with Dorothy L. Sayers, she prevented from disintegrating during World War II. Malleson published her autobiography, *Three-a-Penny*, in 1940, and wrote numerous short stories, which were published in several anthologies and in such periodicals as *Ellery Queen's Mystery Magazine* and *The Saint*. The short story 'You Can't Hang Twice' received a Queens award in 1946. She never married, and evidence of her feminism is elegantly expressed in much of her work.

By Anthony Gilbert

Scott Egerton series

Tragedy at Freyne (1927)

The Murder of Mrs
  Davenport (1928)

Death at Four Corners (1929)

The Mystery of the Open
  Window (1929)

The Night of the Fog (1930)

The Body on the Beam (1932)

The Long Shadow (1932)

The Musical Comedy
  Crime (1933)

An Old Lady Dies (1934)

The Man Who Was Too
  Clever (1935)

**Mr Crook Murder
  Mystery series**

Murder by Experts (1936)

The Man Who Wasn't
  There (1937)

Murder Has No Tongue (1937)

Treason in My Breast (1938)

The Bell of Death (1939)

Dear Dead Woman (1940)
  aka *Death Takes a Redhead*

The Vanishing Corpse (1941)
  aka *She Vanished in the Dawn*

The Woman in Red (1941)
  aka *The Mystery of the
  Woman in Red*

Death in the Blackout (1942)
  aka *The Case of the Tea-
  Cosy's Aunt*

Something Nasty in the
  Woodshed (1942)
  aka *Mystery in the Woodshed*

The Mouse Who Wouldn't
  Play Ball (1943)
  aka *30 Days to Live*

He Came by Night (1944)
  aka *Death at the Door*

The Scarlet Button (1944)
  aka *Murder Is Cheap*

A Spy for Mr Crook (1944)

The Black Stage (1945)
  aka *Murder Cheats the Bride*

Don't Open the Door (1945)
  aka *Death Lifts the Latch*

Lift Up the Lid (1945)
  aka *The Innocent Bottle*

The Spinster's Secret (1946)
  aka *By Hook or by Crook*

Death in the Wrong Room
  (1947)

Die in the Dark (1947)
  aka *The Missing Widow*

Death Knocks Three Times
  (1949)

Murder Comes Home (1950)

A Nice Cup of Tea (1950)
  aka *The Wrong Body*

Lady-Killer (1951)

Miss Pinnegar Disappears (1952)
aka *A Case for Mr Crook*

Footsteps Behind Me (1953)
aka *Black Death*

Snake in the Grass (1954)
aka *Death Won't Wait*

Is She Dead Too? (1955)
aka *A Question of Murder*

And Death Came Too (1956)

Riddle of a Lady (1956)

Give Death a Name (1957)

Death Against the Clock (1958)

Death Takes a Wife (1959)
aka *Death Casts a Long Shadow*

Third Crime Lucky (1959)
aka *Prelude to Murder*

Out for the Kill (1960)

She Shall Die (1961)
aka *After the Verdict*

Uncertain Death (1961)

No Dust in the Attic (1962)

Ring for a Noose (1963)

The Fingerprint (1964)

The Voice (1964)
aka *Knock, Knock! Who's There?*

Passenger to Nowhere (1965)

The Looking Glass Murder (1966)

The Visitor (1967)

Night Encounter (1968)
aka *Murder Anonymous*

Missing from Her Home (1969)

Death Wears a Mask (1970)
aka *Mr Crook Lifts the Mask*

Murder is a Waiting Game (1972)

Tenant for the Tomb (1971)

A Nice Little Killing (1974)

Standalone Novels

The Case Against Andrew Fane (1931)

Death in Fancy Dress (1933)

The Man in Button Boots (1934)

Courtier to Death (1936)
aka *The Dover Train Mystery*

The Clock in the Hatbox (1939)

The Vanishing Corpse

Anthony Gilbert

An Orion book

Copyright © Lucy Beatrice Malleson 1941

The right of Lucy Beatrice Malleson to be identified as the author of this work has been asserted in accordance with the Copyright, Designs and Patents Act 1988.

This edition published by
The Orion Publishing Group Ltd
Orion House
5 Upper St Martin's Lane
London WC2H 9EA

An Hachette UK company
A CIP catalogue record for this book is available from the British Library

ISBN 978 1 4719 0968 9

www.orionbooks.co.uk

CHAPTER ONE

Miss Laura Verity, a 50-year-old spinster, late of London, S.W.5, was determined to die. She made her plans for this event with her usual thoroughness and simplicity. Visiting her lawyer, stockbroker and banker, she settled her affairs in a manner least likely to prove troublesome to her heirs, and told her landlady that she was obliged to go into the country for a time on account of her health. The landlady, Mrs. Loveday, said, well, yes, she'd been remarking to Loveday that very week that Miss Verity didn't look herself at all, quite washed-out she was, and what she needed was a proper change.

"That," said Miss Verity, "is what I intend to have."

She contemplated the future without much regret. She had had a narrow childhood, a hard youth and a penurious middle-age. Now she was too old to work, her income had dwindled, she would inevitably sink from the comparative respectability of two furnished rooms to a dubious bed-sitting-room, and would eventually be compelled to apply either to the Relieving Officer or her sister, her sole relative, for aid.

"Either of which courses would be quite out of the question," she told herself firmly. "Besides, there are far too many people cumbering the earth as it is."

She gave serious thought to her main problem, the locus and manner of her departing. She would never, she knew, have the courage to fall from a height, cast herself before an oncoming train or cut her throat with a bread-knife. Poisons that were painless were impossible to get hold of; the same objection applied to a revolver.

"Besides," she warned herself, "it would make such a mess and one should remember those who come after."

At about this time a notorious lady took her own life by cutting the veins of her wrist while seated in a warm bath. This seemed to Miss Verity an admirable notion. Razors were easily come by; a warm bath was a daily ritual. Only she felt the need for privacy. It would not, for instance, be either kind or discreet to die in Mrs. Loveday's house. There is a superstition among those who rent furnished lodgings that a house where a suicide has taken place is unlucky, and they will, therefore, shy from coming there. Mrs. Loveday's lodgings had to support both herself and a workshy Mr. Loveday.

"Besides, it would make a very drab headline," Laura told herself. "Woman found dead in Earl's Court bath-

1

room." A woman found dead in a lonely cottage would please a far greater public, though pleasing the public was scarcely the thought uppermost in Miss Verity's mind.

"I should like a little time to rest and consider," she reflected. "I should like to feel myself mistress of the roof under which I sleep. All my days I have spent in other people's houses. Now for a little while I will have a house of my own."

In an advertisement in the "Church Times" she read of a small bungalow, suitable for artist or writer, two and a half miles from a large seaside resort, possessing all the amenities of civilization and none of its drawbacks. The cottage was described as surrounded by beautiful wooded country, standing not far from the sea, while a line of omnibuses passed at the foot of the lane. The rent asked was absurdly small. When Miss Verity saw the cottage she understood the reason for this. It was not only a mere bungalow—two rooms, a kitchen and a very primitive type of bathroom, it was as lonely as though it were situated on a desert island, standing up a winding quarter-mile drive, where the trees and shrubs had not been cut back for a quarter of a century. Originally, no doubt, it had been possible for cars to reach the door of The Nook, but now nothing larger than a bicycle could make its way up that precarious path. The omnibus service consisted of a number of ramshackle little buses running at irregular intervals between Periford and Brighton, the town in question. There was no shop for more than two miles, but there was a farm a mile or so distant, where eggs and milk could be obtained.

"Will it be possible for them to be delivered to my door?" Miss Verity inquired.

The owner of the cottage, a woman called French, was dubious.

"Mrs. Home might send her Rosie, but as a rule you would be expected to fetch them yourself. Mrs. Home is a rather nervous woman, and is always imagining that the woods are full of danger. That, of course, is absurd. But I know she keeps them behind their own fence and will not even let them play in the woods."

Miss Verity considered. "If I decide to live here I shall be as lonely as a witch in a fairy-tale," she assured herself. "No one will come from the village, unless it is the postman, and as I shall give no one my address, even he will not disturb me. Why, I may remain here for years before I am discovered. I must remember to leave some definite clue as to my identity."

Aloud, she said, "It is certainly an isolated spot. But your visitors . . ."

"I have none. I chose this place because it is like a desert island surrounded by trees instead of water."

"You did not build it yourself?"

"It was built by an artist who felt the same need to escape from his kind that I do. If solitude is what you want you will never find a place more to your mind. You'd hardly know you were living in a human world."

"I should hardly be surprised to find wolves in these woods," said Laura fantastically. "But no doubt that seems to you quite demented."

"Only the human variety prowl here, and that seldom. I personally have never been disturbed."

Miss Verity looked thoughtfully at her hostess. She saw a tall muscular woman with a weather-beaten face, cropped hair under a felt hat with a dilapidated feather stuck in one side. (She picked that feather up in the woods, decided Miss Verity sagely), large work-worn hands and the kind of feet most useful for the kind of life she had chosen; her voice had a rusty note as from disuse; her clothes were of some rough tweed material; she paid no attention whatsoever to her appearance and clearly had never heard of powder or nail varnish.

"As a concession to convention, I keep a cracked old bowler hat hanging in the hall," said Miss French with a queer lop-sided grin. "They say that keeps tramps off. I shouldn't have thought so myself. Men are far softer than women, don't know how to say No except to their own wives." Her mouth tightened. "Now if you are interested, let me explain the various stoves and lamps. There's no water from the main, of course, and naturally no electricity or gas. But I've contrived to live here for twenty-five years, so I dare say you can manage for a few weeks."

"A few weeks?" Laura sounded a little startled.

"How long did you wish to rent it?"

"I thought three months at any rate."

Miss French pulled at her bony jaw with a hand on which there glittered unexpectedly a fine diamond ring. "Three months? I don't know that it'll be convenient for me to be away so long as that."

Miss Verity assumed an equal obstinacy. "I should want it for three months," she said firmly.

Miss French shrugged her shoulders. "Oh, very well. After all, I dare say it will make no difference, three months or six."

"Living alone so long has certainly turned her brain," reflected Laura, following the woman into the minute kitchen. Here, suddenly, she went down on all fours.

3

"You need to get down on your hands and knees to light this lamp," she explained. "It heats the bath water It takes twelve hours, but it's quite simple really. Here's the chart—put rain-water in, a drop or two in the valve and fill it up. Every fortnight. From this tap. There's a separate lamp for boiling water for kettles. They use this kind on yachts. At least, so I'm told. I've never been on a yacht. Don't pull out the wick. If you do, you'll never get it back." She was demonstrating rapidly and quite incomprehensibly as she spoke. Miss Verity envied her her agility. For all her big bones she seemed able to double up without an effort. After this display she backed energetically out of the cupboard of a kitchen, and proceeded to explain the cooking stove. This was, if possible, more complex than the lamp. As for the sanitation, it didn't seem necessary to understand that, because there didn't appear to be any.

Laura found herself wondering inconsequently how long it was since Miss French had taken off the suit she was wearing. It looked as though it had grown upon her. All this time she had scarcely spoken. The stove dismayed her a little, but she assured herself that she would understand it in time; in any case, she had no intention of allowing such a trifle to deter her from putting her plan into effect. When she was able to stem the tide of Miss French's eloquence, she offered to take The Nook for three months, paying rent in advance. Miss French, with no more pretence of hesitation, accepted the offer, and it was agreed that Laura should enter on her property in a fortnight's time, that is, on Tuesday the 12th March. It was a relief to find that Miss French betrayed no anxiety as to her reason for wanting thus to isolate herself, seeming to take it for granted that any intelligent person would wish to do as she had done herself.

"Or perhaps she is convinced I am hiding from the police," Laura told herself. "Well, it is no matter. In a very short time nothing anyone thinks will be of any importance at all."

It was on a dark night that she took possession of her new home. Owing to heavy falls of snow the trains were all late, and she missed the connection that should have landed her at Periford at four o'clock. In consequence it was almost seven and quite dark when she reached the station. Not unnaturally, she found a strong disinclination on the part of drivers to take her out on such a night. Though the rain held off, the wind screamed like a dervish, bending the tops of the trees where the buds were beginning to swell faintly in black sheaths; it was furiously cold, Laura told herself, clutching a suitcase in one hand, a handbag, a torch and the brim of her hat in the other. The cabmen demanded extortionate fares, on the ground that it was risking your life to go out in such weather at all, and warned her that she would have to accomplish the last half-mile on foot. The shrouded light from the station shone on their sullen faces, giving them a Hogarthian ugliness; Laura felt a pang of pleasure to think that shortly she would have quitted a world where such horrible creatures were tolerated. Since, however, money was now of little value to her, she agreed to their demands and deposited herself inside the dusty vehicle. They drove at a snail's pace down a road as black as death. The only illumination was an occasional lamp, painted a deep blue, that emitted the smallest possible gleam which was almost immediately swallowed up by the darkness. For a short distance houses and cottages lined the route, but soon these petered out in a pair of villas that had never been completed and they found themselves in the open countryside. On their right Laura could hear the boom of the sea; the wind had lashed the waves to a fine fury and every now and again a great burst of water would come thundering on the shingle, and the dispersed stones would rattle and drop as though there were human foot-steps slipping precariously among them.

"Anything might happen here in the dark," she reflected as her cab crawled sullenly through the night. "It is absurd to realize that this is the year 1940. It might be the Middle Ages, with a thief in every shadow and a murderer hiding behind every bush."

The thought was hardly a reassuring one for a woman, no longer young, determined to spend her last days alone in a cottage cut off from civilisation, set in the heart of a wood, whose tree might shelter only Heaven knew what tramps and ruffians. It had been part of her plan to withhold her address from the whole world. Only to her sister, Mabel, had she said that she would be taking a short holiday and was renting a small country cottage as soon as she found one suited to her require-ments.

"I do hope Laura isn't going all queer, the way some middle-aged women do," observed Mabel, handing the letter to her husband, Ernest. "This hiding in a lonely cottage now—it isn't safe for a woman of her age. Just think of all the women who've been found murdered in cottages and bungalows. There was the Crumbles murder and that Swansea case and that woman—I forget her name—who was buried in the moat and no one heard anything of her for ages."

"They all had lovers," said Ernest placidly.

"Well, perhaps Laura's lost her head over some man who's simply playing her up for what she's got. Think of the Brides in the Bath case; think of that man who married twelve women for their bit of property; think of Landru. . . . ."

"Think of Laura," Ernest advised her. "If she's never lost her head over a man all her life, is she likely to start now?"

"They often do—she's just the age. There was that woman in the Moat murder, she was fifty-six, and such a good churchwoman. . . ."

"Oh, well," said Ernest good-humouredly, being tolerant for the two of them, "if that's what she wants to do, it's her life, isn't it? And I must say, she hasn't had much fun."

Laura would have appreciated that. She was often sorry her brother-in-law had married such an unpleasant wife. If he had chosen someone else, they might have met much more frequently.

Laura, however, had forgotten about them as she made her way towards her self-chosen destination. After some time the cab stopped abruptly, and the cabman put his hand behind him and jerked open the door.

"This is as far as we go," he announced, not offering to help with the suitcase.

Laura climbed out, lifted down the case, switched on the torch, counted out the fare, and stood by the roadside with a pang at her heart watching the little red light disappear in the direction of Periford far more rapidly than it had come. Once it was out of sight she seemed alone in an enormous black world. There was no moon and no stars; the wind almost swept her off her feet; the suitcase was heavier than she had expected, and she floundered slowly through the soft sand that was blown in all directions and came flying into her eyes and her mouth when she was sufficiently ill-advised to open it. This she did frequently, having acquired the habit during many lonely years of talking eagerly to herself. The light of the torch was fainter than she had anticipated, and for an instant there crossed her mind the thought that it might go out altogether before she reached the cottage.

"Of course, I intended to be here long before this, while it was still daylight," she said aloud, and then the wind came by and her mouth felt full of the gritty substance of the sand, and in her effort to keep her balance, cross the road and not allow the torch to point heavenward, she allowed her hat to blow off and be whirled instantly into the impenetrable night.

"Well, it must go," she told herself irritably. "It is no great matter. I shall not be requiring hats much longer, but really if I had known what a business it would be to take my own life, I believe I would have stayed on with Mrs. Loveday. Certainly they will bring in a verdict of Unsound Mind, and on my word, I am not sure that will not be justified."

Now, in this bitter night, this darkness, this hostility of the elements, it seemed to her a lunatic's idea to retire from the world as a first step to relinquishing it altogether.

Stumbling grotesquely, she at length felt her feet touch solid ground, as the sand was left behind and she embarked on the quarter-mile drive to The Nook. The path here was so narrow that nothing wider than a bicycle could hope to negotiate it, and even for a bicycle it was perilous on account of the roots of elm trees that surged across the path above the surface of the ground. The torch, burning now with a sullen golden gleam, barely illuminated the pitfalls on the road. All about her she was conscious of that urgency of life so much more powerful in the country at night than in town. There were movements in the trees, in the leafy heaps all about her in the darkness where creatures moved and slithered and fled through the night. Progress was necessarily slow, because of the fury of the storm and the unfamiliarity of the road.

"I should have waited till the morning," she told herself. "In the daylight I could have made my way easily. Now I feel as though the rest of the civilised world had been wiped out and only Heaven knows what horrors may not fill the woods." She paused to set down her suitcase, that she must keep changing from hand to hand on account of its weight; as she did so she dropped the torch and heard it strike dully against the roots of a tree. Crouching, she felt frantically for it, advancing a step, then retreating. She could check her movements by the case that she had set on the ground; she would not move far from it, and indeed in the darkness she dared not do so. A careful exploration, however, warned her that at this point the ground sloped on the left to a hollow filled with damp leaves. She stood irresolute on the edge of this for a moment, wondering how deep was the drift, and whether she might not find herself in a worse plight if she went after the torch than if she attempted to complete the journey on foot without any aid. Cautiously she tried to feel the surface of the leaves; plunging in her arm she felt it sink elbow-high; she drew it out stained and cold from its contact with the leaves,

for the snow had not long melted, and had soaked into
the little hollow.

"It may have rolled a considerable distance," she told
herself. "In this wind one would hear nothing."

And now terror possessed her. No smoker, she never
carried matches. She had had the forethought to pack
an additional battery in her suitcase, but this would be
useless to her without the torch. She moved her feet,
one at a time, in this direction and that, hoping to locate
the missing light; once she thought she had found it,
for her shoe struck against something hard, but when
she delightedly went down on her knees she discovered
it was only a stone. Groping her way back to her suitcase she lifted it, and faced the rest of the journey in
the dark. Her advance was desperately slow, foot by
foot. The drive wound first in this direction, then in that;
perpetually she found herself stumbling over the exposed
roots and flung out her hand to save herself from falling.
The whole world was full of suppressed activity. When
she moved she could hear footsteps following her at
some distance, and when she halted, they ceased also.
There were rustlings in the trees, thick shadows that
would, she knew, prove to be human forms waiting to
pounce upon her as she advanced. Once, when she put
out her hand, it touched something soft and clinging,
and she cried out in terror. For it could only be a
human hand, she thought. She stood very still, waiting
for that hand to be laid on her shoulder, to·grip her
arm, or, stooping craftily, to catch her ankle and throw
her on her face. She thought she detected a movement
on the other side, and knew that they were waiting, the
pair of them, to wind a scarf round her mouth, suffocate
her for the sake of the little money and treasures she
carried in her case. She tried to find her voice, to say,
"I'll give you everything, only let me go." For though
she had come to The Nook to die, she had never conceived
herself as one of those pieces of human wreckage discovered by a passing workman and featured in the evening press.

"A pair of angular legs are seen sticking out of a bush,"
she reminded herself in fastidious disgust, "and presently
the whole, referred to as the trunk, is laid out on a
slab for anyone to inspect for identification purposes.
They will find the most odious explanations for my retreat
here, anything, in fact, except the truth. And now that
I have lost my torch, I am without a weapon of any
kind."

As nothing happened, however, she proceeded on her
journey; not for one instant did she believe she would be
permitted to enter the house alive. Monsters, unknown to

history, lurked all about her; grinning obscenities escaped from asylums, idiots whose desires took the most perverted forms, all these, she was convinced stalked her footsteps.

"All my life I have been wrong," she cried to her heart. "I thought I was made for adventure, and that it was a vicious fate that kept me cooped in towns, but now I know that Earl's Court is my spiritual home, for I am shaking like a leaf from head to foot, and if I could awake and find this all a dream and myself safe in Mrs. Loveday's room, I would willingly take an oath never to leave the neighbourhood again."

Step by step, foot by foot, she advanced. Once a hand reached down out of a tree and caught her by the hair; she gave a desperate toss of her head but she could not shake off the grip. She thought wildly, Perhaps it is an orang-outang. Of course, they are not normally found in Sussex, but anything is possible in this place, at this hour. She remembered the valley where the suicides walk, always with their feet turned inwards so that they shall never travel either to heaven or hell; she remembered the valley of the living dead, who prey on strangers for their food; she thought of the vultures and their cousins, the carrion crows, and she thought, It is true, the thing I have always feared. I have gone mad. This is madness. When they used to say in my childhood that So-and-So was out of his mind, I used to wonder where he could be. Now I know. This is the state of madness. She put up her hand, dashing wildly at the hand that gripped her hair—to discover that it was the small, light branches of a bush caught fast in the net she wore over her head; she tore it fiercely away, leaving the net dangling like a scalp, and went on. All through that nightmare journey she was aware of ghostly companions; one laid a hand on her waist, one brushed against her knees, others touched her shoulder, her arms, set cold fingers against her colder cheek. She was so much absorbed in calming her heart that she walked into the wall of the house before she realised that she had reached it. Setting down the case she began to feel along the wall with her fingers. She knew the shape and disposition of the door; it had two little glass panes, with curtains hung behind them. Presently she touched glass, but this she discovered was a window, not a door.

"There cannot be another house up here," she told herself. "Nor can it have turned itself round since last week." But even as she spoke she realised what had happened. The drive wound round the side of the house, turning sharply to the right by the front door; where she now stood, therefore, was the back of the house.

The back door was made of wood, fitted with a lock to which she had the key in her bag. As she felt for the key-hole in the darkness the wind came pouring across the wide empty fields, tore through the wood and almost swept her off her feet. Then it went shouting down into the valley, and she heard a distant thud as the branch of some unsteady tree came crashing down.

She was so much occupied in finding the right key and getting the door open that she did not observe the light in the front room that went out as she crossed the threshold.

CHAPTER TWO

Stepping quickly inside the house, Laura set down her suitcase and, going down on her knees, flung back the lid. In one corner she had packed candles and matches. Miss French had promised to leave a supply of these, but Laura had the spinster's conviction that nothing could be relied upon to be as she wished it unless she assumed personal responsibility, and had brought these goods with her. Now she was thankful that she had done so. She had meant to find her way round with the aid of her torch, but without it she felt helpless. There would be lamps and candles standing about, she supposed, for her single visit to the cottage had not been sufficient for her to be sure where such things would be. Her chief feeling was one of an intense thankfulness that after that nightmare journey she should be safely under this roof. The solitary aspect of the cottage, the darkness, the lack of comfort, none of these could depress her. She could even rejoice in the ferocity of the wind, the sighing and creaking of the trees, the top of boughs against the window, knowing herself secure.

"I will light the Valor stove and put on a kettle. I have some tea here, in case Miss French has not left the kind I prefer, then I will see what there is in the larder and have a meal of some kind. It must be almost eight o'clock. As soon as I have lighted a candle I shall know the time."

She found the blue box, extracted a candle, and fumbled for the matches. She was still on her knees, looking fearlessly ahead of her, when she looked up and saw . . .

"Oh, merciful God!" she whispered. "This is more than I can endure. What is it? What can it be?" She did not move from the floor, nor could she take her eyes from the small red light that glowed at her through the dark.

It was very small, like a fairy lantern in a child's play. It did not move or flicker, but hung poised in space. The air all around her was thick, so thick it might almost support such a fairy light, yet she knew there could be no such comforting explanation. Then a breath came to her nostrils on that thick black air, and she knew it was a cigarette end she saw glowing at her like the red eye of an enemy through the dark. It was motionless. Therefore her presence here was known, for if he believed himself alone, the smoker would kindle a light, move about freely. And behind that cigarette was a face, a face that would condemn her for no reason but her unwelcome presence here. She waited, still as death. Outside, the fury of the storm increased. The wind tore at the hinges as though it would throw down the door, rattled angrily at the windows; the contrast between that fury and the stillness of the room in which the two of them waited, invisible, taut, desperately vigilant, made her fling up one hand over her mouth to repress a scream.

"He knows I'm here, of course," whispered Laura to her panic-stricken heart. "Of course he knows. Is he waiting for me to move, or what?"

She felt that her slender chance of safety lay in complete immobility. Suppose he had not heard? Then perhaps he would go without harming her. But if he had heard, then it would seem more natural to move about.

"Only, if I did, I might run into him. I wonder what he will do? I shall see that red light move, come nearer, nearer . . . How will he attack me? With the cigarette itself? Perhaps He will stab at me with the burning end—my eyes, my mouth. That is how they blind people, I have heard. Of course, that is what he will do. Blind me so that I shall not know him again." And she wanted to scream out that she was already blinded by the darkness, that she could see nothing, that if he would go she would swear she had heard nothing—only go.

Terror had stiffened her hair; now suddenly courage came to stiffen her spine. She was ashamed of her dread. Nothing worse than death can happen to me, she reminded herself, and it was for death that I came here. She shut her eyes for a moment as though she would collect her pride to defend her in this strait and when she opened them she faced only darkness. The light had vanished!

Then he has gone, she thought. But could even a shadow move so quietly? Or was it my imagination? Or some strange reflection I cannot yet understand? But most likely he had thrown down the cigarette end and put his foot upon it. And now she was in a worse plight than before. She had nothing to indicate the movements of the trespasser. The carpet under their feet was thick enough to deaden footsteps; the darkness was as thick as a velvet curtain. At this moment he might be beside her, behind her; she might feel his hands descend upon her shoulders, encircle her throat. If she stretched a hand perhaps it would touch his, stealing out to mutilate and destroy. She could not afterwards have guessed how long she remained thus, transfixed with fear. Only, suddenly a wind stirred all the draperies about her, laying a hand of ice on her forehead, and she heard the closing of a door. Then, as the wind dropped for a moment, she discerned the sound of footsteps on the hard path, dying presently into the distance.

Slowly, slowly, she rose to her feet. He had gone then, gone without discovering her presence. She put her hand behind her and bolted the back door. Now at last she dared to light her candle and, disregarding the grotesque shadows that it flung, moved towards the front part of the house. As she reached the front door she flung herself feverishly against it, turning the key and drawing the bolt. As she did so she remembered a ghost story of her childhood, of a lady who, put to sleep in a haunted room, had carefully locked and barred both door and windows. Then, as she extinguished the candle, a voice whispered in her ear, "Now we are quite alone!" Now, thought Laura, if after all he did not leave the house, if my ears deceived me, I have locked him in with me.

Lifting the candle above her head, she saw its wandering shadow move round the walls, distorting each angle and picture, making the whole something unreal and strange. A lamp stood on a table close by, and she paused to light this, intending to carry it into the sitting-room and disperse, as well as she might, the sensations of horror and fear that had racked her since she stood by the roadside and watched the taxicab returning to Periford. This front room was the pleasantest in the house; Miss French had furnished it with some comfort and taste, and a large wood fire made it seem cheerful and homely.

"I dare say she has left it laid," reflected Miss Verity. "I will light a match and in a few minutes there will be a fine blaze. Then I can settle down and forget what I have been through. Why, I dare say, by morning I shall be able to laugh at my fears." For Laura was one of those who can display an admirable spirit by daylight, but whose imagination peoples the dark with all manner of monstrous perils. For this reason she would never buy an evening paper, saying that bad news could keep, and that with a new day before her nothing could altogether daunt her spirit.

In this frame of mind, therefore, she lifted the lamp and, carrying it carefully in one hand by its slender stem, she opened the door with the other. As she entered the room she lifted the lamp high so that its light should fill the room. As she did so it came into her mind to wonder what the stranger had been doing in her house, so far from any road.

"Perhaps he was a tramp—or perhaps he was escaping from the police. Perhaps he was as afraid as I. If I had been less concerned with myself, perhaps I could have been of use to him. I should know at least that life is neither easy nor pleasant for many of us." And for a moment she gave herself up to remorse for her own cowardice. "But at the same time it was very odd his being here," she told her heart sternly. "It is all very well to be pitiful, but if he is in trouble with the police he has made himself the enemy of society. One is too apt to forget the victims of these young criminals." And resolutely she put the thought of him out of her head. She stooped and kindled the fire, and soon the yellow flames were shooting up the chimney. They and the lamp that burned with a steady golden glow, gave a great air of homeliness to the room; the cretonne that covered the chairs was of a pleasantly faded pattern, there were books strewn on the tables, and the curtains of deep maroon gave an impression of warmth. Already she could laugh at her fears; she had allowed herself to become panic-stricken, driven half-demented by a few clutching branches, the whistle of the wind, a handful of darkness. It was absurd. Was she not proposing to go down shortly into a greater darkness still? When she was thoroughly warmed and restored, she thought she would set about making herself a meal. As she had anticipated, she experienced a sense of deep pleasure at being alone, so far from humanity in this little house. She put out her hand to touch the walls, looked affectionately at the low ceiling, patterned by the shadow of the flames.

"I shall be happy here," she said. "And the fact that I shall only be here for a short time will set an edge on my pleasure."

The kitchen opened off this sitting-room, and, lighting the stove, she set a kettle on to boil. She found that Miss French had left a whole cold fowl in the larder and a piece of boiled ham.

"It is not easy to shop here and the weather looks very forbidding, so perhaps you will accept this contribution," the absent hostess had written in a fine pointed hand. Miss Verity's heart sang with satisfaction. She set out a tray with the cold food, found butter and bread, procured a teapot and china, and drew the round table in the sitting-room in front of the fire.

"This," she thought, "is what I have always dreamed."

She had set her little luminous travelling clock on the mantelshelf, and before she could have believed it possible the hands pointed to ten. She collected her tray, carried it into the kitchen, washed up by candlelight, and prepared herself for bed. She had left the suitcase in the hall, and this she now fetched along. She had left a kettle on the stove for her hot-water bottle; already in her mind's eye she saw herself curled up in bed, the blankets tucked round her shoulders, one bottle at her feet, another clutched gratefully in her arms, a lamp burning, the wild world shut out, tranquillity and silence within. She opened the door, the lamp in one hand, the bag in the other. The light threw a golden glow on the pale walls. Miss Verity's mind was occupied with the question: Shall I have a cup of Bourn-Vita before I go to sleep? If so, will there be enough milk for breakfast? And if this bleak weather continues, shall I be able to make my way over to the farm to-morrow for a fresh supply?

She was so much engaged in this calculation that she had crossed the room to the wardrobe and set down her case before she realized that here also someone had preceded her.

The girl lay on the bed, her head turned away from the light, her hands clenched, her knees a little drawn up under her. The moving light did not wake her, nor did Miss Verity's spontaneous cry of alarm.

"I must have bolted her in with me," thought Laura. "She has been here all the time. Why didn't she come in? Or hide? How soundly she sleeps."

Without moving she said sharply, "Who are you? How did you get here?"

But the girl made no reply.

"What are you doing here?" demanded Miss Verity, but now her voice faltered a little.

The girl slept on, unheeding. The fact that her unexpected companion was a woman did something to calm the older lady's fears. A young man would have terrified her beyond further endurance, but a girl was another matter. She wondered whether she could be ill, why she was here at all. It was all most strange. Grasping the lamp more firmly she advanced to the bedside.

The girl's face was turned to one side and half-buried in the pillow. Round her neck she wore a blue scarf; a ring glittered on her finger. Miss Verity saw all these things before she saw the face itself. When she had done that she moved away quickly, feeling very sick. Instinct made her set down the lamp on an adjacent table before any accident could befall. Then, slowly, her eyes still fixed on the bed, she moved across the room. But she asked no more questions. She knew it was useless; the girl had not answered her first ones, because it was no longer possible.

After a long time Miss Verity straightened herself and looked round. A hissing from the kitchen warned her that the kettle was boiling over and she ran quickly from the room, leaving the lamp behind her. When she realised this, she fumbled frantically for a candle. She had the feeling that she must obtain some other light instantly, before some further horror took place. In her mind's eye she saw the dead hand steal <u>out</u> and extinguish the lamp; then in the darkness the Thing would come sliding through the room and into the kitchen.

"Certainly I am going mad," whispered Miss Verity, scrabbling for the matches. Glancing over her shoulder she could still see the lamp alight in the farther room. Making a sudden dash she reached the threshold; the body lay on the bed as it had done for more than two hours. It hadn't moved. It would never move again.

Miss Verity, having turned out the kettle, forgetting the purpose for which it had been boiled, came back and stood at the bedside. Her reason, that had been momentarily paralysed by her discovery, now began to move. It was obvious that the body had been there all the time she had sat so comfortably beside the fire, dreaming rosily of her tenancy here. She had not, as she had endeavoured to persuade herself, imagined that little red glow; the face behind the cigarette had not been the face of a harmless tramp or some curious hiker—no one knew better than Laura the fascination of an empty lonely cottage—it had been—her mind flinched from the words—a murderer. For the girl hadn't died a natural death. The blue scarf was no longer the decoration it had been when its owner tied it carelessly round her throat some time earlier in the day; it had become an instrument of death. It was, indeed, tied so tightly that in one place it was completely sunk in the swollen flesh. And for two or three minutes she, Laura Verity—had been alone—in the dark—with a murderer.

"As now I find myself alone with his victim," she added, and the full horror of the situation beginning to open like some poisonous flower, revealing its dreadful heart. "But—I cannot remain here with a dead woman all night. I must—I must . . ." Here thought came to a standstill. She could not imagine what her next step should be. Had this taken place in S.W.5 she would have called the police—by telephoning if she had been alone, or have shouted to Mrs. Loveday, and told her to get a constable. - But at this cottage there was no telephone. There were no neighbours; there was no policeman for a couple of miles. There was no mortuary, no hospital—in short, there was nothing.

"Then, if the police cannot come to me here, I must go to them," she decided simply. But that again was out of the question. By morning she might feel courageous enough to walk out of the house and down the drive, but for nothing she could conceive would she unbolt the door to-night.

The alternative was to remain in vigil until daybreak. It is absurd to be afraid, she told herself. The poor creature is dead. She can do me no harm. I can leave a candle here, and take the lamp into the sitting-room, where the fire is still burning, and I have no fear of falling asleep. Why, millions of people have slept in a house, even in a room, where a dead person is lying. But, she discovered, it was not the fact of death that made the situation so unnerving, it was the manner in which it had come. To watch by a dead person was not terrible, but to watch by the body of someone who had been strangled put a very different complexion on the affair. Nevertheless, it was obvious that she had no choice. Leaving a candle on the dressing-table, she softly closed the door and went back to the sitting-room. But it was impossible to rest. She kept turning her head over her shoulder, expecting to see the body, with its head sagging dreadfully on one side, come stealing through the doorway. When presently she moved her seat so that she faced the door, she was certain that it beckoned at the windows, that were now at her back. She glanced panic-stricken left and right, expecting to see it watching her from a dark patch of shadow. Each time the curtains moved in the wind, she believed her last hour had come. She no longer felt herself alone; she heard footsteps in the hall, in the next room, behind her back, everywhere. Though she struggled for good sense, she felt herself compelled to rise and stealthily to open the door of the death chamber, to reassure herself that the corpse had not stirred. The candle gutted wildly in the draught of the door, flinging on the ceiling a monstrous shadow of a fallen head with a grotesque decoration like a pair of rabbit's ears protruding under the chin. That, she told her leaping heart, was a reflection of the ends of the scarf where it had been knotted round the dead woman's throat.

The unreality of the position robbed it to some extent of its horror. She was afraid, true, but if she could have realised it completely she would have gone out of her senses. For instance, it never occurred to her that she could be in any way connected with the crime; she never thought that her story would not instantly be believed. She was already planning to return to London while inquiries were prosecuted. She could not imagine being shadowed, or placed in a dock, or having her motives or personal life questioned. Not until about eleven p.m. did she understand that it was useless for her to lie awake, planning how to phrase her story to the police, because she would never get as far as the station. The murderer would see to that.

By this time she had returned to her chair by the fire, and covered herself with a rug. Sheer exhaustion had dulled the edge of her panic. Besides, human nature is notoriously adaptable. And the end was in sight. In a few hours she could walk out of this house, down the drive, into the village and put the matter into authority's competent hands. So she had thought. But now, with the suddenness of a conjurer producing a rabbit from his hat, her mind assured her that, foolish though murderers may be, they are not quite foolish enough to allow a solitary witness to live to tell the police the truth. Between now and dawning something else would happen at The Nook. And this time it would happen to her.

CHAPTER THREE

As that realisation dawned, hope died in her. She remembered Poe's dreadful story of The Pit and the Pendulum, the red-hot walls gradually closing in, the bitter knife descending nearer and nearer to the unprotected breast. Of course she would never be allowed to tell her story to the police. Probably at this moment the murderer crouched under her window, down the window. He would wait, she supposed, until she had extinguished the light. Yet could he expect her to remain in the dark with that lolling Thing on the bed next door? He could not hope that she would not discover it. I must just have arrived a few minutes too soon for him, she told her despairing heart. If I had been a little longer he could have disposed of her somewhere—the coal hole or the woods themselves, perhaps. In such weather only a fool would go wandering through that wilderness. Of course he did not know the cottage had been let. Miss French assured me she had little communication with the rest of the world. And he would think of this place as suitably lonely for a meeting. Perhaps he did not really intend to kill her. Perhaps it was a lovers' quarrel and it turned out tragically. I wonder why he did not leap upon me while we were waiting in the dark?

The answer to that, however, was soon found. Of course, the murderer had no notion of her identity, of her strength, of the dangers she might present. She might even be a man of superior powers.

"And does he know now? But certainly he does. I went round securing the windows; he would see my shadow by the light of the lamp I was carrying. He must know I am a woman, small, and of no particular strength. In fact, I have often been told I look remarkably like a hen, and the biggest coward on earth will have no fear of that ridiculous bird. Then no doubt he is watching me through the glass." And so great was her panic that she could even believe him to possess supernatural sight, and so penetrate the thick curtains that covered the windows and perceive her where she sat bolt upright in the cretonne chair by the fireplace.

As though in answer to her conjecture there sounded at that instant a low steady knocking at the pane. Knock-knock-knock-let-me-in. So she translated it. She sat rigid, with clasped hands. There were no shutters, no bars to these windows. A broken pane and the interloper would come leaping over the sash.

"Who was ever fool enough to build a bungalow in such a spot?" she wondered. But then she recollected that determined criminals can scale any wall, penetrate any door. Had she lived on the top of a skyscraper she would be insecure. "Only," she told herself, "I should feel safer, and therefore I should be less defenceless."

. The pitiless tapping continued. Tap-tap-tap. Miss Verity began to feel hypnotized. In a moment, she knew, she would rise and cross to the window and stare out at her enemy. She lifted her voice.

"Go away, if you are wise," she called. "I am armed."

As she spoke, she heard the door behind her swing softly open.

She knew at once that it was a trap from which there was no escape. When she turned her head to face the intruder from within, the man tapping on the glass would seize his opportunity and break through. It is a compliment that they think it necessary to have two of them pitted against me, she told herself valiantly. Leaping to her feet she whirled round—to face a black emptiness. The door swung ajar; beyond it lay the darkness of the hall. And in the hall lurked whatever it was that had opened that door. She stood irresolute. The tapping, of course, had been intended to distract her attention from possible movements in the house. If—when—she went into the hall she would certainly be stunned, possibly murdered outright. It seemed improbable that anyone would visit this house for weeks, perhaps not until the end of the three months of her tenure. She had paid a cheque in advance, and neither she nor Miss French were casual correspondents. No postman would call, no trades-man, no visitor. So, ears strained for a sound behind her, eyes vainly attempting to pierce the darkness ahead, she waited.

The tension became more than she could bear. She moved suddenly to the window, unhasped the sash, flung up the pane.

"Come in," she said furiously.

Nothing happened at all. A new suspicion stabbed her. Taking up the lamp she moved back to the open window. A spray of lilac blew inwards in the angry wind.

"So that is my tapping ghost. And what of the second ghost in the hall?"

Holding the lamp at arm's length she walked boldly through the black door. In the event of attack the lamp was a formidable weapon. It would, probably, set the house alight, but that might provide an opportunity for escape. The hall was absolutely empty. There was no one hiding in the bedroom, where the corpse lay un-touched; the candle had guttered badly. It was obvious that, in spite of Miss French's protestations about the draught-proof condition of her house, the wind did pene-trate; there was a long waxen winding-sheet down the side of the candle. That, as Laura knew, meant a death, and she shivered. But perhaps one death was enough. Perhaps it did not portend her own.

At midnight she decided to turn on the last news of the day. She had brought with her a miniature dry-battery set that, she had been promised, would last for three months without renewals. "And after that I shall have no need of it," she reminded herself tranquilly.

It brought her a great sense of companionship to hear the familiar voice of the announcer, although the news he had to give brought no particular comfort to her heart. But it made her feel as though she were really at home.

"This is the B.B.C. Home Service. Here is the midnight news." Laura listened to it all, eagerly drinking in every word. She even kept it on to hear a police message that followed the news.

"Another pedestrian who has crossed the road with the lights against him, no doubt," she told herself.

"We are asked by the police to broadcast the following warning. To all householders within a fifteen-mile radius of Brighton, Sussex, Andrew Stroud, a homicidal lunatic, escaped about midday from a private asylum in the vicinity and is still at large. He is a man of powerful physique and exceedingly dangerous. The public is warned to avoid woods and solitary places where he may be in hiding." The voice died away and there was now nothing to be heard.

Perhaps she fainted for a little while. Afterwards she could not be sure, for the shock of that announcement filled her with a dread that nothing could dispel. The common sense she had summoned to her aid would be useless against a maniac. When she was able once again to take stock of the position she feverishly twiddled the knobs of her wireless set. Somewhere, surely, someone was still talking. It didn't matter what gibberish he spoke. Probably, to a maniac, all tongues were alike. Peculiar sounds emanated from the wireless.

"So long as there is any noise he may believe I am not alone," breathed the desperate woman.

But presently the wireless became completely silent and so did her nervous endurance. The thing she could not have believed happened. Oblivious to corpse, terror and the appalling danger that she now feared menaced her at every instant, she slept.

When she woke it was morning. Light filled every cranny of the room in which she sat. She looked round her dazedly. Nothing had happened, after all. Then, common-sense asserting itself, she decided that a responsible criminal would certainly not linger around the scene of his crime, but would vanish as soon as possible before the alarm could be given. It had been a stroke of ill-luck for him that she should arrive precisely when she did, but was she really such a source of danger to him? She could lay information about the body, but she could supply no details. She had not so much as set eyes on the murderer. No, she told herself, ashamed of her earlier panic, certainly he will not be waiting round here. He will leave me to make such explanations as I can. He can hardly hope that I shall myself be suspected, for the taxi-driver can testify to the hour of my arrival and to the fact that I came alone.

Her fears largely dispersed, she compelled herself to re-enter the death chamber and bend more closely above the body. It was not a pretty sight, the tongue protruded, the eyes started from their sockets, the colour of the face had changed from girlhood's pink and white tints to a dreadful bluish shade.

"She is quite young," reflected Miss Verity pityingly, "And I think she must have been pretty. I wonder what it is she is holding so tightly in her hand?"

She had never read a detective story, and she knew nothing of the iniquity of touching a body before it has been seen, examined and photographed by the law. She therefore compelled herself to open the tightly-clenched hand and abstract from the chill fingers a scrap of paper of grayish hue that it contained. On this slip of paper, that had clearly been torn from a larger sheet, were some words in noticeably black ink. They formed part of a sentence, and read . . . "Of course I will marry you. Harry."

"That kind of murder," decided Miss Verity fastidiously. She had no sentimental sympathy for girls like this. They knew, or should know, their way about, and if they got into trouble they had only themselves to thank. It seemed to her fairly obvious that Harry had changed his mind. He had brought her here and decided that death was the simpler way out. Or perhaps there had been a quarrel—only why, inquired Laura sensibly, come all this way just to have a row? It seemed absurd.

She smoothed out the scrap of paper and, after a moment's consideration, put it in her handbag, as proof to the police that something serious had really occurred. She had been told that there were numbers of half-crazed men and women who went about notifying non-existent crimes, or even accusing themselves of murders that were at the time engaging the attention of the police. She had no desire to be numbered with these. This scrap of paper, then, should be her passport to a fair hearing.

She moved across to the window and pulled back the curtains that she had drawn so light-heartedly the previous night, before she had realized that she was not alone in the bungalow. To her surprise she saw that snow was falling in large light flakes from a grey sky. It lay like a covering mantle on the leafless boughs and like a carpet on the ground. The effect was one of sheer loveliness in that wooded landscape.

"Day dawns in heedless beauty," quoted Miss Verity, softly, transported by the scene and forgetting for the instant the horror within. In any case, morning had brought its customary courage to her heart. She no longer believed in the nearness of the murderer; instead she swam away on a daydream, in which a prominent detective, perhaps one of the Big Five, said, "Well, it was a pretty bit of work, I grant you, but if it hadn't been for Miss Verity's coolness and pluck I doubt whether we'd ever have laid the scoundrel by the heels."

She made herself some tea and toast, fastened the front door and with only a small tremor stepped out into the forest. The snow was falling more heavily now; it blew in her face and she had to put her head down to walk against it. Now and again she paused to brush the flakes from her coat, but it only settled again an instant later.

"I shall look like Father Christmas by the time I reach Periford," she told herself with a smile. The effect of the snow among so many trees was a little bewildering; every now and again she would believe that she spied someone moving in the distance, but a moment later she would be reassured. Before she had gone forty yards her footprints had been obliterated; so the snow would blot out any other footprints there might be.

Miss Verity had not been gone long before the murderer came back to the scene of the crime. Taking a key from his pocket he opened the front door and stepped into the hall. But once in the house it was a shock to realize that between the commission of the crime and the present instant someone else had been in the cottage. He did not remain long, and as he left the house the clock on the parlour mantelshelf struck ten.

* * * *

On the whole Laura quite enjoyed her walk down to the main road. Though she would not have acknowledged the fact, she was in some odd way intrigued by the position. She had lived since childhood in a routine so monotonous and unbending that even horror was a welcome change. Being used to taking life as it came, she had already accustomed herself to the circumstances of the crime, though she was thankful for the scrap of paper in her bag. She felt it so improbable that anyone would be able to believe such an affair happening to her insignificant self that she was glad to have something tangible to back up her story.

While she waited on the high road for the infrequent Periford bus a car came travelling in the same direction at a high speed. The driver was a short, fat, common-looking man with a round check peaked cap pulled down well over one eye. Seeing Miss Verity he drew up, and pushing his head out of the window, shouted, "You waiting for the Periford bus?"

Laura looked as though she had been carved in ice. "Yes," she replied.

22

. "I'm going into Periford," said the man. "I'll give you a lift if you like."

"I suppose he thinks I'm a complete fool," thought Laura disdainfully. "Of course he knows why I am going into Periford, and he has made up his mind that I shall not get there." And aloud she said, "No, thank you. I'm in no particular hurry. I will wait for the bus."

"You know there isn't one for five-and-twenty minutes?" the man suggested. "You'll be as frozen as Lot's wife by that time. What's the matter with my car? Or don't you trust my driving?"

"I prefer to wait for the bus." In spite of her much-vaunted courage Laura's teeth began to chatter a little. The road was deplorably empty; the snow, falling faster than ever, made a sort of screen behind which a man could quite easily hide his identity.

"Afraid of bein' compromised bein' seen with me?" the man grinned. He had a mouth like a fish, she thought, one of those fish that have deadly teeth in their jaws. Snap, snap, and off come both your arms. She noticed his hands, too. Big hairy, freckled hands, the sort of hands that could close like a vice round your throat, or draw a scarf so tight, so tight that breath would be choked out of you and you would lie helpless, murdered by your own muffler, hidden behind some tree, for days perhaps before anyone discovered you. She folded her coat more closely round the white silk scarf she wore, and stepped back a pace.

"I do not care to accept favours from strangers," she said distinctly. But she thought "If he opens that door. if he gets out and comes towards me, what chance have I? I could scream but who would hear me? I could struggle, but he is like a gorilla. Probably no one saw him come; the snow will cover the tracks both of himself and of his car. Certainly I came down here to die, but not like this."

The coarse-looking man whistled, nodded, pushed back the cap he had tilted a little by way of salutation and to her inexpressible relief drove away. She turned to watch him. The road was straight almost the whole way to Periford; if he stopped or turned the car she would be able to see it happen. She supposed him, if honest, to be a commercial traveller, though how anyone could be persuaded to give such a man an order she could not imagine. Commercial travellers in her opinion should be smart, deferential, sober and energetic; this man looked none of these things. But here she wronged him.

Fearful of being accosted by another motorist, Miss Verity decided to walk in the direction of Periford; she would hear the rush of the oncoming bus and could turn and signal in plenty of time. If she were walking, it was less likely that anyone would speak to her. The snow began to thicken; now it was difficult to make headway; the wind had risen and blew the flakes violently into her face; she bowed her head and felt a snowflake land on her neck, melt and run down her spine.

"I shall get bronchitis," said Miss Verity aloud. Looking up she saw a black and white bird, like an advertisement for whisky, come flying out of the trees on her left.

"A magpie," she exclaimed. "One for sorrow . . ." and she looked round hopefully for a second. She had proceeded for about half a mile when she heard a sound behind her and, turning, saw the little green bus come dashing along at a tremendous pace. She turned, waving her hand, but it seemed to take no notice.

"Stop!" she yelled at it, feeling rather like Canute giving orders to the sea. To her amazement it stopped.

"It's all right, lady," said the driver-conductor reproachfully. "I ain't blind—nor deaf."

Flushing at the rebuke, Laura climbed the two steep steps and sat down.

"I was so afraid you might pass me," she explained. "You were going so very fast. And walking is so difficult in this snow."

He nodded amiably. "Been waiting long?"

"About twenty minutes. I'm a stranger here and don't know the times of the buses."

"Where are you going?" He had his file of tickets ready.

"Periford."

"North or South End?"

"I—I don't know. The police station."

He looked at her sharply. "That's North End. Fivepence."

"Will you tell me the best place to get off?" she inquired, humbly, taking her ticket and her penny change and sitting erect on the first vacant seat.

"I'll tell you."

She wondered what he was thinking. Actually he supposed she had lost an umbrella or a pet cat or some such trash. Anyway, he quickly forgot her, occupying himself with thoughts of his young lady who was coming with him this evening to price things in the shop windows. Behind Laura, two girls' voices rose youthful and clear.

"I wouldn't be surprised if it was a woman," said one. "She'd need to be strong."

"Some of these little women are like snakes. You'd be surprised what they can do."

"What's that they're talking about?" Laura asked the driver.

But he didn't hear.

The two young women went on discussing the "freak" they had seen at a travelling show the previous night. No thought of murder was in the mind of either.

"How does anyone know already?" wondered Laura. "And why should they think it was a woman? I suppose someone saw me going up the drive, and they think— they think—oh, but they couldn't. It's impossible. I'd never seen the girl before." And memory said, "That's what all murderers tell you." The nightmare sensations of the previous night began to overwhelm her again. She questioned her own wisdom in going to the police. Mightn't it, after all, be wiser to slip back to the cottage, repack her bag and vanish? She wasn't an important person. No one would worry much as to her whereabouts. Even Mabel didn't care really. She could go to some pleasant boarding-house in Worthing or St. Leonards, and mingle with the crowd. Nobody would even be aware of her identity there. She would be just one more shabby, elderly female without ties. But though she considered this plan, she discarded it. When the body was found, the driver of the cab might remember bringing her last night, and it would seem very strange that she should disappear, leaving nothing behind her but a dead body.

"Not even my own body," she reflected with a kind of grim humour.

The young women got off at South End; Laura looked at them curiously. Young, smart, a bit common, you saw millions of them. If she saw them again to-morrow, she wouldn't know either of them.

The bus took her through the town, that was pleasantly bustling, and seemed a thousand miles removed from the grim scene she had left. Even her suspicions about the driver of the car that had wanted to give her a lift seemed rather foolish now. But as she ascended the steps of the police station and pushed back the swing-doors she seemed to realize for the first time the immensity of what she was going to say. She didn't believe they would take her seriously.

She walked into a room marked "Inquiries" and saw two police constables, a sergeant and the driver of the mysterious car. He was still wearing his cap, rather less over his eyes now, and seemed completely at home. Instantly Laura knew the truth.

"He is the murderer. He has come to give information. He realises I have been at the cottage; he wanted to put me out of the way. When he realized I couldn't be hoodwinked by him he came here ahead of me to try and throw suspicion on myself." She threw up her chin.

"Please," she said, drumming her fingers on the counter.

One of the constables came towards her. "If it's about that Pomeranian," he began.

Miss Verity could throw back her head no farther, but her voice was contemptuous.

"It is not," she replied distinctly. "I have never cared much for foreigners."

There was a roar of laughter from the ill-mannered man in the tweed cap. The constable merely shrugged his shoulders. Goofy, he decided. The place seemed swarming with them. Quite harmless, probably, but a nuisance to everyone who had anything to do with them. They harried lawyers to make wills disposing of property they didn't possess. They believed they were persecuted, they wrote anonymous letters to themselves—put 'em all to sleep if I had my way, he thought.

Miss Verity once more engaged his attention. "I have come," she announced, "to lay information about a murder."

The only person who seemed impressed was the man in the cloth cap; he took a step in her direction. The constable seemed no more interested than if she had reported the loss of a pair of gloves. "I knew it," was what he was thinking. "One of the loopy ones. I can always tell." For he belonged to the new school of detectives, who measure a man's psychology and without clues or circumstances can tell you at once if he is the person who left the blood on the seventh stone or carved up the old lady in the garret.

"Murder!" repeated Miss Verity, more loudly. "By the way, I understand that a constable is not sufficient for such a case. It should be a sergeant at least." She looked round and saw the sergeant. "This is a very serious matter," she said.

The sergeant came forward politely. "Yes, madam. You said a murder. Can you give me the details?"

"That is why I am here." She paused, then exclaimed suddenly, nodding towards the driver, "Don't let that man go whatever you do."

The stranger came forward. This time he took his hat right off, and she saw that he had very little hair.

"Lady," he told her earnestly, "you wouldn't be able to put me out. Crime is my bread-and-butter."

"I can quite believe it," said Laura icily. "Well, then." Turning away from him, she addressed the policemen. She told her story concisely, but even as she did so she was aware that it sounded like some romance from the films. She was thankful that she had thought to bring the scrap of gray paper. When she laid this on the desk, the sergeant spoke for the first time.

"You say you took this out of her hand?"

"Yes."

"You shouldn't have touched the body."

"If I hadn't brought something, you might quite well have thought I was a lunatic. It doesn't sound a usual sort of story."

"It could be, Benton," chuckled the fat man. "It could be."

Benton took no notice. "And we should have been notified at once. As it is, there's a good twelve hours lost. So much more chance for the criminal to make his getaway."

"There is no telephone in the house. As I have explained, I had had the misfortune to lose my torch. The nearest house is a mile distant and I am not sure of the direction. The last bus to Periford had gone two hours earlier. I had no weapons, and the murderer was probably waiting outside to hit me over the head the instant I emerged. In that case you would have had two bodies instead of a body and a witness. I fail to see how that would have improved the situation."

"She's got you, Benton," chuckled the fat man. "It wouldn't. Come to that, what would you do yourself in the lady's shoes?"

There was a moment's silence. No one seemed to dispose to answer that question. Miss Verity put another.

"Is this person a member of the police force?" she inquired, indicating the stranger.

"Not yet." He answered the question himself. "But we ought to be introduced. My name is Crook, Arthur Crook, and I'm a lawyer. No case too hot to handle is my motto. They call me the Criminals' Hope and the Judges' Despair. And if you ask me whether I'm always on the side of truth and justice, the answer is No, I'm not. All the nobility of the world back truth and justice; I always had a sort of sneaking feeling for the underdog. Y'see," he approached Miss Verity and spoke earnestly, "if you're in the right you still need all a lawyer can do to prove it, but if you're guilty and you know it—well, you do see, don't you? You need everything you can get. That's the way I figure it out."

"You mean, you'd defend a murderer?"

"None of my clients are murderers. They pay me to prove they aren't. I'm like any other workin' man. A fair day's work for a fair wage. That's all. If ever you should be wanting me . . ." But she shrank back.

She had her own idea of what lawyers should be like. Some resembled her own Mr. Bradley, tall, elegant, white-haired, with white slips to his waistcoat and a monocle on a broad black ribbon; and others were thin, serious men with the acknowledged "legal" face. They never, never looked like bookies' touts with a big coarse face and a pot belly and short muscular legs.

The sergeant had been issuing instructions. He looked at Laura as if he held her responsible for the whole thing.

"It's a pity about that bit of paper," he said. "You may have destroyed a valuable clue."

"That's only the police making excuses in advance," Mr. Crook assured her. "Don't let them get you down. It's the uniform, of course. If I'd worn a uniform, you'd probably have got into the car like a lamb this morning. I know. Women are like that."

CHAPTER FOUR

The policemen were looking at one another in what she thought was a rather peculiar manner. Then the sergeant said, "We'd better be getting along. There's been enough time lost as it is."

There was a police car waiting at the entry as they came down the steps. Behind it was Mr. Crook's less showy model. He climbed in and took his place at the wheel.

"Anyone want a lift?" he offered.

"You coming, Mr. Crook?" The sergeant sounded a bit dubious.

"Ever know me to refuse a bit of free entertainment? to say nothing of the chance of a job of work? Besides, this lady may need me—professionally, of course."

Laura turned with instant dignity. "If I should require the services of a lawyer—and I see no reason to suppose that I shall do anything of the kind—I have a solicitor of my own, a perfectly good solicitor," she repeated impressively.

Crook, however, refused to be impressed. "They ain't always the best kind," he assured her. "Anyhow, he's not on the spot. Take it easy, Miss Verity. I know more about the police than you do. People talk about police protection, but it's protection from the police that innocent people want more often. If there's anything more dangerous than the official conscience, please the pigs I never meet it."

The police gave Laura a seat in their car and they all went back along the high road. The snow had ceased falling, and was gathered in dry ridges along the road; the scene was a charming one, the sun shining on the snow-covered roofs and branches of trees. Periford is an old-fashioned market town with a Square, dominated by the Dragon Inn, and on the swinging sign with its ferocious green emblem the snow was heaped. Laura, however, had no eye for her surroundings. She was trying to accept the picture of herself in a car with three policemen.

"I forgot to tell you, you can't take a car up that drive," she observed suddenly. "We shall have to walk."

"There's a bypath, steep but much shorter," said the constable. "The car will be safe enough in the road, and we'll walk."

Nobody else spoke. Laura was beginning to experience that sense of unreality again. Even on the films you did not walk into a cottage and find a strange woman dead on the bed. And if this kind of thing was beyond the pale in the cinema, it was certainly incredible in real life.

"I feel like Bertram," she told herself. (Bertram was her brother, a missionary in distant parts.) "When he was asked if he believed in the Apostles' Creed, he said, 'I know it's true, but I don't believe a word of it.'"

The police car ran very smoothly, and Mr. Crook bounced cheerfully behind until they reached a narrow path with a blue painted signpost inscribed "Private Road to The Nook only. Private Property."

"Not that it is," the sergeant remarked. "But Miss French wasn't what you might call matey. The fewer people she had around, the better she was pleased."

The policemen and their passenger and the intent Mr. Crook alighted from their respective cars and picked their way up the slippery path. The snow had not yet begun to melt, for here the hedges made a deep shade, but already Laura perceived the print of a cat's feet on the powdery surface. She felt like someone in a fairy tale, and abandoned herself to the sensations of the moment. Besides, it took her all her time to make the

ascent; the snow covered various protruding stones and
little hollows, and she stumbled once or twice, until the
vigorous Mr. Crook came sturdily up behind her and
propelled her up the path with a greater familiarity than
she altogether cared about.

They went through a small gate marked The Nook and
along a winding path that shortly led them to the front
door of the cottage. Miss Verity produced her key and
admitted them.

"It's in this room," she said, touching the door-handle
with manifest reluctance, but refusing to accompany them
into the room. She felt suddenly she couldn't bear to
look at that swollen dreadful face again.

A minute later the sergeant emerged from the death
chamber and caught her rather roughly by the arm.

"Look here!" said he. "What's this? A practical
joke?"

She stared. "I don't understand . . ."

"Don't you? Well; I don't understand, either—don't
understand why you brought us up here on a fool's
errand."

"It's not a fool's errand. I don't care how much you
dislike it, if there's been a murder, the police have to
find the murderer."

"If there's been a murder done," agreed the sergeant,
with an unpleasant inflection. "Only in this case there
hasn't."

"She couldn't have killed herself. At least, I never
thought she could. But even if she has, you . . ."

"That'll do," said the man grimly. "You know as well
as I do that there hasn't been a murder committed, and
there isn't any body lying on the bed."

She was so much taken aback that for a moment she
was deprived of speech. She stood there, looking like
a rag doll, her body sagging against the lobby wall.

"Not there! Oh, but it's you who are mad. She's lying
on the bed with her head turned away and a blue and
red scarf knotted round her throat."

Mr. Crook's voice sounded from her other side. "What
the sergeant means is that she isn't there now. This is
where you can help us. I suppose you're sure she was
dead?"

Miss Verity shuddered. "If you had seen her face!"

"Well, somehow she's been spirited away."

"That's all poppycock," said the sergeant angrily. "What
I want to know is—where is she now?"

"What do we keep a police force for?" Crook asked
casually. "Why not look under the bed?"

The sergeant, however, was still staring at Laura. She

threw his hand off her arm and ran into the bedroom. The counterpane was pulled neatly up over the pillow. There was no sign of any body anywhere in the room!

"Perhaps you think whoever murdered her came in here when you were out and took her away," the sergeant continued in his unpleasantly suggestive voice.

"A very good idea," applauded Crook. "It could be, you know, my dear fellow, it could be."

"How do you suggest he got in? None of the windows is broken."

"Perhaps he came by the door. Perhaps he had a key or perhaps he was one of those enterprising fellows who can work miracles with a little bit of wire."

"And what about her clothes? Where's her coat? and her hat? You're not suggesting she came through this sort of weather just in . . ."

"Keep it clean, sergeant," said Crook hurriedly.

"She wore a long blue coat, and I dare say she had this scarf over her head. The one with which she was strangled, I mean. That would answer your question."

"You're asking us to believe that, while you were out, someone came here and collected her like a parcel for the laundry?"

"I dare say it does sound improbable, but find a better answer if you can. After all, she was here and she's gone. It's not my job to find her. I didn't put her there."

"That's the spirit," approved Cook. "The lady's right, you know. She hasn't got to find the deceased."

"The point is this." The sergeant looked steadily at Laura as he spoke. "No one but this lady has seen the body. We've had no inquiry for a missing young woman. There's no sign of a body here and no forced entry. There aren't many places where it could be hidden . . ."

"On the contrary, sergeant, there are so many places I don't see how you can hope to vet. 'em all," put in Crook, in his aggressively cheerful way. "What you mean is, there ain't much room in the cottage. I'm with you there."

There was so little room that it took them no time at all to search; there were a couple of casual lean-to's in the garden and they examined these also, but entirely without result. By this stage it was clear to Miss Verity that they believed her not so much malicious as crazy. There were people who perpetually tormented the police by admissions of crimes they had never committed, and they presumed that she belonged to this class. Perhaps they even thought she believed her own story.

"How long were you planning to stay here?" the sergeant asked her.

"Three months."

"Alone?"

"Yes."

"What about servants?"

"I can look after myself. Anyway, I fail to see what this has to do with . . ."

"Any relations?"

"Fewer than most people." Miss Verity spoke with grim satisfaction. "And those I have don't trouble me much."

"What's the name of your next-of-kin?"

"Why do you ask me that?"

His red pencil flickered. "Matter of routine."

"It isn't," she declared flatly. "It's sheer curiosity and I'm not going to justify it. No one knows my address here and if I can help it they're not going to."

"Any special reason for that, Miss Verity?"

"I want to spend the last few weeks of my life in peace."

"The last few weeks!" He repeated the words sharply.

"Probably. I expected to be here three months at the outside."

The policemen exchanged significant glances. Goofy—not a doubt of it. That's what those pregnant glances meant. Either naturally mental or one of those hysteria cases, who hunger for a bit of publicity before they're shovelled into the inevitable tomb. No sense in telling such a story, of course, but these crazies never saw a step ahead. Some queer desire for the limelight. Understandable, perhaps, when you thought of the lives they had probably led, but one hell of a nuisance for the police.

"Giving false information is an offence in law," the sergeant warned her.

She faced up to him without an instant's hesitation. "I did not give false information, and I defy you to prove that I did. That body was there. You can tell me till you're blue in the face that it isn't there now. I can see it isn't. But it was. You simply swear it wasn't because you haven't seen it, but have you ever seen the Pyramids?"

"I don't see," the sergeant began, but she bore him down.

"I can see you haven't, but you don't say they don't exist for that reason. You're prepared to take other people's words for them, but you won't take my word about this body."

"You're the only person to see it, Miss Verity . . ."

"You're forgetting something," she interrupted sharply. "Someone else saw it."

"Who was that?"

"The murderer."

There was a moment's silence, broken by Crook. "Nice work," he observed judicially. The policemen refused to be impressed.

"We'll be going," said the sergeant in a voice of thunder. "If you should see any more of the body, be sure to let us know."

They went off, like outraged heroes, Crook bowling gaily after them. In spite of her anger and bewilderment Miss Verity could not help smiling. He looked so very queer and unprofessional running alongside those tall men in blue.

But when they were out of sight she sought desperately for some solution to the mystery. The body had been there when she left the house that morning—the body was there no longer. Clearly, then, during her absence someone had entered the house and removed it. The only other person who could have known it was there was the murderer. She was therefore forced to the unwelcome conclusion that the murderer had a key to her house.

"He might descend upon me at any minute," she whispered. "Perhaps he's waiting outside now, waiting for the policemen to go and me to be left alone."

As this thought flashed through her mind, she heard a step in the hall. Before she could turn her head, a voice said, "Hands up!"

She swung round, panting with apprehension, to meet the sharp green eyes of the little cockney lawyer.

"Thought your number was up that time, didn't you?" he remarked with a grin. "Never mind. That's my way. See things as a joke."

She struggled with her rising fury. "It is not a joke, and no one but you could conceivably have thought it was. It's a murder that nobody but me is going to do anything about."

"I wouldn't be too sure of that," said Crook, suddenly serious again. "You're a dangerous woman, you know."

"Dangerous? To whom?"

"Why, to the murderer, of course. I'll take my oath he didn't expect you last night. When he realized you were here—or it could be that he didn't know until he came back this morning—yes, it could be. He'd know then, because he'd see ashes in the grate. . . ."

"I had no time to put things straight before I left," interrupted Miss Verity with dignity. "Naturally, I like my house to look spick and span, but not considering murder a joke, I thought my first duty was to inform the police of what had occurred."

"Ever hear that self-preservation is the first law?" inquired Crook. "Your first duty, my dear, is to yourself. You're in a tight spot, and you may as well recognize it."

"Did you come back to tell me that?" asked Laura colourlessly.

"It occurred to me you mightn't quite appreciate the position. You've upset a nice trim little murder, and the man who did it has the entry to your house. That's worth thinking about."

She turned to him eagerly. "You believe me, don't you? You don't think I'm crazy or out for publicity? The body was there. I don't know where it is now, but when I left the house this morning it was on that bed."

"Oh, I believe you," said Crook obligingly. "It's my job to believe people. That's what I'm paid for."

"But—are your clients always innocent?" She sounded a little sceptical.

"Always." Crook's voice was as firm as the rock of ages.

"They must sometimes be in the wrong," she urged.

"Officially, I never defend a guilty man. I'd be so ashamed of myself, if I did—but you're an intelligent woman and you get my point."

She was rather afraid she did.

"Now, I've got a proposition to make to you," the lawyer continued. "Pack your grip and get out of this place before it comes too unhealthy for you."

"Leave the cottage?"

"You weren't thinking of staying, were you? You're the only possible witness for the Crown if the corpse does inconveniently reappear: you don't suppose a chap who's committed one murder is going to shy at a second? He might put you out anyhow, just to be on the safe side."

"That would be exceedingly dangerous for him."

"Not always. Might make it look like a suicide. Fit in very neatly with the police's present views. And if that should happen—well . . ." he shrugged his shoulders. "No one knows you're here, no one knows your nearest relative. You take my tip and get out."

"Where?"

"I'll find a nice place for you. Only get out of here while you still can."

She leaned against the window-sash, looking over the expanse of wood and hollow, snow-besprinkled, that spread as far as she could see. The sky was heavy with unshed snow; there would be another storm soon.

"And if there is," pointed out Crook, answering her unspoken reflection, "you may get snowed up here and no one will be surprised not to see you for a couple of weeks maybe. After which time they might be glad not to have to see you."

She paid no attention to his prophecies. She was leaning against the window, staring at something that rivetted her attention. She put out her hands and tugged at the window-sash.

"It's bolted," said Crook sharply. "What's the matter? If you want to get out, there's the door. Or do you think the window's safer?"

"It's not that. Look there." She pointed to something beyond the window.

Crook lounged up beside her. "What's got you?"

"Do you see—on that bush by the front door. I didn't notice when we came in—a bit of stuff? Blue and red pattern. I tell you, that's part of the scarf she wore. So it means it means . . ."

"It means most likely she went out by that same door as she came in. Only this time the murderer accompanied her," Crook finished for her. "Well, well, that'll give our sergeant a bit of a shock." He pushed up the window and leaned out, looking in either direction, as though he expected to find something. "Pity about this snow," he went on, withdrawing his head. "It's covered all the tracks. Still, the odds are he'll have put her down rather than up. No man's going to be such a mug as to carry a dead weight—and you don't know what dead weights the dead are, Miss Verity—up a slope if he can dispose of her equally well by going down. I'd say there were plenty of pits and hollows down among those trees where a body could lie for weeks or months without bein' found. It's goin' to be heavy snow for days to come."

He turned towards the door.

"Where are you going?"

"Don't you want your reputation justified in the eyes of the law?" demanded Mr. Crook. "To look for that body, of course."

"You don't know it's in the wood."

"Where else do you think it will be?"

"He might have taken it away in a car."

"And bumped into another car at the first turning, and been asked what the something something he was carryin' a corpse as passenger for. Or he might have to stop for petrol, and some chap think—you've no idea how nosey they can be—it looks a bit queer to have a blue-faced lady for your girl friend. No, no, I'll lay my good name, and that's my fortune, believe me, that the little girl's sleeping her last long sleep in the shade of the immemorial elms."

He closed the window and turned back to his companion. "Ready?" he inquired.

"Ready?" stammered Miss Verity. "For what?"

"Well, aren't you coming out with me to look for the lass?"

"You mean, in all this snow?"

"There's going to be more snow soon, and then it'll be harder still. Don't your good name count with you at all?" He seemed genuinely amazed.

"Nothing a mere policeman says can affect my good name," Laura informed him coldly.

"That's all you know. What the police can do in this country would surprise you. Besides, when you get a chance to wipe their eye, you're not surely going to play Nelson and let it pass by on the other side."

This crazy mixture of metaphors kept Laura dumb for a moment trying to disentangle the sense from the chaff. When she realised that she was being invited to go nosing for a corpse as a dog noses for a bone, she drew back in horror.

"But—I couldn't."

"Just as you say, lady. Well, I think I'll take a peek round myself."

Miss Verity awoke to the fact that, although she had been terrified, though she hated the thought of murder and shuddered afresh to remember the swollen face that had lain on the pillow all night, she was by no means satisfied to leave the rest of the story to this—interloper. She said, therefore, without any change of tone, "If you wait until I have put on my goloshes (for she had removed these on entering the house in the company of the police), I will come with you. After all, this is my affair."

"Just so," agreed Crook blithely. "It's a pity we don't either of us know more about the lie of the land. The body will be thrown down into some pit where the snow will cover it."

"The snow will soon melt," murmured Laura primly.

Crook squinted up at the lowering sky. "Soon wouldn't be my word for it. That snow's coming down like the Assyrian on the fold of the righteous. It may lie up here for weeks; we're pretty high—and if you get a frost on the top of that, as you very likely will, a body could stay in cold storage for weeks more. I don't say she wouldn't be dug out eventually, but you wouldn't know, not having the experience. how hard it is to run a chap to earth after three months. Y'see, he may have got out of the country, changed his appearance altogether,

dyed his hair—anything. No, no, we want to find this
body double-quick, you take my word."

Hunting for the proverbial needle in a bundle of hay
seemed to Miss Verity child's play compared with finding
a body in this waste of snow-covered woodland. There
was nowhere any footprint to be seen, which showed,
said Crook, that X must have come up to the cottage pretty
soon after she herself had left it, and been away, with
his work done, before the snow stopped. Laura was
surprised at the height they were above the road. Her
progress last night had been so slow she had not realized
that all the time she had been steadily climbing. Long
before they came to any conclusion regarding the disposition of the corpse, Laura hated Mr. Crook as she
didn't even hate the murderer. The snow he had phophesied
began to fall, and with the snow came a cutting wind
that seemed to freeze where it touched. It was like having a frozen hand laid on your cheek, your breast, your
every limb, she thought. She stumbled, half-mad with
rage and a kind of fear, after the leader. "It's no use,"
she muttered fiercely to herself, over and over again, "we
shall never find anything in this snow. We'd better
wait." But when she said this aloud, Crook reproved her
sharply.

"I'm a lawyer. Know what that involves? If I was to
stop now I'd feel I was an accessory after the fact"

He warned her to take care how she went, and to
fling her arm round one of the tree-trunks if she felt
herself slipping.

"If you started to slide on this," he added with a grin,
"you could bump to Kingdom Come and no one could
help you."

At last they found themselves on a side-path, a mere
ledge of snow-covered earth, with a deep drop into a
circular pit.

"Pity about the snow, it's so deceptive. Can't see
how deep that goes. But I'll tell you one thing that's
queer. See those trees?"

He pointed to some tall trees that had obviously suffered badly in last night's storm.

"Lost a lot of branches," Crook continued. "See the
white pith of the boughs? Well, then, where are they?"
She looked at him, frowning, not comprehending. "The
branches," repeated Crook, with forced patience. "The
branches that were broken off. Of course, they could
have been swept into the pit, but there hasn't been enough
snow to cover them completely. No, if you ask me, I
should say they were dragged to the edge here and
deliberately thrown down to hide something else that

had been tipped over the edge. Besides, even last night's
wind wasn't powerful enough to move great boughs, and
these weren't twigs by any manner of means."

Against her better feelings, in defiance of all those prin-
ciples that had upheld her throughout her uneventful
existence, Miss Verity felt a strange forbidden thrill o
excitement pour through her. Murder was horrible, but
there was something fiercely exhilarating at feeling herself
one of the only two persons who knew that a murder had
been committed—no, she corrected herself, one of three,
for of course the murderer was aware of it. She tried to
put something of this into words.

"Beginning to get you, is it?" asked Crook. "You know,
I wondered if it might."

Something in his tone made her turn sharply and look
towards him. He was standing on the lip of the crater
a short distance from herself. There was a crafty gleam
in his eyes; his mouth, she thought, was like a rat-trap;
a hard unscrupulous face. No, he wouldn't care that a
girl had been murdered. He wouldn't care if I fell over
this minute and was never found again. She saw that
he was smiling and had begun to make his way towards
her, and suddenly she knew what was in his mind.
She had only a moment, she felt, in which to save herself.
They were so far from any sign or sound of life that no
one would hear her if she screamed. Physically, she
was no match for him; she had only that morning refused to give the name of the next-of-kin to the police.
No one knew where she was, except those same police
who, if she mysteriously disappeared, would shake contemptuous heads and say, Goofy, clean goofy. Only had
to look at her to see that. And then her story about a
corpse. . . . Oh, Crook had played his cards well, leaving
the cottage in the company of the police, stealing back
after they had returned to Periford. No one would have
seen him return, no one would guess what she herself
now knew to be the truth, that the dead girl's murderer
was now standing just above her unhallowed grave, pre-
paring to hurl a second woman in to join the first.

He had been so clever, she thought, edging away from
him, wondering if she had one chance in a thousand if
it came to flight. In her mind's eye she saw them dodging
and doubling among the trees, saw her foot catch in some
snow-covered root, felt those great freckled hands, that
had already pressed out one woman's life, close re-
morselessly round her throat, and she tried to cry out,
but only produced a mere shred of sound that could
not have been heard even on the path above them.

"Look out," exclaimed Crook, darting towards her. She leaped backwards, felt her foot sink into snow and crumbling earth, the solid ground melt, knew that she was falling, falling . . . It hadn't even been necessary for him to lay a finger on her. Instinct made her clutch wildly at the crater's edge, and she found herself gripping a hardy growth of ivy that crawled over the lip and was itself anchored, like a cancer, to a tree a short distance away

"Hold on," yelled Crook, stooping over her. She saw that he had one arm round a tree, and the other came round her shoulders, gripping her like a vice. "Don't both want to go over," he explained, puffing like a grampus. She was kicking out wildly for foothold, and by some miracle one foot caught in a loop of bramble, so that for an instant she was no longer a dead weight on Crook's arm. With a great heave he pulled her up; somehow between them they scrambled her over the side of the pit, a dishevelled undignified figure, her clothes in disorder, her hair unlooped round her ears, one hand badly scratched, one golosh missing.

"What made you do that?" demanded Crook. "Haven't we got enough trouble to suit you? You amateurs!" Then he grinned. "Good thing we haven't got an audience" he observed. "We look as though we'd been having a roll in the snow."

Fortunately her pious upbringing and experience prevented her from understanding what he meant by that, but she felt both ashamed and bewildered. Now her suspicion, so rigid a moment before, was melting After all, he had dragged her up, when he could easily have hurled her to her death. Perhaps he wasn't the murderer, after all. Crook, meanwhile, had taken a large white cotton handkerchief out of his pocket and was tying it round the trunk of a tree.

"We'll never find this place again if I don't do something to mark the spot," he explained. "The snow will level up the whole place soon, and it won't be safe to search. But even if we have to wait, we can find out where she lies. Because if we can't dig her out the murderer can't either. Well, my suggestion to you, Miss Verity, is to pack your case and come down to the town and have a quiet life for a change."

She was glad enough to accept this proposition. With some difficulty, chilled and wretched, the damp snow soaking her feet, aware of her miserable appearance, she trailed after him until they reached the cottage. The packing took a very little time; she had taken only a few toilet articles from her bag and these were soon replaced. As they went through the hall, she found herself glancing hurriedly left and right for fear that the murderer had effected some new change during the past hour; but it seemed obvious that no one had entered the cottage. Slipping, stumbling, clutching blindly at trees, certain that she was suffering from frostbite, she followed him down the steep path to the road. He packed her into the seat besides the driver, casually tossing her luggage into the back. Then he got in himself and drove off. Looking at her sideways he thought, "I can't think how it is some chaps always find themselves rescuing the young and beautiful from distress, while I always get landed with a red-nosed spinster with about as much S.A. as a fish. Still, it's safer that way. Look on the bright side all you can." And then he discovered that he had left his handkerchief tied to a tree, and that the presence of a lady in the car, even so unprepossessing a specimen as the unhappy Laura, had its disadvantages.

CHAPTER FIVE

The Royal Crescent Hotel, at Brighton, is an immense structure. Whether you admire it or not depends on your taste. Miss Verity thought it dreadful. It had five hundred bedrooms, and was built on American lines, with straight white balconies jutting out all the way up.

"I couldn't stay here," she said at once. "It looks like a kind of glorified Sing Sing."

"Easy to tell you've never seen Sing Sing," was Crook's unemotional reply. "I suppose what you hanker for are two nice little furnished rooms in a side-street. Don't you see, that's just what you mustn't have? You want to be in a large public place. Then, if anything should happen, you'll have people all round you. You've tried a solitary lodging and look where it got you. Don't suppose you're out of the metaphorical wood just because you're out of the actual one. And don't agree to see any strangers in private."

Miss Verity bridled. "Seeing that I shall only have a bedroom here, if I decide to stay, I should certainly not be likely to do that."

"Well, don't forget you're up against someone whose life is not merely in danger, but who probably values it more than you seem to value yours. I'm staying here myself—well, I don't foot the bill, of course—and you can get in touch with me at any time. Here's the telephone number of my room—456—easy to remember. You're 478—so we're on the some floor. That's a good thing, too. Now I've got to get ahead with the job I was doing before all this happened. But you remember what I've told you, and take care."

His manner more than his words aroused her apprehension. It was ridiculous, she told herself, to suppose that any harm could befall her as she walked in the streets or crossed the road, but was it really her imagination that a car driven by a dark young man with a brown hat pulled well over his eyes almost ran her down? And when she was looking in a jeweller's shop, harmlessly choosing birthday presents that would never be hers, was it just coincidence that he should emerge and stand looking at her oddly for a moment before crossing the street and getting into the car that stood in the car park opposite?

After a momentary indecision she pushed open the door of the shop and made some inquiries about an inexpensive enamel ornament she had seen in the window. While she was examining it, she asked idly, "Wasn't that young man who had just been here called Baxter? I thought . . ."

"I couldn't tell you, madam," said the assistant dryly.

"I wish I knew. His mother is seriously ill, and no one seems to know where he is." Miss Verity was genuinely horrified to hear this falsity trip so lightly off her lips; as a rule, she was as truthful as her name. But at the same time she felt excited at her own ingenuity.

"Well, as a matter of fact, his name isn't Baxter," the assistant assured her.

"You're quite certain?"

"Quite certain. We've just been doing a little business with him—a matter of a ring—so naturally we've got his name on our books. A gentleman called Fennel."

She nodded, doubtfully. "How very disappointing! His mother is a great friend of mine. I'm afraid he hasn't been a very satisfactory son—Hugh Baxter, I mean. There really is a likeness, but of course young men do look very much alike."

"Well, I can assure you this gentleman is Mr. Harry Fennel."

She almost dropped the purse she was opening, to pay for a brooch she didn't want. ". . . of course I will marry you, Harry." Mr. Harry Fennel! She wanted nothing but to get back to the hotel, find Crook and give

41

him this fresh clue. She could barely wait for her change to be brought, the brooch to be wrapped up. She fairly ran out of the shop.

"Queer old bird," said the assistant, and instantly forgot her.

There were several people in the hall of the hotel when she came hurrying in, but she paid no attention to any of them. She had got to get hold of Crook without delay; in her earnestness and her certainty that she was on the right track she gave no thought to the impression she might make. She dashed up to the reception desk, saying excitedly, "Where is Mr. Crook? He is staying here. Is he in his room?"

Reception clerks are practically surprise-proof. This one betrayed no grain of astonishment at her peremptory manner, her gloved hands clutching the counter edge, her eyes fanatically bright.

"I'll ring through and ascertain for you, madam."

She drummed her fingers impatiently on the desk. He must be there, insisted those restless fingers, he must be there. But he wasn't.

"Did he leave no message as to when he would be in?"

"I believe not, madam."

"How tiresome? It's most urgent." For the young man might leave Brighton at any moment. She moved sharply away, almost cannoning against a newcomer approaching the desk. She swerved with a mutter of apology, glanced up and met an intent pair of eyes fixed on hers.

The clerk at the desk said briskly, "Mr. Fennel? Your call came through, sir. The gentleman says to meet him at the place agreed at nine o'clock."

Laura heard the words and instantly discovered their true meaning. She had no doubt whatsoever that the young man was the Harry who had written to the dead girl. The appointment for this evening was probably part of a plot to dispose of the body before the police could intervene.

"Somehow he knows that I am on the track," she assured herself. "If not, he would be satisfied to leave it where it now is, for in the ordinary course of events he would be unlikely to find any safer hiding-place. But I know where the body is, and so does Mr. Crook, so he is taking the first opportunity of placing it elsewhere." She reflected that all the time they had been walking this way and that through the woods this morning they must have been observed.

"I have no doubt that if I had been alone I should by this time have joined that wretched girl, under the snow," she told herself. "A man like that will stick at nothing—nothing. Why on earth is Mr. Crook not here? This is the critical moment. It is essential for him to be on the spot." She walked restlessly up and down her room until the occupant of the room below, who was lying down with a bad headache, looked furiously at the ceiling and swore to herself that to-morrow she would leave the place altogether. After a while it occurred to Laura that the meeting was not to take place until nine o'clock, by which time Crook might have returned. Meanwhile, there were several hours to be got through, and it might be as well for her to spend them in some sort of company. If Harry Fennel knew she was on his track he might prove as relentless in disposing of her as in his treatment of the unhappy anonymous girl. She took up the telephone and rang with forlorn hope to Crook's room, but there was no reply. Rather at a loss, she set down the instrument and fell into a reverie, in which, more or less single-handed, she captured the murderer and vindicated the dead girl. It would be strange, she thought, if, after a lifetime of commonplace detail, I were to leap into prominence, just when I had made up my mind that there was nothing left worth living for. She caught sight of herself in the glass, and instantly her dreams faded. In the hundreds of novels that she had, in her time, read aloud to cantankerous employers, the middle-aged woman had always been immaculately dressed, curled and mannered; she had never had uncompromising gray hair drawn back over her ears and fastened in a Swiss bun effect on her neck. Nor had she colourless lips and a worn skin. Miss Verity did not suppose there was anything she could do about the latter, but among the amenities of the hotel was a hairdressing salon. Even women who thought lipstick and rouge fast had their hair professionally dressed. Perhaps in the salon there would be a woman of approximately Miss Verity's own age who wouldn't be bored at the prospect of a middle-aged customer, as these scented, powdered, rouged young women would. Perhaps she would have a few moments to spare to discuss a possible change of style. In her imagination Laura Verity saw herself emerging chic, trim, transformed. She rang for the electric lift and was carried down to the hairdressing department. This surprised her by its size, and by the number of clients being attended to at this moment. A slim young beauty at the desk said aloofly, "Have your an appointment, madam?" to which her prospective client replied with some asperity, "Certainly not. I am staying in the hotel."

The young woman flicked through the pages of the book and said, "If you could come back in half an hour, I think . . ."

"I don't wish to wait," said Miss Verity in a final voice.

"I'm afraid there is no one free at the moment. . . ."

"There's no one in cubicle number four," remarked Laura disagreeably, perceiving an open door and an empty chair.

"Miss Lawrence is expecting a customer at any moment."

"Let her wait instead of me."

The girl looked not merely shocked but disgusted; at that moment, however, the telephone rang and she turned to answer it. Laura heard one side of the conversation.

"Yes, madam. I see. No, that is perfectly all right. Ten o'clock to-morrow with Mr. James. Yes, madam, I will book it."

Hanging up the receiver, the speaker turned back to the expectant Miss Verity.

"A client has unexpectedly had to cancel her appointment," she announced. "If you will go into cubicle No. 9 Mr. James will be along in a few minutes."

Miss Verity looked dismayed. She belonged to the school of respectable middle-aged womanhood that finds something a little improper about unpinning one's hair in front of a man. Still, there was no doubt about it, a great many society women did this without apparently impairing their virtue, and what a society woman could do in London, Laura Verity supposed she could do in Brighton.

Mr. James was young, dark-skinned, a trifle dagoish, she thought. His own hair had a slick permanent wave, and he spoke on a high nasal note.

"What for you, madam? Shampoo and—er—set, or just an iron wave?"

Miss Verity hesitated. "I wanted to discuss—that is, I thought I might find someone here to suggest a new way of dressing my hair—something a little less—a little less severe. Up till the present I have been engaged on work in London that has necessitated a very simple form of hairdressing, but now . . ."

"Now you feel you'd like something a little more feminine? I feel sure you are right, madam. That form of hairdressing is definitely old-fashioned."

Miss Verity was a little startled by the word feminine. It was one to which she had become early accustomed.

"If you wish to acquire a husband, my dear, you should be a little more feminine," her mother used to say.

"Husband fiddle-faddle," said her outspoken grandmother. "Laura can do a great deal better on her own account. I never found a husband anything but a nuisance and an expense."

But in any case Laura had never had much time or opportunity to acquire a husband. Certainly there had been young men in the houses where she had acted as companion, but there had been something staid and aloof about her even in her twenties, and anyway, none of the young men experienced the smallest desire to contract such a mesalliance as marriage to a penniless companion of no particular parentage would involve. Hearing the word brought back those days with a rush, the disappointment she had crushed down, the jealousy when her contemporaries announced their engagements, her fear, hardening into certainty, that she was destined to be an old maid, and then the happier years when she could accept her destiny and even be glad she wasn't her sister, Mabel, whom matrimony had made as sweet as a bitter fruit.

"Perhaps you could think of some way . . ." she offered nervously, still thinking of those young men in flannels and boaters, rushing through the hall to the river or to the cricket ground, always, always leaving her behind in the big rooms that seemed so quiet when they had gone.

Mr. James did not look hopeful. He unpinned the thin coil, spread it disdainfully on Miss Verity's shoulders, held it up and let it fall, as who should say, Well, really, I don't know what you expect me to do about this. After a minute, during which his client experienced acute humiliation, he said, "The best thing I can suggest, madam, is for you to have it cut and washed with a rinse, and then waved with an iron. Then, if you like the style, you can have it permed next time you come in."

"Cut?" whispered Miss Verity.

"It isn't possible to do anything with it while it's this length." In the mirror she could see his face, the face of a young man faced with a boring piece of work, anxious to get through it with bare civility. Suddenly she was ashamed to be plain and dull and unadventurous. Young men, she thought, have no notion of the power they have over middle-aged women; if they had they would be a little more kind.

Mr. James produced a pair of scissors that he flashed professionally, and a moment later she felt them severing her hair from her head. She wanted to cry out, to tell him to stop, but she bit her lip and said nothing. Snip-snip, snip-snip, surely he was depriving her of every lock of hair and she would look like a convict. She essayed a tiny joke.

"You will leave a little on my head, won't you?"

The young man did not even look up. "It must be tapered," he explained carelessly. "Unless hair is very thick or long you have to do something to make it presentable. A neat roll is the best for you. You'll be pleased with yourself when it's done. After all," it was his turn to make a joke, "birds' nests went out a long time ago."

She sat meekly until at length he had trimmed her to his satisfaction. Then she could not forbear a glance over her shoulder, to where the cut hair lay on the floor. It seemed to her there was a tremendous lot of it. After all, it might be gray and thin and lank, but it was hers; it had enabled her to look a lady for years and years; the little that remained would make her look like one of those grotesque dolls you see in rich drawing-rooms, a few puffs and curls round a vacant face. But she said nothing, and Mr. James came back with a broom, carelessly brushing away her hair, and setting a towel on the basin edge and inviting her to bend forward. While he massaged her head with the lather he carried on a cheerful conversation.

"You suffer from a very dry scalp, don't you, madam? A little oil massage is what you require. Or rather, a course of oil massage. Oh, I'm not suggesting you should start that to-day. There wouldn't be time, anyhow. I have another client here already. But how about a friction?"

"I don't think so," gulped Miss Verity as well as she could, feeling that those strong slim fingers would soon penetrate her skull and then nothing would matter any more.

"If you take my advice, you will. When did you last have a friction applied?"

"I always wash my own hair," explained Laura with all the dignity she could command.

"It's funny how ladies that wouldn't think of trying to make their own clothes seem to think they know all about their own hair," remarked Mr. James in tones of simple bewilderment. "You go to a dentist when you want a tooth stopped, don't you? But your hair's every bit as important as your teeth. More, in a way, because while everybody comes to false teeth sooner or later (Miss Verity winced; it had been sooner in her case), there's no reason why you should ever come to false hair. It's all a matter of foresight. Ladies think they can save the cost of hairdressing, but they don't allow for the time when they'll have ruined their hair and have to start thinking about transformations. And a good transformation is one of the most expensive things going. It costs a lot to start with, then you must have three or four, because one or two are always with the hairdresser, being brushed and made up; and somehow people always get to know when hair isn't genuine. Mind you, M. Charles, where I was before I came here, made a very realistic transformation. A piece of real artistry, but even so, if your hair never comes down in the least or gets a hair disarranged, and particularly when it never starts changing colour, your friends begin to get suspicious."

He had jerked Laura backwards and was now towelling her scanty gray rats'-tails as he spoke.

"A nice friction is worth a lot to anyone with hair like yours," he continued. "Mind you, I don't say we can work miracles, but you can't go neglecting your hair for the better part of your life and then expect it to look as if it was a prize-winning head, but there's a lot we could do, and a lot we'd like to do. After all, the way your hair looks affects our reputation. I wouldn't like it to be said that a lady left my salon looking as if she'd been pulled through a hedge backwards. Now, madam, I'll just put you under the dryer while I shampoo the next lady, and as soon as you are dry I'll give you a friction to tone up the scalp and set the new hair growing—I noticed a lot of split ends while I was cutting you, and that's always bad—and then an iron wave, and you won't know yourself when you're finished."

"Perhaps I shall wish I did," replied Laura, essaying a second little joke that fell as flat as the first. She was terrified of the drier, but Mr. James was having no nonsense; he took her head in his hands, arranged it in the right position, set the monstrous metal helmet over her, slapped down a couple of illustrated weeklies, pushed wads of cotton-wool behind her ears and departed.

At the door he turned. "Can I send a manicurist along to you while you're under the drier?" he suggested.

"What for?" Laura was startled into exclaiming.

"Some ladies like to save time by having their finger and toe-nails done while their hair dries," explained Mr. James.

"I can at least look after my nails myself," replied Laura cuttingly, and he shrugged and went out. Laura was quite indignant. Toe-nails, indeed. She remembered her governess's teaching. Toe-nails should be cut square and the skin pushed down every day immediately after washing. Dry very carefully between the toes to prevent the formation of soft corns. She looked at her finger-nails. Not for worlds would she submit herself to most scathing comment. They were clean and well-kept, but a rheumatic strain accounted for cracking of the surface and a certain brittleness that caused them to break off at the least provocation. Drawing a long breath of relief because the young jackanapes would be occupied trying to swindle some other woman for the next quarter of an hour, she opened one of the papers.

The manicurists had their tables just opposite the line of hairdressing cubicles. There had been several women sitting at the little tables, dabbling their fingers in little bowls, talking with animation and confidence to the girls, all of whom were beautifully painted and waved and most of whom were young and pretty. Gradually Laura's attention faded from the uninteresting magazine, with its shiny pictures of notabilities she had never met and for whom she didn't care a jot, and began to be absorbed by the conversations that came clearly through the thin curtain.

"Fifty-six and he's twenty-nine," said a piercing female voice, "and they've gone for their honeymoon to some desert a million miles from anywhere. Well, sooner her than me I said, when I heard. Take my word for it, the next thing will be she died of fever away from every human creature but her husband, and he'll be a rich widower with the pick of the London girls for a second choice."

"You're right, madam." There was no doubt about it; the two women were both convinced of the truth of what they said. A foolish infatuated elderly woman had bought a young husband; therefore she must expect to be murdered.

"And they don't even sound distressed," thought Laura, in horror. "Murder's become a part of natural life. And yet I read the other day that only seven people in every million are murdered."

The voices went on. "She'd had two husbands already," said the client in conspiratorial tones.

"I dare say it becomes a habit," agreed the girl. She wasn't really interested, Miss Verity realized; it didn't matter to her how many people were murdered, unless they happened to impinge on her personal life. She had her own interests, her own friends; other things didn't really count. Then a new voice took up the tale. This time it belonged to a man. Laura was startled. She had not realised that men could come down here, or indeed that men had their nails manicured at all. And suppose some hussy should elect to have her toe-nails done and there was a man at the next table? All very risque, decided Laura with a toss of her head that brought it into sharp collision with the frame of the drier.

"You generally have Ivy, don't you?" said a girl's voice. And the man answered, "When she's here. Is this her day off?"

"No. That's what's so peculiar. Yesterday was her day off, and we expected her back this morning. But she didn't come or a message or anything. Mr. Turtle's ever so annoyed. He says even if you must go sick you could ring up."

"Perhaps she hasn't gone sick."

"That's what someone else was saying. Well, young Ivy's only got herself to thank. Always gadding about with someone. Look at that traveller in the hosiery she's always going about with. What's the sense, Ivy? I said to her. You know he's married, with four children, and his wife wouldn't divorce him anyway. First thing you know you'll be in trouble, and what'll happen to your job then?"

"Liked her bit of fun, did she? Well, I suppose it's not very exciting manicuring rich women's nails for a living."

"It's what a lot of us have to do," retorted the girl in tart tones. "Anyway, she could easily get a steady fellow, and they're all right here about married women working so long as you don't use your married name or start a family. She could have had a home and everything, only she's silly. It 'ud never surprise me to hear she was found in a ditch one of these days."

"You have a very vivid imagination," said the man. "I don't suppose anything's happened to her."

"Unless she's gone off with the traveller. Oh, she could have. She's like that. I remember when I saw her setting off, looking so saucy in her new coat and a blue and red scarf tied over her hair. . . ."

Miss Verity waited for no more. Pushing back the drier, she peered resolutely round the curtain. Fortunately she had no notion of the appearance she presented.

There, at a little table, sat Mr. Harry Fennel having his nails manicured! Throbbing with excitement, Miss Verity pushed the electric button which said Service, and looked round for her hat. She couldn't wait another moment. Now all her suspicions were crystallized. Fennel was the murderer and he mustn't be allowed to get away. Ivy was employed at the hotel, she always did his nails, they had been going about together, he had got her into trouble and had taken the simple way out. (It did not occur to Laura that a good many men have found it simpler to marry the girl than risk hanging on her account.) In response to her frantic ring Mr. James appeared, looking outraged. These dryers were supposed to be fool-proof but with a woman like Miss Verity anything might happen. He saw her standing excitedly by the basin, her hair hanging limply round her crimson face.

"I can't wait," she told him flatly as he entered. "A most important appointment. My hat."

"Madam!" he sounded horrified, as indeed he was. "It is impossible . . ."

"Rubbish! This is far more important. What about my bill or will you put it on my account as I'm staying at the hotel?"

"You can't possibly go out looking like that," said Mr. James severely. Thus admonished, Laura glanced carelessly in the glass, and drew back with a cry of dismay. Who was this extraordinary little creature with steel-blue hair hanging in tails round a flushed face?

"What have you done?" she demanded furiously.

"Done? You agreed yourself it must be cut. Of course, until it's curled you can't tell. . . ."

"I don't mean that. I mean the colour."

"The colour?" He stared.

"Yes, yes, yes. You've made it blue."

"Just a rinse," said Mr. James coldly.

"I didn't ask for a rinse."

He came a little nearer, drawing the curtain behind him. "You don't appear to understand, madam. When hair has been systematically neglected for years, something must be done to improve it, so far as possible. Naturally, one cannot do a great deal with hair such as yours, but a strong rinse and a good permanent wave would give it some distinction."

"But—it looks appalling." She tried to think of herself lying in her shroud with a lot of blue curls round her yellow face.

"Wait until the irons have been through the hair. You will be delighted with the result—yes, delighted. And now, madam, you are not yet dry." Gently but inexorably he forced her back into her chair, readjusted the drier, picked up the discarded papers and placed them on her lap. "It will require at least another five minutes, possibly ten, and then I will curl it."

Miss Verity's spirit was, temporarily at least, broken. Ivy might be lying dead at the foot of a pit and her murderer seated at a table over the way, but not even Crook would listen to a blue-haired woman who hadn't even been curled. She admitted defeat, and concerned herself with photographs of a bevy of plain young women surrounded by puppies.

After what seemed far more than ten minutes Mr. James returned, laid some heating-irons on a gas jet, and proceeded to toss Miss Verity's steel-blue locks into twirls and corkscrews. She was so much alarmed by this that she shut her eyes tight so that she should not have to watch an operation whose eventual results she would, she knew, dislike.

"There, madam," said Mr. James, sooner than she expected, removing his irons with a flourish and standing back. "You will agree that's an improvement."

She opened her eyes nervously; facing her was a woman with a neat steel-blue roll and some small curls clustered on her forehead.

"The aim is to show the forehead," Mr. James continued. "Your forehead is your best point. You should, therefore, expose it. Now, if you find you like this style of hairdressing I can book you an appointment for a perm. next week. Shall we say Tuesday? Would ten o'clock suit you?"

"I shall not be here at ten o'clock on Tuesday," expostulated Miss Verity, wondering who the blue-haired woman could be and deciding already that she didn't care about her.

"There are rapid trains from town? Perhaps you would prefer a later appointment?"

"I am not going to have my hair permanently waved. I was simply filling in time. Will you tell me what I should pay for this?" He told her and she gave him the exact silver. It never occurred to her to offer him a tip.

CHAPTER SIX

Back in her room she telephoned frantically to Mr. Crook, but without result. It occurred to her that he might be somewhere in the hotel, writing letters, she murmured, not yet understanding that the only place where Crook ever found himself at home was a bar. However, the hall porter assured her that Mr. Crook had gone out.

51

"But he may have come in again," she persisted. "Please send a boy round. It is very urgent."

"Mr. Crook came in some time ago, and went out again. No, he left no message as to the time of his return. No, madam, I am sorry."

She thought she detected a disapproving note in the flat official tone.

"I suppose he thinks I'm running after the man," she reflected. "Though I can't imagine any woman ever wanting to have more to do with him than she could possibly help."

She consoled herself as best she could by deciding that in all probability Crook would return for dinner, but when she came downstairs at half-past seven there was no sign of him. She dared not ask again at the desk, but she managed to slip a casual query to the waiter.

"I don't know whether you know him by sight. He's short and . . ."

The waiter assured her, with a smile she did not quite understand, oh yes, they all knew Mr. Crook, but he hadn't come in to dinner. He often didn't come in to dinner. A very popular gentleman, Mr. Crook.

"I wonder what he meant by that," thought Miss Verity, uneasily. "I dare say he has a very peculiar reputation, and I am probably endangering mine by asking for him so often."

It was, however, a consolation to realize that it was still possible at her age to endanger a good name in which no one had ever displayed the smallest interest; and with that thought she turned away to look for the dining room. It had, at various times, been Miss Verity's ambition to stay at a really smart hotel. On her rare holidays she had never been able to rise above a guest-house, where no one dreamed of changing for dinner and everyone sat at a communal table. But now, she thought, when I am so near the end of everything, one wish at least is about to be fulfilled. It was a pity she hadn't thought about changing to-night, but then if she were to accompany Mr. Crook in the evening her blue taffeta would look definitely out of place. Anyway, she was wearing her most modish blouse, white satin with minute black buttons down the front, and a tailored frill at the throat.

"To-night I shall have a table to myself," she assured her rather nervous spirit as she paused outside the door of the big room. "I shall be able to choose my meal instead of having something slapped down in front of me by a perspiring maid, with an opportunity to snatch a potato and a spoonful of greens from a communal dish as it travels down the table. There will be flowers instead of a tarnished cruet. Perhaps I shall even indulge in a glass of sherry or a little white wine." For an instant she found herself regretting that her only acquaintance at the hotel was the loud horsy Mr. Crook, and resolved to make it known from the very first that their meeting had been accidental. It would be a pity if the other guests gained the impression that he was her choice of friends. Naturally, she could not avoid being seen with him in this exciting—hastily she amended the sentence—this appalling affair, but surely there would be other guests more to her mind with whom she could enter into conversation in the freemasonry of the lounge.

All this time she had been standing by the doorway, more or less blocking the entrance, waiting for someone, probably the head waiter, to come forward and guide her to a table. If she allowed him to see by her manner that she was "good for a handsome tip," as her father used rather vulgarly to observe, he would doubtless give her a well-placed one. She waited optimistically, therefore, shoved in a well-bred manner from side to side by other guests, until at length a waiter, who had summed her up at once and knew that ten per cent. on the bill was the utmost he could hope for, came forward, saying with rather perfunctory politeness, "One, madam? This way, if you please."

"I am—staying in the hotel," she explained a little breathlessly, following him as he threaded his way expertly among the tables. This, she thought, was not quite fair; she had intended to sail through the room like a languid swan, instead of which she was like Alice chasing after the indefatigable Red Queen. The waiter paused at a small table in a corner, an obscure little table where unimportant visitors could be accommodated, a table, moreover, already occupied by a single lady.

"Madam does not object?" he said politely. "The hotel is so full that separate tables for one are practically impossible."

Miss Verity felt horribly cheated. If she'd been a young man like Harry Fennel or a woman in an evening gown she wouldn't have been pushed into a corner like this. Instantly in her mind she halved the handsome tip she had intended to bestow. But because she had been brought up to show good manners she could only murmur something about expecting a friend, a fib to which the waiter naturally paid no attention.

"So many people from London are staying here," he told them both, pulling out Miss Verity's chair.

Laura looked at her companion, and her heart sank yet further. A woman of the world, a duchess, an adventuress even—she would have objected to none of these, but the lady already seated belonged to a type which which she had been familiar all her days. Heartily betweeded, shod in enormous brogues, wearing a hat that seemed the twin of Miss French's—oh, you saw her striding all over Earl's Court, leading dogs, changing library books, giving wretched shop assistants hell if they hadn't got precisely what they wanted—indeed, one might as well be having dinner with Miss French, decided the disappointed, the cruelly disappointed Laura, as she reluctantly seated herself and, with none of the anticipated thrills, took up the menu. It didn't occur to her to wonder whether her companion—a virginal hearty if ever there was one, as Mr. Crook observed the moment he set eyes on her—objected to having her table shared. Anyway, she knew that for the most part people like that didn't care. They liked to talk, to throw their weight about, to impress their personality on anything soft enough to retain the impression, "and I," confessed Laura sadly, "shall be like wax in this woman's hands. . . . Before the end of the meal she will have annihilated me. Already I can see that she thinks my hair ridiculous, though actually her own close crop is even more so. I remember how my father used to say he detested all women who aped men, thereby losing the good qualities of both sexes."

To cover her discomfiture she took up the wine list, an action that instantly attracted the attention of the wine waiter, who ran up and stood obsequiously at her side. Miss Verity was in a quandary. She knew nothing about wine, and had no idea what she ought to order. Indeed, she scarcely knew the difference between red wine and white. Nor did the waiter make any effort to assist her. He stood there, waiting, but displaying none of the obsequious attention of which she had dreamed. In a flurry, Laura pointed to a name under the heading Burgundies (Red).

"Half a bottle of No. 62," she said. It was the first time in her life she had ever given such an order.

The wine arrived before anything else and as soon as it had been poured out she began nervously to sip it. Sooner or later, she knew, her companion would begin to speak, and her nerves were taut, waiting for that alarming instant. Sure enough, she did not have to wait long.

"Often drink that muck?" demanded the lady in a loud masculine voice. "Most unwise."

"Muck?" Miss Verity could scarcely believe her ears.

"All the wines they serve in hotels like this are muck," continued the voice, without any consideration for the feelings of the staff or of the other diners. "You ask the waiters what they drink themselves and order that."

"As a rule," faltered Miss Verity, "I drink only water."

"Good wash for the kidneys," agreed her extraordinary companion, and then the soup came, and Laura could turn her attention to that. She could feel herself scarlet from head to foot. Even the tips of her ears were burning.

"You here alone?" the other went on. "It's a rum place, isn't it?"

"If you don't care for it, I wonder you stay," exclaimed Laura, desperation giving her courage.

"No worse than any of the others. I only arrived last night and this was the first place I saw. You just come?"

"I—well, actually I only arrived to-day." She twisted her head over her shoulder, for she was seated with her back to the door, to see whether Mr. Crook had come in. "My lawyer engaged a room for me. I am here on business . . ."

"Never trust lawyers. Always swindle you. People that can't manage their own affairs should be in lunatic asylums."

"I am sure she thinks that is my rightful destination," thought poor Laura, tackling sole vin blanc, and finding it remarkably like the cheap fish they served at the one-and-sixpenny go-as-you-please meals in Earl's Court. "Indeed, she looks quite capable of driving me into such a place." And she said unexpectedly, "I wonder—I am very sorry, you will think it so strange— but I wonder if you would mind changing places with me? I am expecting a friend . . ."

"Tell me what she's like and I'll tell you when she blows in. Sorry I can't change, but I've got Highland blood. Never sit with my back to a door. Probably stabbed in the back through treachery (here she rolled her R's till Laura nearly jumped out of her seat) in a previous existence."

"Now she will talk about reincarnation. It is always something," Laura reflected, and hurriedly she inquired, "Do you know it well—Brighton, I mean?"

"Just told you, I only arrived last night." She looked round. "Not so bad, really, as hotels go."

Miss Verity, who thought it at least as frightful as Craigavon or Mon Repos, where she generally put up, only murmured weakly, "Rather—large, don't you think?"

"I like 'em large. The larger the better. Big place full of people. Don't like little solitary places. Dangerous." She hissed the word like a swan intent on driving off an invader. Laura suddenly remembered how very dangerous solitary places can be; but she wasn't feeling particularly safe here.

"Buckler's the name," the other continued. "How about you?"

"My name is Verity—Laura Verity."

The big woman stared, then broke into a great horse-laugh. "So that's what it is? I knew it was something."

Laura coloured again. "I'm afraid I don't understand."

"Stage, eh? Well, of course. No one living has a name like that." Though she didn't say so, Laura knew she was thinking, "And only fast women on the stage have blue hair. She shivered and drank a hearty mouthful of wine. She had inadvertently chosen a good brand of burgundy—or good as hotel burgundies go—and before she had drained the second glass her mood had changed. She found herself forming phrases in her mind to confound the tweed-cloth bully—no imagination about clothes, the eternal brownish mixture that never looks smart even when new, and these had seen their best days at least a couple of years ago. She tossed her head and poured out a third glass of wine. Her original intention to offer Miss Buckler a little had died a speedy death. She was no longer a poor little down-trodden companion, but a resolute woman who would help the police to track down the perpetrator of a dastardly crime—her few visits to the cinema returned to strengthen her determination. She smiled a little patronizingly.

Presently Harry Fennel came in and sat down at a table well within her purview. She watched him with some anxiety, wishing that Crook would return. Her companion's voice, in no whit abashed, startled her from her contemplation.

"That's no good, m'dear," it said. "Old girls like you and me better keep in the background."

Laura came to herself with a start and a very small hiccough, instantly suppressed.

"I beg your pardon?"

"He's a very pretty young man, no doubt, but there are plenty of younger women to tell him so. Not married, are you? No, I can see you're not. Marriage is like the measles, best contracted in early life. After that, it may be fatal."

"I had no thought of marriage," protested Miss Verity indignantly.

"Wonder if he's as sure as that." Miss Buckler's voice said in effect, "All my eye and Betty Martin to you." Then the waiter appeared, the dinner having suddenly petered out in a not very satisfactory poire melba (out of a tin) to inquire whether the ladies would take coffee at the table or in the lounge.

"Here," said Miss Buckler without ceremony. She had been smoking all through the meal and now she snapped another cigarette out of her case and passed it to Laura.

"Thank you," said Laura. "No. And I will have my coffee in the lounge," she added to the waiter.

The other woman grinned, showing big horse-like teeth stopped with gold.

"I'll keep my eye on him for you," she promised.

Miss Verity made a helpless gesture and hurried out. "Now I do trust she isn't going to be like Miss Hitchcock," she muttered to herself, colliding in her haste with a tall young couple who were just coming in, beautifully dressed in evening clothes. "Oh, I am so sorry, so very sorry. I'm afraid I wasn't . . . Miss Hitchcock used to follow me from pillar to post, wanting me to swear eternal friendship. A very peculiar woman, and I always wonder what it was she saw in me. But she was the same type." It occurred to her, as she took her place in the lounge and picked up an evening paper as a shield behind which she could hide herself and the blue curls that had begun to trouble her again, that Miss Buckler and Mr. Crook would make an excellent couple. It was odd, she reflected, that she who was so precise and mousy, as her sister Mabel always told her, should have attracted the attention of two people both so utterly dissimilar from herself. All the same, though she hoped to elude Miss Buckler to-morrow, she did most ardently wish for the return of her male vis-a-vis immediately.

Mr. Crook, however, did not arrive, and after a little the wine that Miss Verity had taken began to have a most extraordinary effect. She became aware of reserves of courage she had no notion she possessed; she resolved that on the morrow she would say to the waiter, "I am sorry, but I cannot share my table with that lady. You must make some other arrangement. I am recovering from an illness and absolute quiet is essential."

After all, the ordeal she had undergone during the past twenty-four hours might quite truthfully be described as an illness.

Most surprising still, she began to lose her sense of anxiety and strain as the minutes passed and still there was no sign of Crook. By ten minutes to nine she had begun to think that it didn't really matter whether he came or not. She, Laura Verity, was capable of handling the situation entirely on her own account. She felt she would hardly mind if the redoubtable Miss Buckler approached her again.

"Excuse me," she would say, "but I have an appointment."

At that moment, with a clatter of heavy shoes, her dinner companion appeared abruptly at her side.

"Like to come to the pictures?" she demanded. "Time for the last house."

"Thank you, no," returned Miss Verity firmly. "I have an engagement." She was delighted to hear her voice speaking the words so clearly, with such an admirable firmness. "An engagement," she repeated importantly.

"He's just going out, if you were thinking of him," Miss Buckler warned her, with an unwomanly snort of laughter.

Instantly Laura was perturbed. It was essential that she should see the direction Harry Fennel took. If he went straight along the west road then she would, she thought, be safe in assuming that he was making for Butler's Wood, where Miss French's bungalow was situated; but if he turned to the right, then she would own her suspicions unfounded.

She stood up; the hall seemed larger than it had done before dinner; Miss Buckler seemed positively enormous.

"Enormous," she whispered. "Hippopotamus."

"What are you talking about?" asked Miss Buckler suspiciously.

"Poetry," returned Laura with some dignity.

"Enormous doesn't rhyme with hippopotamus."

Laura looked at her scornfully. "I know that," she said. "Now, you must excuse me. I have to ask at the desk if my friend has sent any message."

At the desk the clerk told her that Mr. Crook hadn't arrived. No, and he hadn't sent a message and no one knew when he was expected. He might spend the night in town. Would Laura leave a message? Laura considered. It would be unwise to leave the sort of message that might warn young Fennel she was on his track. She decided to say nothing. Side-stepping rapidly, she entered the lift and was taken to her room. Fitting her small black hat over the blue curls that looked more prominent than ever under the glare of the electric light, it occurred to her that it might be possible to leave a private message in Crook's room. But when she stole nervously along the corridor, the slip of paper in her hand, she found that the door was locked. Undeterred, however, she bent down and succeeded in wedging the paper under the door, where, she thought, he could hardly fail to notice it. It might be unintelligible to a porter or chamber-maid, but Crook was no fool. Crook would know what she meant. Have fresh evidence. Am following undoubted clue. That was what she said. For my this time the wine had come thoroughly into its own, and she was convinced that Harry Fennel was the murderer. She had contrived to glance through the Visitors' Book while she hesitated at the desk, and assured herself that the signature "Harry" on the scrap of paper in the dead girl's hand was identical with the scrawled "H. Fennel" in the hotel record.

It was discouraging, as she returned from her errand, to find the large amused figure of Miss Buckler watching her from the head of the stairs.

"So that's his room?" she remarked. "Y'know, you're riding for a fall. And at your age . . ."

Without a word Miss Verity brushed past her. Her only fear was that she might be too late. She caught the lift as it was descending. She thought she heard the other woman chuckle. "I am making a fool of myself perhaps," admitted the slightly intoxicated Laura, "but it is in a good cause."

The wine had clouded her brain, too much for her to realise that if her suspicions were well-founded she was rushing headlong into the worst possible kind of danger.

The clock was striking nine as she hurried through the hall and into the street. But luck was with her, inasmuch as she espied young Mr. Fennel driving his car out of the garage as she appeared. She was further fortunate in that a bus going in the direction of Periford drew up at its stopping place directly in front of the hotel at the same moment, so that she could keep an eye on her quarry's progress for a short distance. Soon, of course, he was out of sight, but keeping to the main road, so that all her suspicions were confirmed. It was distressing, therefore, that, when they reached the entrance to the drive, there should be no sign of his car. She had alighted from the bus and now she stood irresolute on the snowy roadway. There was no sign of traffic anywhere. Since they had not passed a stationary car, she concluded that he had left it at the foot of the private path, and turned in that direction. There was no car here either, but a little farther on she found it. A dark green car with a little dancing doll at the back window. She looked, with her first tremor of nerves, up and down the empty road. Only now, when it was too late to draw back (or so she believed) did she recognize the foolhardiness of her decision. If Fennel discovered she was on his track he would have no more scruple about putting her out of the picture than of crushing a beetle with his foot. She didn't even blame him. When a man's life is forfeit he must be expected to resort to every kind of means to preserve it.

Creeping up to the car, she peered through the window. In the back were a number of rugs, intended, of course, to conceal the body. It was very dark in the road, and she didn't imagine they would dare flash lamps much in view of their burden. If she were to conceal herself in the car, she might escape detection, discover their destination and their plans regarding the corpse. Fennel might also betray important details as to the commission of the crime. She sent one final glance in either direction, perhaps her last glance of freedom, she told herself, turned the handle (it had not occurred to her that the door might be locked) and huddled down on the floor, with a rug over her. She folded it back carefully from her ears, so that she could hear footsteps approaching. Even though there is snow, she told herself, they are carrying something so heavy they must make a little sound.

There was no luminous dial to her watch, so she could only guess the time, in such circumstances a most treacherous way of measuring it. It had been nine-thirty when they reached the entrance to the drive, and she had walked another ten minutes or quarter of an hour after that, for the roads were difficult on account of snow and darkness. She felt as though she had been crouched in the car for hours, but common sense warned her that it would be a far shorter time than she supposed. She tried to divert her imagination by drawing a picture of the activities of the two men in the dark snow-covered wood. It would be an eerie, a grisly task, she decided, and began to shiver, in spite of the warmth of the rugs that by this time were half-stifling her.

They would tie a rope to a tree—of course Crook had simplified things for them by leaving his handkerchief round the trunk to show them the exact whereabouts—and one of them would lower himself into the pit. He would be soaked by the snow, but he would somehow or other rescue the body and tie it to the rope. The man at the top would have to haul it up; then Fennel himself —she thought of Fennel as the man going down into the pit—would be raised; then they would take the Thing, already showing marks of corruption, and bring it down to the car. They would put it in the back, covered with rugs—I hope I shall not faint at the stench, thought Miss Verity; perhaps it would be wiser to leave the car when I hear them approaching and conceal myself. But then she reflected that she would have no idea where they had taken the body, and also she might be seen scurrying across the road. There was very little cover on the road itself. Besides, the bottle of wine was still potent to strengthen quailing spirits. She waited.

There was no doubt about it—they were an unconscionable time at the job. Laura let her thoughts wander. It was safer, really, than pinning them to the matter on hand. She found that the long wait or the cold or something was making her knees tremble; she began to think almost affectionately of Mr. Crook. So deliberately she tried to think of something else, something not remotely concerned with the murder at all.

She therefore tried to absorb herself in her favourite day-dream, in which she was travelling to the Riviera by the Blue Train. Miss Verity had never in all her life left her native land, but she knew all about foreign travel. No one had ever more assiduously collected coloured pamphlets and posters, or badgered the travel agencies with greater enthusiasm. Sometimes she had even given the impression that she would be returning in a day or two to make final arrangements; she knew the names of all the hotels recommended by Thomas Cook, and their current prices. During conversations, if no one who knew her circumstances was present, she could give an impression of being comparatively widely-travelled. Unlikely though it may sound, she was so successful this evening that presently she actually felt as though she were on the train. She experienced all the sensations of rapid travel, felt rather than saw the movement of the surrounding country (for she always thought of the country going past her window rather than the actual, reverse process), and awoke suddenly to the realization that it was not a dream, that she was moving. As soon as she understood this, she poked her head up from the rug and peered upwards. A young man with a dark hat pulled over his eyes was in the driving seat; next to him, most realistically arranged, was something that she knew was not human. Whenever the car took a sharp corner this Thing swayed stiffly, so that once it even lay against his shoulder. He put out a hand to steady it, and it remained stiffly at an impossible angle, until the next swerve caused it to tilt anew. Miss Verity was suddenly aware of the horror of her situation. She put a hand over her mouth to cover a scream. All her vaunted courage failed her; the effects of the thin cheap wine had disappeared. Now she wanted nothing but to be allowed to leave the car with its grisly passenger, and go back to London—not Brighton, but London, to the house in S.W.5. If I get out of this alive, she whispered, I'll never try and right another wrong all the days of my life. It seemed, however, quite probable that she would not get out alive.

She had no sense of direction; the car went along one road, turned into another. It was far too dark to see signposts or the names of roads; she crouched, with her head twisted uncomfortably on her neck, watching the driver. It seemed to her that he was taking the darkest and most solitary of roads. If only they could turn into a main street, be held up, if only for a minute or so, by a red light, she would seize her opportunity, shout to a passer-by, make good her escape. Or suppose the young man left his car for a minute, as Nature might compel him to do, she would steal out by the opposite side and somehow, though it involved a ten-mile walk, find her way to a town, whence she could return to Brighton. But the young man showed no disposition to leave the car, that ran presently through a residential area. Miss Verity could see chinks of light between drawn curtains behind which people sat carelessly secure without an idea of the drama being swept past their very doors. If you said to them, That car is being driven by a murderer; the companion in the seat beside him is a corpse, and hidden under the rugs is a woman in peril of her life, they would only have laughed, because things like that don't happen.

"And they don't, to sensible people," almost sobbed Miss Verity. "Why didn't I let him get away with his murder? What is this girl to me, after all? She sounds up to no good, and I dare say, if he did murder her, it was no more than she deserved."

The houses were all left behind now, and they were running along a strip of dark road in an uncontrolled area. The car went faster and faster; to her horror the driver suddenly began to speak.

"So you thought you'd spy upon me, did you? Thought I wouldn't guess you were hiding there? Then you were going to make a fool of me in public? Going to tell everyone what I'd done. Clever, weren't you? But just not clever enough. Because, you see, I do know you're there, and you can take it from me, you're—never—going—to—tell—anyone—anything." He drew a deep breath. "Get this," he ordered. "All the people you've been cheating for years are going to get their own back at last; and it's no use crying out, because we're absolutely alone and nobody would hear you."

Laura was too terrified even to scream. Besides, screaming wouldn't help her now. She supposed that in a moment the car would draw up at the side of the road, the driver would dismount, he would open the back door of the car—and what chance would she have against a man who already had one murder on his conscience? Now there were no lights to be seen anywhere; a pall of darkness hung over the world. The moon, that had been shining when she left Brighton, was obscured by a veil of sullen cloud; there were no stars, no footsteps sounded. It was like an uninhabited world.

The car swung round another corner and drew up with a jarring of brakes and a muttered oath from the driver. Miss Verity was thinking. It will be like that man who hit his passenger on the head with a mallet and then set light to the car. Perhaps that is what he will do to me. Perhaps that's how he means to get rid of both of us. And suppose he should only stun me, and I couldn't get out of the blazing car? She almost fainted with horror at this thought. Here, however, she woke to the realization that things were happening. There were lights round them, a great blue car sprawled across the road, shattered glass gleamed in the roadway. There was even a policeman.

"Having fun?" asked the driver, as calmly as though he hadn't one actual and one potential corpse as passengers. "Any damage?"

"Only to the car. Which direction are you going, sir? This gentleman's in a hurry—wants a lift."

A big man, wrapped in a brown check overcoat came forward, speaking with a strong nasal twang.

"I'm in an allfired hurry," he said. "Of course, this had to happen to me to-night."

"Want a lift?" inquired the young man casually. "If you can fold yourself up in the back, you're welcome."

Here Miss Verity found her voice. "Constable!" she screamed. "Constable!"

As though they were marionettes jerked by a string, the three men turned simultaneously. They saw an astounding apparition; a short elderly lady, with a smutted nose, a black hat perched crookedly above one ear, bluish curls on her temples, a crumpled suit, a white terrified face, was gibbering at them from behind the window of the car.

The American was the first to recover. "Say!" he said. "Are you asking me to share the back with that? Does it bite?"

"Who the hell are you?" asked the young man, simply.

Laura paid no attention to him. "Officer!" she repeated,

struggling for dignity, unaware that her appearance denied her the smallest hope of success. "Arrest that man."

The driver of the car came round and opened the door. He inspected Miss Verity as though she were a new kind of beetle and he a naturalist who had chosen beetles for his hobby.

"Would you mind telling me what the something something you're doing in my car?" he demanded.

"Officer!" She still refused to answer. "That man's a murderer."

The policeman looked in bewilderment from one to the other. "Are you the B.B.C.?" he inquired.

"Not exactly." The driver produced a card with the speed of a conjurer discovering a rabbit. "Here's who I am."

"Never mind who he is," clamoured Miss Verity. "Ask him who—what—he's got in the front seat. Just look at it for yourselves—only look."

"Yes, look," echoed the driver.

The constable flashed his light and the three men crowded forward. There was a general roar of laughter.

"Well, I'm damned," exclaimed the American. "Didn't know women were as short as that in this country."

Against her own will Laura lifted her head. The bullseye lantern was shining on something that looked as though it had been lifted from a shop window. A beautiful waxen face, a curled red wig, pearls round a long wax throat, no rug but a black opera cloak round the waxen shoulders, a white scarf over the head—Laura could not believe her eyes. She opened her mouth, stammered, looked helplessly from one-man to the other, was silent again.

The policeman looked at the card in his hand. "Len Sinclair and his bit of stuff," he read. "This your bit of stuff?"

The young man grinned. He was not, Miss Verity now saw, in the least like Harry Fennel. He was slim, rather foreign-looking, with very bright dark eyes.

"You've probably heard of me," he was saying. "I'm taking Lulu up to town—we've got two shows at the Palaseum to-morrow. I came down to-night to give a private entertainment at a local house. The old chap had seen me in London and set his heart on having me down, so, as my show doesn't start till to-morrow, down I came. If I'd known, though, what the roads would be like or what might happen to me before I got back, I'd have turned down his proposition—cold."

"And this lady?" continued the constable stolidly. "Where did she come in?"

"I'd be obliged if you'd ask her. One thing, I haven't stopped at all, so she must have been in the car when Lulu and I boarded it." He turned to the shuddering Laura, and there was a note of genuine kindliness in his voice as he said, "If you wanted a lift, why couldn't you ask for one, instead of hiding yourself as you did? And what's all this about me being a murderer?"

"That's simple enough," said the policeman grimly, and the tone he used to Laura was the reverse of kind. "You ought to be ashamed, a woman of your age. Haven't you got anyone to look after you?"

She tried, incoherently, to explain. "He'd gone out—I didn't know where he was—I thought I'd come without him . . ."

"You'd better come along o' me," said the policeman grimly. "You can do the rest of your explaining to the sergeant."

"You don't think I'm drunk?" exclaimed Miss Verity, suddenly furious with exasperation.

"I wouldn't be surprised to hear you'd had a little drop," countered Mr. Sinclair blandly. "Well, didn't you?"

"If you're insinuating I can't take a little wine with my dinner without becoming intoxicated—I shall instruct my lawyer to act for me. And now, will you kindly convey me to a telephone. I have to ring up Mr. Crook."

"Mr. Crook?"

"Yes. He is staying at Brighton. I must get in touch with him at once." She turned, with a fragment of recovered dignity, to the young man. "I am extremely sorry I got into your car, but I believed it was the car of the man who killed that poor girl."

Even the American forgot about the urgency of his train and joined in the questions.

"What girl?"

"The girl I found dead in my cottage—the cottage I had rented, that is—the day before yesterday."

The policeman looked flabbergasted. "What's all this about a murder? We haven't been informed."

"You'd better ask Mr. Crook. He believes in it. I suppose you have heard of Mr. Crook?"

The man nodded. "We know about him. But he's not asked us—still, that's not his way. Likes to put one over on the police if he gets the chance."

"Let's all go along to the station," clamoured Len Sinclair. "You'll have to report this car smash, and this gentleman wants a lift, and we can't leave the lady by herself in a howling wilderness. Besides, she wants to telephone."

So, a queer enough procession, they made their way to the local police headquarters.

CHAPTER SEVEN

All this took place at Critchley Sutton, a small compact town about twenty miles from London. As the procession filed into the station, the sergeant glanced up, frowned, then saw the American citizen and his expression changed.

"What is it?" he demanded. "D. and D., house-breaking, blackmail, or a kidnapping affair?"

"Most likely the last," grinned Sinclair. "That is, if it's possible to kidnap someone without meaning to."

"Sort of kleptomania," contributed the American helpfully.

The policeman gave the facts; the sergeant looked sternly at Laura.

"You ought to know better at your age," he said. "Haven't you got anyone to look after you?" Exactly as the policeman had done.

"If you will kindly ring up the Royal Crescent Hotel, I will ascertain whether my lawyer, Mr. Crook, has returned."

"Crook, eh?" chimed in the irrepressible Sinclair. "That's a phony sort of name for a lawyer."

"Suits him," said the sergeant laconically. "You've heard his motto. I only defend the innocent. And the rum thing is his clients always are—technically—innocent. I will say we've never caught Crook but yet, which only shows you how much truth is really worth."

"I might make a note of the name," suggested Sinclair. "You never can tell when Nature may not get too strong for you, and I'd like to know that if I should bat another gentleman over the head there's someone to stand between me and the little covered shed."

The American here intervened, asking that particulars might be taken regarding his car, and some arrangement made for its removal. It was his first visit to England, and he knew nothing of English procedure. The policemen were, therefore, exceedingly considerate, as is the English manner towards guests. When these preliminaries had been dealt with he took his leave, saying cheerfully he hoped they'd find the body and everything would be all right.

"And you let this be a lesson to you," he added to the astounded Sinclair. "In my country they could have you up for treating a lady like that."

"Loopy," said the sergeant in soothing tones as the door closed.

"Just an American," amended Miss Verity. "Is that my call coming through?"

By good fortune Mr. Crook had returned to the Royal Crescent, and came at once to the telephone. The sergeant would have explained the position, but Miss Verity took the instrument out of his hand.

"I think I shall explain this best," she said. "Mr. Crook, this is Miss Verity speaking from Critchley Sutton Police Station. There has been a development in The Nook murder. Would it be possible for you to come here immediately? I don't care to discuss this sort of thing by telephone."

"There won't be another train to-night," gasped the constable, staring at Miss Verity in horror.

"Mr. Crook has his car." She looked at Sinclair. "I don't know whether the police will want you to stay," she began, and he took her up cheerfully, "I don't know that either. But I know I want to. I want to see this Crook chap. I want to hear the whole story. After all, I am in it."

"Only by accident."

"Most people get mixed up in murders by accident. That's all right. The night's young and my bed would have hysterics if it saw me before 3 a.m."

Mr. Crook covered that forty miles in just under the hour. He said he knew all the short cuts and the un-built-up areas where a man wasn't compelled to a crawl that would shame a snail. He arrived at about half-past eleven, beaming and unruffled and packed with energy.

"What's it all about?" he said. "I hope you haven't told them too much."

"I haven't told them anything," said Laura. "I thought it best that you should be present."

"It looks like an action for trespassing," added Sinclair with unimpaired good humour. "Y'know, I'd no idea a murder could be so exciting."

Laura began her story with the finding of the body in the bedroom of The Nook and ploughed resolutely on to the events of this evening. Crook could not deflect her nor the sergeant hurry her. She made statements —in particular in regard to Harry Fennel—that made Crook blench, but she paid no heed. Only when she came to recount the events of the past two hours, her own terror when she heard Sinclair's threats, her passionate eagerness to escape, did her voice tremble a little.

"And is that the lot?" demanded the sergeant before Crook could speak, as her voice shook into silence.

"How much more d'you expect for your money?" Crook wanted to know.

"So you thought I was threatening to murder you," marvelled Sinclair. "I'll say that must have given you a turn. Well, thanks a lot. This is going to put me at the top of the bill."

"Sure?" drawled Crook.

"How d'you mean—sure?"

"There's more than one way of telling this story, just as there's more than one person goin' to tell it. It might be made to make you look a thunderin' ass."

"I'll chance it," said Mr. Sinclair cheerfully. "Well, thanks a lot," and he, too, was gone.

Laura turned to face the indignant gaze of the sergeant.

"I wouldn't have believed it," he said. "Do you realise you've got nothing—nothing on this man, Fennel? Just because his Christian name's Harry and he smokes cigarettes you're identifying him with the murderer."

"You forget that he knew the girl at the Royal Crescent."

"We don't even know that the body is the girl at the Royal Crescent. No one but you has even seen the body. He could bring a slander case against you if he knew what you were saying."

"It might hurry the police up at that," was Crook's dry comment. "Don't you let them fluster you, sugar. You've done mighty well. If I believed in Providence I'd say you were inspired to get into that car 'to-night. It's kind of made the police open their great sleepy eyes and take notice. Now, then, how about it? This lady and I believe there's a body buried in a pit in some woods near Periford, and we demand that the police shall make a search. We know that a girl is missing from Brighton Hotel, and the scarf she was wearing the day she vanished corresponds to the scarf worn by the dead girl. We've given the Periford police one chance and they muffed it. This is another. If there's any chance of their muffing that, too, you can take it from me the public will want to know a thing or two." He turned back to Laura. "I was half expecting this," he told her. "Your new friend at the Royal Crescent heard me asking for you at the desk, and told me you were hot on the trail. So, instead of going out again, I just hung around."

"I left a note," murmured Miss Verity.

"You'll have to tell me about that presently. Anyhow, Fennel has been back an hour or more. Now, then," he turned to the sergeant, "if you want us, you'll know where to find us."

The sergeant unwisely ignored him. "Haven't you any friends who could look after you?" he demanded of Laura.

"She's got me and for the present I propose to stick closer than a brother. Don't you pay any heed to him, Miss Verity. You're a positive gold-mine. You remember that and stick your chin in the air as high as it'll go."

"I am afraid they all considered me mad, as certainly Miss Buckler does," observed Laura meditatively, as she climbed into the disreputable car. "Perhaps you agree with them, but at least you have the good taste to keep your opinion to yourself. It may be, of course, that I am unreasonable to expect anyone to believe in a body that no one but myself will admit to having seen, but what conceivable motive could I have for vacating a cottage that on first appearance seemed to suit me admirably? And you must acknowledge," she added with sudden fire, "that, though the body is not yet forthcoming, up to the present remarkably little search has been made for it."

"Negligence on the part of the police?" suggested Crook, with a grin. "That 'ud be a pretty card to play."

"Are they going to do anything about it?" the lady went on.

"Certainly they are. They're goin' to have the whole country at their throat if they don't. What do we pay the police for? To shut their eyes when murder is committed and allow the dead to go unavenged? How's that for a headline?"

"Are you a newspaper proprietor as well as a lawyer?" inquired Laura respectfully.

"The next best thing. I have—let me whisper it—A Friend At Court."

This friend he proceeded to call up on his return to Brighton. "Cummings? No, no, I want Mr. Cummings.

Engaged? Nonsense. Tell him Crook's on the line and there are dirty doings in Brighton. That'll fetch him." He smiled a smile of superior wisdom while he waited. A long drawling voice sounded at the other end of the wire.

"Mud-raking again, Crook?"

"You know as well as I do the municipal authorities pay their dustmen better than their district nurses. I've got an exclusive story for you."

"Have you knocked all the local reporters out with a beer bottle? I wouldn't put it past you."

"For some mysterious reason they haven't got wind of it. I can't imagine why. But, then, bein' only a lawyer, I wouldn't know what instinct it is that warns a newspaper man when to go out and be a vulture."

"I hope it's a murder," said Cummings, callously.

"Certainly it's a murder, though whose murder I'm not permitted to say."

"Meaning you don't know?"

"How right you are! According to my lady friend down here, she's a poor little working-girl who spends her time polishin' the nails of the rich."

"Male or female rich?"

"I get you, Cummings. In this case, my friend believes the male rich. Said to have a rovin' eye between-times."

"And she's paid the penalty? In other words, died the death?"

"So I'm assured."

"Meaning it's a case of disappearance?"

"There's one disappearance, so far unaccounted-for. That's the murderer. There's one corpse that's also a disappearance. No one's seen the body but my client. That's the trouble."

"Meaning no one else believes in it?"

"Precisely."

"And this is where I come in?"

"Couldn't be better put."

Cummings chuckled. "You leave it to me, old boy. Just a rough sketch of the lady's story, that's all I ask. We can deal with the trimmings."

The next morning the "Daily Record" had magnificent headlines surging right across the front page. Cummings said he didn't cater for the cultured, the educated or the well-bred. He said he took his orders like everybody else; and, he would add modestly, he did his best to give satisfaction. On this occasion he had, to use

Crook's expression, done them proud. All across the
front page the story roared.

VANISHING CORPSE DISCOVERED BY MYSTERY SPINSTER.
THE BODY ON THE BED.
Brighton Girl's Tryst With Death.

"A little vulgar, are they not?" demurred Miss Verity
when Crook brought the glaring sheets to her notice.

"So's human nature," was Crook's hearty response.

"But—quite so vulgar as that?"

"Cummings knows as well as I do that when you've
got a living to earn you can't afford high brows or high
hats. You must be ready to touch your own to the
chap that supports you."

"That must be very exhausting for Mr. Cummings,"
suggested Miss Verity. "I see that the 'Record' has
two million readers."

"All likin' their jam spread about an inch thick. Besides, it isn't only the public, it's the police. It 'ud
take a couple of German tanks rolling up to their own
front doors to make some of these chaps wake up to
the fact that there's a war."

Miss Verity declined to continue the argument, but
bent her attention to the paper.

Is body discovered by London spinster Laura Verity
that of missing manicurist Ivy Green? inquired the
"Record's" crime expert. Ivy, a slight pretty girl
with a penchant for male society, has not been seen
by her family or anyone else since her afternoon out
on Tuesday last. Her employer, Alfred Turtle, of
the Royal Crescent Hotel, Brighton, expected her to
come on duty on Wednesday, the 13th, as usual. Deep
mystery envelops the story of her disappearance unless . . .

Here, in accordance with the practice of the editorial
staff of the "Record" the paragraph abruptly broke off,
and in huge capitals the public was adjured to

READ LAURA VERITY'S OWN STORY.

Laura Verity, fifty-year-old spinster of Earl's Court,
London, tells mysterious story of dead girl found on bed
in solitary country cottage. Ten p.m.—wild night—isolated bungalow—no telephone—no neighbours—body on
bed. Miss Verity describes her agonised vigil by the
body of an unknown girl, an experience that has so shattered her nerves that, under medical advice, she is receiving no visitors. Even the Press are excluded. But
readers may be convinced that when the ban is lifted

the first man past the door will be the "Record's" crime expert.

WHAT WOULD YOU HAVE DONE?
MISS VERITY'S DESPERATE DILEMMA.

To stay or not to stay—beside a murdered corpse through a dark and endless night. That was the frightful choice facing Miss Verity on the night of Tuesday last, the 12th instant. Outside perhaps lurked the murderer awaiting his second victim; within was the foully-murdered body of a young girl. For what appeared like an eternity she waited until at last day broke. Never was a human soul more thankful for the returning sun . . . At this juncture Miss Verity laid the papers aside.

"I really cannot see why the "Record" should wish to interview me," she observed. "They tell my story for me far better than I could tell it myself. They have even invented a sun in a snowstorm, an innovation that would never have occurred to me."

"The Press don't allow little things like that to trouble them," Crook told her. "Anything about Len Sinclair there?"

But fortunately (from Laura's point of view) Mr. Cummings had decided to draw a veil over that incident.

"Not because of your feelings, honey," Crook assured Miss Verity. "Only—it don't do a public man any good to have his name mixed up with a murder—see?"

CHAPTER EIGHT

"It is a strange world," reflected Laura, with no marked originality. "When a tragedy really takes place and I approach the police they merely assure me that I am mad; but when a completely absurd incident occurs they instantly begin to take notice and turn out in their hundreds."

This was perhaps a rather higher compliment than the police deserved. They did not turn out in the spectacular numbers suggested by Laura's reflection; but once the Press had the story well in hand it was impossible for them any longer to ignore its possibilities. They officially closed the wood to the public and, with long faces and scarcely suppressed oaths, got to work.

"Well, there's no question of us being on the dole between now and Christmas," remarked one constable to another. "The snow's been falling heavier and heavier ever since the 13th; we'll be able to burrow halfway to Australia before we find this body."

"Always supposing there is a body," agreed the other.

"That chap, Crook, said he tied a handkerchief to a tree."

"That'll be a lot of help," acknowledged his companion sarcastically. "Can't be above two or three hundred trees here."

In any case, the handkerchief was not forthcoming. "What d'ye expect?" demanded Crook. "There was plenty of time for the amateur to take a walk in the woods before the pros. got down to the job. If you ask me that handkerchief of mine is decoratin' some private sleuth's museum. And he won't come forward and come clean because he'll be afraid of gettin' a couple of years for obstructin' the police in the performance of their duties."

"It's a phoney case, anyhow," grumbled the police. "There's enough slopes and ravines in that wood to make a very nice Ivor Novello picture, if you ask me. And we're supposed to dig 'em all out."

"Perhaps your luck'll be in," suggested Crook hopefully, departing on other business.

Miss Verity was shocked to find that he could devote himself to any other affair than this disappearance of Ivy Green.

"Surely you have been asked to assist!" she exclaimed. "Are you not going to accompany them to the woods?"

"When you know me a bit better you'll understand that I never do a job of work anyone else is prepared to do for me," Crook assured her. "Besides, it might look suspicious if I was the one to find the body. Remember what they taught you in the nursery? Them as hides knows where to find. No, no, let the police get on with the job and you take my tip and go to bed for three days. Your life won't be worth living if you don't."

Miss Verity said indignantly that she had no intention of running away; she said her conscience was clear; she said she had left London for a holiday; she said she had never had any opportunities to spend days in bed throughout her hardworking life; she reminded Mr. Crook that you can't teach an old dog new tricks.

Mr. Crook grinned. He said he'd be sorry for any dog that didn't anyhow try and learn. He added that the hotel would be lousy with the police all trying to trip her up. He said significantly that if young Fennel really was concerned in the girl's death, the farther she

(Laura) kept away from him, the better for her. It was, however, none of these arguments that eventually persuaded Laura to take his advice. It was the bare fact that he had spoken the truth. . It shortly appeared that it was not possible for her so much as to cross the road to admire the breaking of waves on the beach—and Miss Verity was one of the large army of human beings who derive a real pleasure from this harmless pastime—without someone brushing against her, apologising and saying quickly, Miss Verity, isn't it? I represent the "Daily Boom" or the "Morning Star" or some such journal—never, she noticed with regret, "The Times," to whom she was prepared to accord an interview—and then the speaker would break into a quick-fire of questions, to all of which she would reply with commendable firmness, instilled into her by Mr. Crook, "I am sorry, but I have nothing to say. If you desire any information, you must approach the police."

"We've got their statement," the young man would urge, "but there are other things our readers want to know." And they would even inquire into her personal habits and whether she liked taking lonely cottages, whether she had ever done so previously, and if so, if that occasion had been marked by some astounding development.

To all of which Miss Verity would reply woodenly, "I really couldn't say. No, really, I can't."

"If you ask me, the joke's on the police this time," said the lanky young man from the "Sun" to the plump elderly reporter of the "Moon." I don't believe there ever was a body."

"Where's Ivy Green, then?"

"Where a lot of bad girls go—having a bit of fun on her own."

"If that's so, she'll bless the old lady, giving her all this space in the Press."

Inside the hotel it was just as bad. Laura now had more "contacts," as Cummings would have expressed it, than she could well deal with. Mr. Crook seemed to have left Brighton for a few days and to be devoting himself to other urgent affairs in London, for he was a man with a large and ever-growing practice among a section of the community for whom many more timid lawyers were afraid to act. But the other guests at the hotel were always asking the most ridiculous questions. What had she felt like when she found the body? Hadn't she been frightened? Well, of course, she'd been frightened, said Miss Verity impatiently. She wasn't accustomed to finding bodies on her bed six days out of seven.

"Very sinister, indeed," remarked Miss Buckler, to anyone who would listen. "I can't help feeling that an innocent woman would never have spent the night in the cottage."

"But surely you are not suggesting any connection between Miss—er—Verity and the dead girl?" breathed Mrs. Burton-Smythe, late of Ealing, her whole plump person quivering with pleasure. "Of course, it's all most peculiar . . ."

The police thought it peculiar, too. They came and went like an April sun. You never knew when you mightn't knock up against one at the foot of the staircase or in the manager's room. They talked to Mr. Turtle, who couldn't tell them anything; they interrogated Ivy's colleagues, who said in chorus that Ivy was ever such a good girl, but you couldn't help being what you were and men did follow her about. She'd had some friends, of course, but she wasn't engaged, and she was just out to have a bit of fun. And when you realised how hard you worked in a place like the Royal Crescent, it wasn't fair to blame a girl.

"Did she have any special man friend?" asked Inspector Relph impatiently. He was a short man with sandy hair and a great dislike of the man in the street. The average citizen seemed quite incapable of answering simple questions; he was forever going psychological and putting forward theories of his own. And the women on the whole were worse than the men.

"Now, that Tuesday afternoon. Let's stick to that," he implored. "When this girl went off duty, did she tell anyone what she was going to do?"

"Said she was going out with a boy friend."

"She didn't mention his name?"

"Not likely. Anyway, with Ivy it was hardly ever the same one two weeks running."

"She went off alone?"

"Her sort of friends didn't come and wait for her. She always met them outside."

"Can you tell me the names of any of them?"

Here, instead of behaving straightforwardly and giving him a list of names and possible addresses, the girls all behaved like mares shying from a bit of paper blown across the road. Their memories failed them; they simply couldn't remember, she never mentioned names.

"Come, now," said Relph. "There was a married man, wasn't there, a man you'd warned her against? Who was he?"

After a lot of hesitation they supplied him with the name. A man called Johnson, a traveller in cosmetics. The Royal Cresent did a good trade in cosmetics and scents and hair lotions in the beauty parlour of the hotel, and this Johnson supplied various powders and creams. Relph got into touch with him in his home in Kilburn. Johnson was a good-looking man in a rather flashy way, with an assured manner and a faded-looking wife a few years older than himself.

"Miss Green? Oh, one of the girls at the Royal Crescent. Yes, of course I remember her. I used to see her when I called."

"When did you see her last?"

"I dare say the last time I was there."

"You used to see her away from the premises sometimes, didn't you?"

Johnson looked a little embarrassed. "There was nothing to that. Just took her dancing once or twice, nothing more."

"When did you last see her? I mean, the actual date?"

"I suppose—oh, about a fortnight ago when I came to the hotel."

"You only saw her in the hotel?"

"That's all."

"You didn't see her at all on the twelfth?"

"I wasn't near Brighton on the twelfth."

"No doubt you can tell me where you were."

"Look here," Johnson began to bluster, "what are you driving at? You don't suppose I had anything to do with her disappearance, do you?"

"We've got to eliminate every possible suspect," said Relph in a wooden voice. "That's the only way we can hope to learn the truth."

"Well, I can tell you I was in London, as it happens. The boss had a staff meeting—he does it every now and again—King and Country—you know the kind of thing. Cosmetics are important, but freedom's more important still. If any of you younger men feel inclined to try and join the colours, you have my blessing. Lot of use it is anyone trying to speak out of his turn in this war, but the fact is they've taken his two sons and I suppose it sort of riles him to see anyone under thirty still in a civvy suit."

"What time was that meeting?"

"Three o'clock."

"And when was it over?"

"Half-past four. He wanted to hear about our records, check them up with the same period last year. Matter of fact," he added gloomily, "he's not as good as he used to be. He's got a pretty sound connection, but the war hasn't done him any good. Some of these hotels, for instance—he's always specialised in hotel business—empty as a deserted graveyard. You can have a whole floor to yourself. Well, folk don't like it, and you can't blame 'em."

"So he was really hinting that he was proposing to shorten his payroll."

"Something of the kind. That's got nothing to do with the girl, though."

"Any likelihood that you might be on the list of the axed?"

Johnson coloured, then faced round angrily. "All right, all right, have it your own way. Forsyte's notion was to let the men go who'd be wanted for the army in any case, and cut down the commission of the others. But even that doesn't affect this girl. I tell you, she was nothing to me . . ."

"All right. What did you do when the meeting was over?"

"Hung about till the pubs opened and had a couple. I needed them. About a quarter to six I dropped into a newsreel cinema. At seven-fifteen I went out and had dinner at a pub, and afterwards I went to the dogs. And if you're going to ask me for an alibi for all that, I haven't got one."

"Thanks very much. All routine stuff, you'll understand." Relph nodded to indicate that he hadn't anything else to say. He didn't see much likelihood of nailing Johnson. He could get the police in the metropolitan area to confirm the story as late as four-thirty. After that—well, you can't expect miracles, even of the police, and although he knew the name of the pub where Johnson had had his drinks, and the other where he had dined, it wasn't probable that anyone would particularly remember him. He had said that he dined alone, and didn't know anyone at the dogs.

Relph got out a time-table and began to calculate. Supposing Johnson had left London when the conference was over—there was a train just before five o'clock he could have caught. That would bring him to Brighton at six. Miss Verity had reached the cottage some time after seven. Did that give Johnson time to kill the girl? It seemed to Relph that it was possible, though not probable. To begin with, why should they choose Miss French's cottage for their rendezvous? So far as anyone could learn, Ivy Green had not known Miss French, and indeed all evidence seemed to point to the fact that that extraordinary woman had known no one. It seemed unlikely that they would know the cottage was empty at 6 p.m., and indeed, but for a mischance, Miss Verity would have arrived before that hour. And even if Johnson had arranged to meet the girl at 6 o'clock—an unlikely enough premise in itself, since he could not possibly know what time he would get away from London—they would scarcely settle to meet in a wood after dark. No, Relph thought, Johnson could fairly be ruled out. He next turned his attention to Harry Fennel. All that could thus far be urged against Harry was the fact that he had known the girl and occasionally taken her out.

Harry, tackled by the police, admitted the latter fact rather grudgingly.

"I can't pretend to have known her very well," he said. "I used to see her at the hotel, but I've only been there about seven weeks. She was pretty and amusing, and her only relation was a gruesome old aunt somewhere. There was nothing in it, you know. As for whom she meant to meet that Tuesday, I've no idea."

"Did you see her on that day?" demanded Relph.

"No, but I saw her the day before. I had a manicure . . ." He looked a little sheepish.

"You were in the habit of having manicures?"

"Well, no, but I've spent a good many years, since I was seventeen, in fact, in New Zealand, and I never thought much about my hands. But when I came over here, thinking I might get into the army, I realised how bad they were. As a matter of fact, the first time I had them done it was a sort of joke—a wet afternoon, and I didn't know anyone, so I went downstairs and this girl was so friendly. She was good at her job, too. You wouldn't believe the miracle she worked on those busted nails of mine. I'm quite presentable now."

"And when you saw her on the Monday?"

"She talked a bit as usual. I said, 'What are you doing to-morrow?' and she said, 'If you want to date me, you're too late. I'm going out with a friend.'"

"'Take care of yourself,' I told her, and she threw up her head and laughed and said she knew her way about, thank you. I suppose she did, though she could be reckless. I asked, 'Is it someone new?' and she said,

'Nobody you've ever met.' And then she looked a bit queer and added, 'I do like a uniform.' 'Well,' I told her, 'it's not my fault I'm not wearing one.' That's all she said. It doesn't amount to a row of pins."

"And on Tuesday itself—you didn't see her?"

Fennel shook his head. "I went up to play golf in the morning, a practice round. I had a date with a friend on the Wednesday, and I'm not the golfer I'd like to be, so I took my clubs up to the West Hilton Club and messed about as long as I could see the ball. About five I knocked off and had a drink at the club-house. There wasn't anyone there I knew, and presently I came back here."

"Do you remember what time you came in?"

"A little after six. I thought I'd got plenty of time for a bath before dinner, so I went up and soaked and read an evening paper till about half-past seven, when I came down to dinner."

"I see. Now, there's one more thing. Did Miss Green ever tell you anything personal, I mean about her friends . . .?"

"I've told you, I hardly knew the girl."

None of this got Relph much farther. No one at the hotel remembered seeing the young man come in at six o'clock, but that didn't mean he wasn't telling the truth. In so big an hotel it was unlikely that one particular guest would attract attention unless he behaved in an unusual way. He was able to corroborate the story of the visit to the golf club, but since Fennel had only been going round alone no one remembered the precise hour at which he had left the premises. Nor did the barman recall seeing him.

"But there'd be quite a number of members in the bar at that hour," he explained honestly, "and I wouldn't notice an overseas member particularly. He might quite easily have been there."

Since Fennel claimed that he had travelled to and from the club by car it was useless to examine the conductors of the local bus, so all Relph's questions left him very little farther on. Indeed, there seemed no strong reason to suppose that the mystery would be solved until, at least, the girl's body had been found. Neither her aunt nor Mr. Turtle's other employees could tell him anything of value, while the queer old woman, Miss Verity, clung to her amazing story and could not be shifted in the smallest degree.

By the time the Press campaign was forty-eight hours old, Laura had realised the wisdom of Crook's advice.

Quite apart from the reporters, who almost drove her crazy, there were the other guests at the Royal Crescent. These had increased in number considerably since the story began to leak out. Turtle, who had begun by feeling outraged at the amount of publicity his hotel was receiving, suddenly perceived that it was excellent for business; it might or might not be coincidence, but the fact remained that his hotel was packed out for the week-end. Everyone asked, blatantly or in secret, according to their respective temperaments: Who is Miss Verity? and when they had been informed found some excuse for coming and talking to her. Laura began to feel demented. She still had no private table and Miss Buckler did nothing to tranquillise her.

"One way of making a lot of friends in a short time," she remarked in her outspoken way. "Can't think how you stand it, all these strangers pushing and prying. Drives me mad. Always did. Watching and questioning, and following you round. But perhaps you're enjoying it."

"I absolutely loathe it," replied Laura in dignified tones. "It's absurd to blame me because someone killed the girl in a house I had happened to rent, and I have already given my version to the police. I have complained to Mr. Turtle on my lack of privacy, but he says he is helpless. There is only one thing to do. Mr. Crook was right. I must remain in bed."

"Not forgetting this is a respectable hotel, are you?" chuckled Miss Buckler.

"With instructions that no one is to be admitted."

Actually Laura was furious about the situation. "Considering I only propose to cumber the earth for another three months, of which one week is practically exhausted, I should have thought I might be allowed a little peace during that time," she declared passionately. "Surely I shall lie in the grave long enough without having to waste precious time lying in bed at the Royal Crescent."

There seemed, however, to be no alternative. Crook was spending most of his time in town, and by this time the curious and sometimes inimical glances flung in her direction were beginning to have an unpleasant effect on Miss Verity's nerves. She sent for Mr. Turtle, therefore, and informed him that she was indisposed (as indeed I am, she reassured her conscience. Indisposed to see any more of these detestable people), and would be spending the next two or three days in her room.

"I shall be glad if you will see that I am not disturbed," she added. "As for telephone calls, unless these come from Mr. Crook, I do not wish to receive them."

Mr. Turtle said Certainly, madam, and I quite understand and gave the necessary instructions. The people who had booked double suites because their jaded imaginations were tickled by the whole affair felt cheated. It was a stupid season socially, the war saw to that, and Brighton generally had not felt so pleased since the day that the tide washed up a magnetic mine, and they had to send to Plymouth for an expert to put it out of action. Even with Miss Verity out of sight, they could still exchange views among themselves, reminding one another of similar murders of girls in lonely cottages; the moralists got the most fun out of the tragedy, as moralists generally do, but a fairly good time was had by all.

Meanwhile, Miss Verity reposed very comfortably on a Dunlop mattress and enjoyed a succession of delightfully cooked and served meals brought in by maids, the like of whom she had never seen at Mrs. Loveday's. Every now and again she asserted herself by taking up the room telephone and ringing down for something out of hours, less because she wanted it than because it was an undreamed-of luxury to be able to give orders. And it was certainly a comfort to be free from reporters and Miss Buckler.

But Crook was not the only person on earth possessed of common sense. Passive resistance, he had said impressively to Laura, that's your card at the moment. But there are other cards in the pack to be played by the enterprising, and on the third morning of her voluntary incarceration Laura was told, to her surprise, that the doctor had come and would be glad to know if she was ready to receive him.

"The doctor? I'm not expecting any doctor."

"He says he was sent in by Mr. Crook."

Laura relaxed. How clever of Mr. Crook, though only what one would expect of a lawyer, of course. Naturally, people would begin to be sceptical if she remained in bed and had no accepted disease. This doctor was Crook's intelligent way of shutting people's mouths. Probably by this time they were exchanging mysterious glances and wondering aloud what the old girl was afraid of.

"Show him in," she said, drawing her neat blue ripple dressing-jacket over her shoulders.

Just as Crook was certainly not quite what she would have expected in a lawyer, so Bennett was not quite what she looked for in a doctor. She had very little experi-

ence of them, except when she had held various com-
panionships to old ladies, to whom doctors were as
necessary as Benger's; on the rare occasions that she
had been compelled to consult them in her own interest,
Miss Verity had found them to be middle-aged, harassed
men of no particular character, except that they were
far too busy to spare her much time for the little she
could afford to pay.   Dr. Bennett was tall, dark, wore
glasses and a neat beard and moustache; indeed, he resembled Laura's secret picture of a head B.B.C. announcer. He carried the usual small bag that he dumped
down on a chair, and came to the bedside. Miss Verity
was glad to realise at the outset that he was not one of
these modern men who claim to cure every ailment by
psychological methods, informing you that you have cancer (or tuberculosis or arthritis) because your parents
had a heated argument over your probable sex before
birth—or didn't live happily together after it.   He accepted her prostration as a perfectly natural thing in
the circumstances, and assured her that she need not be
anxious.   It was only to be expected.

"Mr. Crook suggested it might be as well for me to
pay you a visit," he said in rather husky tones.   "I
understand you have had a bad shock, and it has in-
capacitated you for the time being."

"I don't really think I need medical treatment," said
Miss Verity, honestly.

"Perhaps a tonic," suggested the doctor in soothing
tones.

"As Mr. Crook is aware, the only tonic I require is to
be left alone instead of being pestered by these vulgar
journalists," retorted Laura with some spirit. "My father
always warned me that it was a vulgar profession, consisting so largely, as it does, of perpetually inquiring
into other people's private affairs.   It stands to reason
that such a way of getting a living must have a dele-
terious effect on the mind."

"Oh come, Miss Verity," said the doctor good-humouredly.   "It's their bread and butter, you know."

"I dare say the proceeds of jewel robberies are a
thief's bread and butter," Laura observed dryly, "but the
State does not encourage him to pursue his profession."

"And, in any case, a certain amount of publicity is
necessary, if the criminal's to be found."

"The criminal can scarcely complain that there has
been too little of that," she assured her visitor.   "And,
in any case, there are two sides to such a question."

"You are naturally upset by what has occurred," soothed the doctor. "It is all quite natural. It must have been a terrible shock."

"It appears to be providing a number of other people with considerable entertainment," was the difficult patient's reply, delivered in a tart voice. "In that sense, I am a public benefactor."

"You are clearly a woman with a good deal of courage," Dr. Bennett flattered her. "I understand you remained all night in the cottage with the body. Not many women would have been brave enough to do that."

"It was a question of rival horrors, and I am not yet crazed or heathen enough to believe that a corpse can do as much harm as a living murderer."

"I have no doubt you were wise."

"The fact that I am still alive proves that."

"I suppose the police have been troubling you," suggested Dr. Bennett.

"On the contrary, they have refused to believe my story, although force of circumstances have compelled them to move at last. I ask you, is it reasonable to suppose that a woman of my age and position would invent such a tale?"

"You're quite sure you weren't the victim of a delusion?"

Miss Verity sat more upright. The wings of her blue dressing-jacket flapped apart in indignation. "So that's the latest idea? Are you sure Mr. Crook did send you? Are you sure you didn't come from the police? It would be an easy way out for them, save them a lot of work, because once they've found the body they're still only on the bottom rung of the ladder. They've still got to find the murderer—whereas, if I'm suffering from a delusion, they needn't lift another finger."

"Tut, tut, tut," gasped Dr. Bennett. "Tut, tut, tut. I really can't allow you to excite yourself like this. Your pulse now . . ." he groped for the wrist Miss Verity reluctantly conceded to him, "you simply can't afford to allow yourself to be upset in this fashion. Now," he drew a large watch out of his pocket and looked at it intently, "as I thought—a little too fast, but that's only to be expected."

With the apparent intention of putting her at her ease he asked one or two more questions about her "ordeal." Hitherto Laura had only heard the expression used in connection with the newly-born, and she had a faint sense of impropriety when it was employed in relation to herself.

"If you are trying to make out that I imagined the body, you can abandon the idea," she said presently. "There has never been any sign of madness in my family —my mother's sister, Kate, was a little eccentric perhaps, but every family has someone not quite like the rest. And in any case the police have the slip of paper; they can hardly suggest I put that into the dead girl's hand."

"The—er—paper?"

"Yes. Probably the solution will turn on that. Anyway, it's the police's job, not mine. And now I suppose you're going to prescribe a tonic."

"You know our little ways, don't you?" asked Dr. Bennett with a wry smile.

"I have kept in good health for more than fifty years because I have never had time to be ill. I can't give you the name of my town physician because I don't possess one, and if I did he would be too busy to waste time on a woman who doesn't need his services. If it satisfies you, if you think it'll please Mr. Crook, to send in a bottle of tonic, I've no objection. Any more than you care whether I drink it or pour it down the basin."

"I don't propose a tonic," said the doctor mildly. "But a few tablets—a bromide solution in that form—which will have the effect of—er—settling the constitution. Delayed shock is more dangerous than the other kind, and you'd be more than human if you weren't suffering from what happened to you. In fact, it would have had far more serious effects on the average woman. Now, I want you to take two of these tablets every two hours. You'd better take the first two now. I'll give you a little water to wash them down. You're suffering from a certain amount of blood pressure. I shall call again to-morrow. . . ."

"Call every day for a year if you like," interrupted the obliging Laura, "but not on my account. I haven't the slightest intention of taking your tablets."

The doctor made a vague comprehensive movement. "My dear lady . . . As a medical man . . ."

"Oh, I don't think so," said Miss Verity amiably. "Really, I don't. Just at first, perhaps, I believed in you, though even then I thought it strange that Mr. Crook shouldn't have mentioned that he was sending you in—but when you tried to take my pulse with your thumb I knew you were an impostor. You see, there's a pulse in the thumb, in everybody's thumb, so what you felt might have been your own pulse beating rather than mine. If you ever set up as a doctor again," she went on, with a smile tender with malice, "remember you take a pulse—so!"

She grasped her right wrist with her left hand.

"Thumb underneath to hold the wrist steady, fingers on the pulse itself. It's dangerous, in these days of A.R.P. lectures and First Aid, to make an elementary mistake like that. Everyone knows those simple first rules."

Her visitor's discomfiture was complete. He did his best to laugh it off, but Miss Verity showed him no mercy.

"As for those aspirin tablets you were going to give me, it would be a pity to waste them," she added sweetly.

Dr. Bennett, poor fish, stood pulling miserably at his elegant beard.

"Do take it off," Miss Verity pleaded. "I should so like to see what a newspaper representative—it is the "Daily Record," I think. . . ." But even she hadn't the heart to continue. "I must admit it was most enterprising," she acknowledged, relenting a little. "If you hadn't made that blunder about the pulse I might even have been deceived. But though I'm sure you don't mean me any harm—after all, I'm part of your bread and butter, aren't I?—I don't think I'll let you experiment on me. I mean, even bromide can prove upsetting. And now that we've established the fact that you're not a medical men, really your presence in my room becomes quite improper."

The unfortunate man was completely put out of countenance, but he tried to carry off the unfortunate situation with a laugh.

"Ha, ha! Very sharp of you, Miss Verity. Any time you want a job you drop in on us—22 Shoe Lane—you can't miss us. We're built on the American model—steel and black glass. Well, I don't know what my editor will say, but don't suppose you've seen the last of us."

"I suppose you'll come disguised as the corpse next time," she riposted. "Well, thank you for a very amusing interview. But, you know, you were really too interested in my adventure at the cottage. Doctors in these busy days simply haven't got the time to listen to all that personal chatter."

After she had gone she rang for the chambermaid. "Dr. Bennett insists on my remaining extremely quiet," she said. "I am to see no one, except Mr. Crook, if it is urgent. I shall be glad if you will make it clear I am not to be disturbed unless I ring. I am very tired and want to sleep."

But after the girl had gone she took the precaution of locking her door and then, withdrawing the key, of stuffing the lock with tissue paper, so that a master-key would be useless. She had not credited the Press with so much driving force. And next time she might be a little less wide-awake.

When Mr. Crook marched into the lounge that evening he was surprised to find Miss Verity sitting erect and apparenlty much entertained at one of the small tables. She even had a small glass of some pale yellow liquid beside her.

"You're supposed to be in bed," he told her in curt tones.

"I felt I might be more immune from attack in the lounge."

His heavy brow creased. "What's biting you?"

"That doctor you sent in . . ."

"Doctor? I sent no doctor."

"Just what I thought. But he said he came from you."

"All poppycock. You've been diddled, honey. . . ."

"Not nearly so much as the representative of the 'Daily Record.'"

Crook put back his head and burst into a roar of laughter that made one nervous lady snatch at her knitting in the belief that an air raid warning had just been sounded.

"That's a hot one. But you scotched him?"

"I didn't feel you would take such a step without warning me."

"You're a good partner," Crook told her admiringly.

"He seemed to think quite well of my capabilities. He said any time I wanted a job in the newspaper world I could go and see him in his black glass and steel office . . ."

"What's that?" said Crook sharply. "I thought you said the 'Daily Record'."

"I think so."

"You're an optimist," snapped Crook. "Wait here a minute."

Amazed, she saw him fling away into a telephone booth. He was away a few minutes; when he returned his face was dark with apprehension.

"Well, it wasn't the 'Record,' " he greeted her. "Didn't see how it could be. The 'Record's' got the grubbiest offices in Fleet Street."

"Then who . . .?"

"Did he offer you a nice little drink?"

Miss Verity suddenly turned pale. "He said—he wanted—Mr. Crook . . ." her voice sank to a dreadful whisper. "Who was that man?"

"Take it easy," Mr. Crook besought her. "You've done fine up to date. Don't go to pieces now."

"You think he was—the murderer?"

"It could be," Crook acknowledged. "You know as well as me it could be."

For an instant Miss Verity covered her eyes with her hand.

"Now, then," Crook encouraged her. "You better spill the beans, hadn't you? You and me are the Allies, remember. We've got to work together, night and day. We're in a tough spot, sugar, and don't you make any mistake about it."

CHAPTER NINE

The smell of powder, they say, stimulates the war-horse to battle. Danger from an unexpected quarter may arouse in the meek of this earth impulses of which they have never been aware, driving them on at a reckless speed towards a goal whose nature they suspect, but whose terrors they are prepared to face, if necessary alone. It must be confessed that Miss Verity was not altogether satisfied with her man of affairs. Certainly he had told her they were allies, and had bought her a second drink, but after that he had gone out as usual, merely warning her to take care of herself and remember she was a big girl now.

"If it had not been for my foresight I should probably be a fresh source of inquiry to the police," Laura told herself indignantly. It was perhaps natural that she should feel more apprehensive about the murderer's next move than Crook, since her life was at stake, whereas he had nothing to lose but his reputation. And a man as coarse-fibred as he had shown himself to be does not, Laura thought, set so much store by reputation as the daughter of a half-pay Colonel, even though she may have had to earn her own living all her life. Mr. Crook would never have written,

"I could not love thee, dear, so much
Loved I not honour more."

"He tells me to be careful and to stay in bed," Miss Verity told herself with some indignation, "but he never provided any defence against such an attack as was made upon me this morning. Upon my word, it seems to me that the sooner this ruffian is laid by the heels the better, and as Mr. Crook seems occupied with so many other matters it might be as well for me to take a hand myself." She remembered, certainly, the unfortunate consequences of her last attempt to solve the mystery, but she stoutly maintained that, but for the Len Sinclair incident, the police might not even yet have been incited to take up the case.

Lying awake during the night a certain number of details in connection with the case returned to her mind, and she formulated one of those fantastic theories that do sometimes, by some process entirely divorced from logic, contrive to be true. So far as she could judge, there could be no possible danger to herself in making a few local inquiries. She would be careful not to be out alone after dark, and she would not allow herself to be side-tracked. If the facts supported her new suspicions, she would confide in Crook, and leave the actual work of proving the case in his hands. In the meantime, it was refreshing to think of herself as no longer a pawn in his game.

She set out, therefore, after breakfasting in bed, wearing her usual dark suit and small black hat, and carrying an umbrella, despite the promise of a fine day. For she might meet cows on her journey, and although to Miss Verity, as to so many women, all cows are bulls, no matter what their functions, she believed equally implicitly that the rapid opening and closing of an umbrella will drive off the fiercest cattle. Thus equipped, she caught the little bus at the pierhead and travelled as far as Butler's Wood. She dismounted near the private footpath, and began to ascend. She had not gone far before she came upon a small group, consisting of a young man, a young woman in slacks, and a policeman. All three were talking with animation, but it seemed to her that as she approached their voices dropped, until, by the time she had come abreast of them, they were quite silent. She glanced sideways at them as she passed, and was surprised and a little dismayed to recognise the young man as Harry Fennel. She made the barest sign of recognition and plodded valiantly upwards. The snow had frozen over, and it was difficult to walk fast. If the police intended to search every drift, reflected Miss Verity grimly, they had their work cut out.

You'd have to cut through some of those snow banks with a pickaxe. She had not gone very much farther when she heard the sound of footsteps behind her, and a minute or two later Harry Fennel's voice called her name.

"Miss Verity?"

She stopped dead, her heart suddenly dropping in her breast. Why was he following her like this? She looked rather miserably at her umbrella. A bull might be alarmed by so feeble a weapon, but a young man who already had one crime on his conscience was a far more potent foe.

"Miss Verity, stop one minute. There's something I want to ask you."

She could feel herself trembling. During the last few moments she had negotiated a bend in the lane, so that they were now out of sight of the policeman and the unknown girl. They were not, she supposed, entirely out of hearing, but she could hardly scream for assistance before any violence had been offered her.

The young man came nearer. "What is it?" asked Laura quickly.

"I want an explanation from you," he said, and though the words sounded simple enough there was something sinister about the manner in which they were delivered. "You've not been a very good friend to me," Mr. Fennel went on in meaning tones. "So I just thought I'd ask you what it all meant."

With each word he seemed to approach nearer and still more near.

"A friend?" quavered Miss Verity. "Why, we don't know one another at all. We just happen to be staying in the same hotel, don't we?"

"Yes," agreed Mr. Fennel. "That's all. You never set eyes on me before—did you? Did you now?" he added more intently as she remained deprived of speech.

"I—no, of course not."

"Of course not," he agreed in a pleasanter tone, "and that makes it all the more curious."

Miss Verity had backed as far as she could, and now she missed her footing and stumbled against the hedge. Fennel stretched out his hand to steady her; Laura barely suppressed a scream.

"I don't understand you," she muttered, looking desperately up and down the path.

"I'm wondering whether it was you who put the police onto me," he suggested. "And if you did, why you thought of me? It's a perfectly simple question, and there ought to be a perfectly simple answer."

Miss Verity pulled herself together. "There is," she agreed. "But I can't tell it you now. I—have an engagement and I'm already late. But this evening—at the hotel——"

To her relief he seemed to accept this solution. "About six?"

"About then." Crook was generally back by six. It should be all right.

"I didn't expect you to admit you'd turned the police onto me," he told her in candid tones. "I can't imagine what on earth . . ." There was now a look in his eyes Miss Verity had begun to recognise. A bit loopy, it said. Dangerous if not restrained. She straightened her back.

"I'm keeping you from your friends," she panted. "And as I told you, I am late myself . . ." Would he guess what she was doing here? Whom she was coming to visit?

If he did he didn't seem interested. With a cheerful nod and the reminder, "Six o'clock to-night, then, and don't try and fob me off with that amateur policeman of yours," he turned and was gone. Laura stood perfectly still. She heard his voice speaking and the girl's in response. The policeman seemed to have disappeared. Miss Verity increased her pace. She was too far off to hear what the couple were saying, but she felt that the farther away from them she could place herself the better. A few minutes later she struck left into what were called Harper's Woods; here the path was so crooked that she sometimes lost sight of it altogether and began to note outstanding trees or fallen trunks, in order that she should find her way back. Her goal was the farm whence, in happier circumstances, she would have fetched her milk and eggs, and she had almost despaired of discovering it when an abrupt turn brought her in sight of an enormous snow man, wearing the usual dilapidated billycock hat.

"The farm cannot be far off," she told herself, her heart lightening, for this was clearly the work of the children of Mrs. Home. And indeed within a very few minutes she heard the familiar clucking of hens, and then came in view of the house itself. "Farm" was a rather grandiose description for the little building of black staves, with its enclosures of poultry securely wired in. Where they kept the cows she could not imagine, though afterwards she realised that she had by this time almost reached the top of the wood; above the ranks of trees was open pasture land, and here the cows grazed. Shivering with the cold, for it seemed to her as though the temperature at this height was lower than ever, Miss Verity made her way up to the gate in the paling that surrounded the farm and looked round for a bell. I wish I had a fur coat, she thought inconsequently. No wonder the Esquimaux . . . and then perceiving no bell she timidly opened the gate and stood just inside. But I'll never have one, she went on, still referring to the coat. It wasn't important. Lots of women went to their graves without owning such a treasure.

"Yes, please," said a small voice and she found herself facing a girl of about thirteen, who seemed to have appeared from the ground. This, she supposed, was Mrs. Home's Rosie.

"Can I speak to your mother?" she inquired, a little diffidently. The habit of years dies slowly, and she was afraid the woman would put her down as a Nosey Parker.

"I'll see," said the child. Miss Verity came up to the porch. No matter how many warm clothes you wore, you felt skinned in such a temperature.

Inside the house were Mrs. Home and her three younger children, the smallest of whom, a boy of four years old, was roaring lustily. He wanted to go out and play in the snow.

"D'you want to freeze to death?" demanded his mother, unsympathetically.

"Yeth," roared the small boy.

Mrs. Home pushed him rather roughly aside and came forward to greet her visitor.

"Yes, miss. Bobby, if you don't give over screaming I'll give you something to yell for."

Rosie tactfully hustled the child out of sight, though not out of hearing, and Miss Verity explained that she had been walking and had missed her way and was very cold, and wondered if she could possibly have a cup of tea. Seeing from the woman's consternation that this was not a good beginning, she added quickly, "Or perhaps you could let me have some hot milk. It is a long way back to the road, and I am afraid of catching a chill."

Mrs. Home's face cleared. "I could give you that with pleasure. Rosie!"

Rosie's voice yelled back, "Yes, Mum."

"The lady wants a glass of hot milk." She looked round the untidy room, trying to find a chair to offer the visitor. Eventually she pushed a headless doll called Hitler off a horsehair couch, shoo'ed away a cat that looked as though it might give birth to kittens at any moment, and invited Laura to sit down. This Laura did rather gingerly.

"Thank you so much. I'm afraid I've come farther than I intended. What very extensive woods these are. Don't you find it a bit lonely here?"

The woman nodded. "If it wasn't for the children I'd feel buried alive."

"Your husband . . ." ventured Laura.

"Don't see much of him. Too busy. Still, there's not much time to mope."

"I should think not, with your big family. Though I expect your eldest girl helps you a lot."

"Rosie's none too bad," agreed the woman indifferently.

"I walked up that footpath from the main road," Miss Verity continued. "There seems to be a lot of policemen about. Are they looking for spies, do you think?"

The woman uttered a rusty-sounding laugh. "I'd be sorry for any spies that got caught in this part of the country. No, miss, as a matter of fact they're looking for the body."

"The body?" Laura tried to look horrified, surprised and interested. Her common sense told her that the woman would be only too glad of an opportunity to talk, if she didn't suspect an ulterior motive.

"Yes. There's a cottage in Butler's Woods—well, you wouldn't see that, of course, because the police have closed the woods to the public. A Miss French lived there for more than twenty years and nothing ever happened—she used to get her milk and eggs from us—but she was going away for a bit of a holiday and she let the cottage to a lady from London. And the first night she arrived there was a body there."

"You mean, the lady from London . . ."

"No, no. She's all right. But she says she found the body of a girl. Mind you, no one else has seen it, but the police are looking. . . .They'll look till Christmas if you ask me."

"You mean, you don't think it's there?"

The woman shrugged. "Well, it's funny it should walk off the way she says it did."

"But what would be the sense of inventing a body?" asked Laura earnestly.

"Can't tell. P'raps she's one of these actresses from London. They say they'll do anything to get their names in the papers."

Here, fortunately, Rosie appeared with the hot milk in a glass, carefully balanced on a blue saucer. Mrs. Home stood up.

"Oh, please don't go," urged Miss Verity. "I am so much interested in what you were telling me."

Mrs. Home waited until her daughter had returned to the younger children and went on, "I remember when I first married, fifteen years ago that was, and we came here, they found a body in one of the hollows, just bones. He must have been there years, they said. They never found out who he was."

"You think it might be years before this one's found?"

"Always supposing there is a body."

"It's all most exciting," said Laura, beginning to sip her milk.

"Like a film, isn't it? Odd, though, that it should happen the minute Miss French left. There's some—my husband's among them—who think that's queer, too."

"You don't think that Miss French knows anything about it?"

Mrs. Home made an inconclusive gesture. "Mind you, I'm not saying anything. I don't know anything. But what did she want to go away for, she that hasn't stirred out of the place for five and twenty years? Staying with friends, she told me, but they're funny friends that never so much as write to you, Jim Masters, the postman, says he can count the number of letters she's had in all that time on the fingers of his two hands, not using the thumbs."

This aspect of the case had not previously occurred to Miss Verity.

"Of course," continued Mrs. Home, who was clearly enjoying herself, "they do say she was disappointed in love and that's why she buried herself here all these years."

That might be true, but it didn't explain why she should suddenly uproot herself, thought Laura.

"What sort of age was she?" she inquired, in a desperate attempt to keep the conversation going.

"If she'd been hanging since she was fifty, she'd be a long time dead," was Mrs. Home's graphic reply. "She's been coming here for her milk ever since I've been here; from the look of her you'd think she never ate anything else, but they say she would take a basket and skurry round Brighton on Friday, doing her shopping. A long gray weed of a woman, looking as though her clothes had grown on her. You'd think she'd just popped out of her coffin to have a word with you and was going straight back."

"I wonder how she heard of this place."

"She came from Brighton, my husband says, and when she was a girl she was fond of walking. The mooney kind, I dare say. I don't blame the man, whoever he was, not wanting to get tied up for life to that. You'd think you were dead and buried yourself to see her opposite you at breakfast."

"And does anyone know where she's gone?"

"I couldn't tell you, but I don't suppose she'll be best pleased to hear about the body being found on her place. Of course, the London lady didn't stay. She might be a corpse herself now if she had. Why on earth she ever wanted to come beats me."

"Perhaps she'd been disappointed in love, too."

"Beats me how any woman can let a man upset her like that," brooded the farmer's wife. "What I always say is, how can they tell what they mayn't have been saved? Anyway, we never set eyes on this second lady, because she went straight down to the police, and for all I know she's gone back to London again, though Jem says he believes she's at one of the Brighton hotels."

"I should imagine she wouldn't want much publicity. It must have been a great shock for her."

"These actresses are accustomed to shocks. They like 'em. Well, think of the lives they lead. Kissing strange men all over the stage." Mrs. Home, reflected Laura, seemed to have a down on actresses. "'Course, it frightens the children a bit, seeing so many police about, but I don't let them wander in the woods at the best of times. Too dangerous. I believe they've had ever such a job to keep out the crowds, though. Morbid, I call it. All hoping to be the one that finds the body. Still, all they've found so far has been a heap of snow covering some branches, and if you ask me that's probably all they ever will find."

"Why should anyone go to Miss French's cottage?" asked Laura, slowly draining the glass of milk.

"Beats me. P'raps Miss French could tell us a bit more about that. Will you have another glass of milk, Miss?"

"Oh, no, thank you," said Laura quickly. "It was most delicious, but I won't have any more, really. It's much better than I get in my hotel, though it is so expensive."

"I know these hotels. They skim the cream off before they serve the milk, which isn't straight with the dairymen, because they get a name for delivering inferior milk. Still, I know mine's good, if I say it as shouldn't, and what you had was warm from the cow. Seemed a shame to heat it, really."

Laura, who detested the mere thought that milk came from a cow, and liked to imagine it was dropped from heaven in sealed containers, said again, this time a little more faintly, that it was delicious, but she really wouldn't, thank you.

"I dare say Miss French will be coming back?" she suggested, taking out her purse.

"Nobody seems to know where she is."

"She must have left an address for letters."

"She never had none. Still, I suppose somebody knows. It's nothing to me, anyhow, except that I've lost a good customer, and that's a thing none of us can afford these difficult times." She brought Laura her change. "Of course, they do say she was a miser," she threw out casually. "Well, you can never tell. There was a piece in the paper the other day about an old man that begged in a London square for twenty years and left ever such a lot of money."

"Of course, if that story got about," began Miss Verity, and stopped. Because, after all, it wasn't Miss French but the Penniless Ivy Green who had been strangled. Still, she had picked up quite a few hints, and she felt that the bitterly cold journey had been well worth while. At the door she flung out a last inquiry. "I wonder if she took much luggage."

"She can't have taken much. You can't get a car up to the door these days."

Miss Verity nodded. She remembered Miss French opening the door of a press and explaining that she proposed to leave this cupboard locked, since, she explained, she couldn't take all her clothes and papers with her. The police had forced this cupboard when they were examining the cottage in case the body had mysteriously locked itself up inside. But naturally there had been nothing inside it but a very few clothes and some papers in a wooden box. Although summer time had been instituted for some weeks, it was already quite dark when she left the farm. She hurried down the path, getting a momentary shock as she turned the corner and met the snowman. He was really remarkably like Mr. Crook, she thought, and that reflection made her chuckle, and she had reached the high-road before she realised how quickly she had come. Digging in the woods was sporadic now; soon the police would give up for the night. She wondered whether they left anyone on guard or whether the cottage would be available to a daring raider, say, at midnight. Travelling back in the bus she arranged in her mind such pieces of information as she had contrived to glean at the interview, and began to lay plans for to-morrow's activities.

CHAPTER TEN

Her conversation with Mrs. Home had taken longer than she had intended, and it was well after six when she reached the Royal Crescent Hotel. Young Mr. Fennel was waiting for her, a glass of something in his hand. A second glass, presumably for her entertainment, stood on the little round table. Miss Verity had not the slightest intention of tasting its contents, and she began to shake a little at the thought of the peril to which she was subjecting herself.

"Still, he can scarcely offer me violence in this public place," she reminded herself. "I wonder how many people knew that Miss French was leaving her cottage on Tuesday morning? Did Ivy Green know? And is there any truth in the story that the woman was a miser?"

But she said none of this as she murmured a conventional apology for keeping the young man waiting.

"I must just change my shoes," she explained. "They are a little damp."

From her room she telephoned to Mr. Crook, thinking that it might be as well to enlist his aid after all, but no one answered the telephone and after a moment she hung up. A quite unreasonable rage shook her.

"Really, considering the danger we both know I am in, he is remarkably casual," she told herself, drawing out a pair of shoes that looked as though their proper place should be a Victorian museum, so decorated were they with small black beads and ribbon bows. "Well, then, I must proceed under my own steam, as they say in the Navy. And perhaps it is just as well that he is not here. He is like all professionals, believing no amateur is of any use. If I were to offer him my theory he would probably only put back his head and give one of those hearty vulgar laughs of his. Give it a rest, sugar, he would say." She winced at the thought. No, on the whole one was able to look after oneself. It was no thanks to Crook that she wasn't already being measured for her shroud. Taking up a little leather she polished her nose under the impression that she was powdering it, pinned back a wisp of blue hair, and went downstairs.

"I am afraid I must have almost exhausted your patience," she observed politely. "No, I won't drink anything, thank you. I have been walking, it was such a pleasant day, and I have got rather warm."

"Well, it's not what I'd call a pleasant day," murmured Harry Fennel. "Matter of fact, you're looking a bit done in. A drink's just the thing to pep you up."

"Later, perhaps," temporized Miss Verity. "Now, what is it you have to say to me?"

Instantly his pleasant look vanished, to be replaced by one more stern and threatening.

"See here, Miss Verity, I want to know what it is you've got against me."

"I? But that's absurd."

"That's what I feel, but all the same it's you who've put the police on to me, isn't it? Don't say it isn't, because I happen to know it's true. Now, why?"

Miss Verity decided to take the plunge. "Because you were in her confidence, you knew her, you might have been able to tell them the names of her men friends. She did your nails the day before she disappeared, didn't she?. Well, she might have told you what she intended to do the following afternoon."

"She might, but she didn't. Come on, Miss Verity, let's have the truth."

"That is the truth," protested Laura. "Naturally, the police were anxious to get in touch with anyone who might be able to help."

"Quite so, only, you see, I can't."

"They couldn't know that. I quite appreciate," she added quickly, "that they don't even know for certain that the dead girl is Ivy Green."

Mr. Fennel seemed to hesitate for a moment, then he asked, "Do you suppose you could recognize her again?"

A strong shudder ran through Miss Verity's small frame. "After all this time, I couldn't say . . . I think I should know her clothes."

"I mean, if you saw a photograph of her, would you know from that if it was the girl you saw at The Nook?"

"Have you a photograph?"

For answer the young man put his hand into his breast pocket and drew out his wallet. From an accumulation of papers he produced a small snapshot that he handed to his companion. Laura took it gingerly, wondering what his game was, as they say. Perhaps he realized at last how absurd it was to pretend that he hadn't known the girl. All the same, this candour made her additionally suspicious.

Carefully she inspected the picture. "It's not very easy to say," she told him, for this bare-headed radiant young figure seemed to have little in common with the crumpled body on the bed, "but yes, I think that is her."

"Well, that's Ivy Green."

Miss Verity resolved to be as bold as her companion. "This must be so painful for you," she murmured. "Since you were so fond of her . . ."

Fennel seemed to turn the expression over on his tongue. "Fond?" he repeated a little doubtfully. Well, I don't know. It was hardly that. I didn't know her well enough."

"Still, if you carry her picture about with you," insinuated Laura.

"I wouldn't draw too many conclusions from that. The fact is, she happened to show me the snapshot once, and I said, as one does, 'Is that for me?' and she said, 'If you like,' but I've hardly looked at it since. It was only when all this trouble began that I routed it out and thought I'd show it to you to see if you could identify it. But if you've been building romantic castles about her and me, you can demolish 'em. She was a pretty little thing, attractive, too, in her way, and so young, just a kid. She didn't seem to have anyone to look after her, only an aunt in Folkestone, and she didn't get on with her; she lived in a hostel where everyone else was old enough to be her mother, and of course they were always ready to give her advice and read her lectures. I've often thought some of the silly things she did were a sort of defiance, the kind of things children do and get smacked for and so learn better. But there wasn't anyone, so to speak, to smack her; if there had been she'd probably be alive now. She went out with this chap and that, quite openly, because it amused her to think she was shocking the old pussies. I'm certain there was no more to it. I've never believed myself that she cared two straws about this married fellow who occasionally took her to the pictures; she knew nothing could come of it, but it gave her a bit of a thrill; she hadn't any regular boy friend, you see, and you can't have a very exciting life on what they pay girls in a place like this, even with the tips thrown in."

"She certainly seems to have confided in you, Mr. Fennel," observed Miss Verity thoughtfully.

"I wouldn't call it confiding. It was boasting, really, showing off like a child, as I said. Really, she was awfully young for her age. That was a thing that used to worry me a bit on her account, because you know as well as I do that there are plenty of cads about who aren't above taking advantage of anything as silly as Ivy. (How he expected Miss Verity to know this she couldn't imagine, but she felt vaguely flattered at the assumption.) She was only eighteen, you see, and I think sometimes she was damned lonely."

"So you used to take her out?"

"I took her to the pictures two or three times, and dancing once, and I bought her some earrings from that place in the Arcade for her birthday. There was nothing in it. Why, you can see for yourself what a kid she was."

Miss Verity, who had been brought up in an austere manner that had regarded eighteen as being a responsible age, said very little but, "She is rather pretty, isn't she?"

"It wasn't her features so much as her manner. I felt in an odd sort of way responsible for her. You see, I hadn't been in this country long and I came over without knowing anyone, so we sort of drifted together. She was just the kind that comes a fearful cropper through sheer idiocy."

"As she seems to have done."

He looked at her in some resentment. "You're blaming her for getting herself murdered."

"I can't see that it was in the least necessary. If she hadn't gone prying into a house that wasn't hers . . ."

"You don't know the circumstances. Perhaps she hadn't any choice."

"I'm afraid I can't agree there. It can scarcely be imperative for anyone to enter somebody else's cottage. Particularly as the owner was absent."

"I don't suppose she knew that. I don't suppose anybody did. Why should they? Miss French was the sort of person who kept herself to herself. A most forbidding woman."

"That makes it all the more extraordinary that a girl who didn't know her—for I take it, she didn't—should go to such a remote spot in such weather."

"You'd have to ask Ivy why she did that," said the young man gloomily.

"I think she went out to meet a man called Harry."

Young Fennel started. "Why do you say that?"

"Because, when I found her, there was a letter or part of a letter in her hand, and is was signed Harry."

"And that's why you picked on me? But there must be tens of thousands of Harrys in England, and I dare say she knew a dozen herself. Why, I don't suppose it was even in my handwriting."

"I don't know what your handwriting's like, of course," said Miss Verity coolly.

"I can soon show you." He pulled an envelope out of his pocket.

"There's pen and ink on that table," suggested his companion helpfully.

"No, thanks. I always use my own pen." He scrawled a few lines. "Well, was that your precious handwriting?"

"It's difficult to tell, isn't it, especially as you haven't signed it."

He put his name at the bottom. Miss Verity shook her head. "I couldn't say. I dare say it isn't a bit the same. The police would have to compare it, wouldn't they?"

He looked at her, a long, heart-chilling look. "Are you really trying to get me gated for this? You'll be sorry if you do."

Miss Verity stood us. "It's really nothing to do with me," she said. "As Mr. Crook would tell you, the professionals have no use for amateurs, and that is what I am."

"You seem to be able to set the police of half the county by the ears."

"Do you believe in Providence?" inquired Miss Verity unexpectedly.

"Providence?"

"I was thinking that perhaps Providence sent me to that cottage in order to ensure that justice shall be done."

"Justice!" repeated Mr. Fennel.

"You remember what is said in the Bible about the man who put his hand to the plough and then looked back? Well, I don't mean to look back."

He put out his hand and caught her wrist in a grip of iron. "I warn you, Miss Verity, you'd be wise to keep out of this. There's such a thing as an action for slander. If you stop to think for a minute you'll realize how much harm can be done by spreading rumour or—speculation."

"You mean—to you?"

"Perhaps. Just because I like a pretty girl and am a bit sorry for her, doesn't mean I'd murder her. Why should I? It isn't as if I were in love with her or anything like that. As a matter of fact," he added, speaking more rapidly, "I'm hoping to marry someone quite different. Now do you see how much harm you could do me by spreading this sort of yarn? You know what women are like, and if Julia—Miss Addison—hears this sort of talk—well, it's enough to put any girl off."

Miss Verity identified Julia at once—the girl in the blue slacks to whom he had been talking that afternoon. She probably didn't so much as realize that he was on speaking terms with the little manicurist. But—didn't that provide a motive for murder? Suppose the affair had gone a bit farther than he was ready to admit? It still didn't explain why they should have made The Nook their rendezvous, but that objection remained in every circumstance. She asked abruptly, "Did you know Miss French?"

His reaction was instant and unexpected. "Look here," he said angrily, "what are you driving at? Why on earth should I know her?"

"I can't imagine. But I just wondered."

"You'd be safer if you kept your speculations to yourself," he warned her. "Remember what I'm telling you. You haven't an atom of proof, and you go round spreading stories that may ruin me. It isn't wise, you know."

Miss Verity looked hurriedly over her shoulder. If Crook had appeared at that moment she would have hailed him as her guardian angel. But Crook wasn't available. At that very moment, though she didn't know it, he was sitting happily in one of his favourite London bars, talking in a manner that would have made Miss Verity's blood run cold. The only person in sight was Miss Buckler, and though she didn't like Miss Buckler, even she seemed a saviour. "Good evening," she called. Miss Buckler came over.

"We're just having a drink," Miss Verity observed.

"That's all right. Thought from the look of it you were having a row." Miss Buckler was as outspoken as ever.

"Why on earth should we?" asked Harry Fennel. He had released Laura's wrist as soon as Miss Buckler came in their direction.

"None of my business." She turned to Laura. "Come to the surface again, have you? Wondered if you were going to be the next corpse."

"I've wondered that myself," agreed Laura.

She saw Miss Buckler's eyebrows lift. "Like that, is it? Ah, well, we all come to it." She looked down at the untouched glass of sherry. "Who isn't thirsty?" she inquired.

"I'm not," said Miss Verity.

"H'm!" Miss Buckler glanced meaningly from one to the other. "Pity to waste a good drink." Her predatory fingers closed round the glass.

"No, no," exclaimed Laura quickly. "You mustn't have that. We'll order you one."

"I though you said you didn't want it." Miss Buckler sounded huffy.

"I mean," Laura improvised rapidly, "I've had a sip or two already. But of course you must have one. Have one with me."

"Thank you," said Miss Buckler dryly. "I can pay for my own drinks." She was clearly offended. Young Fennel did nothing to help. He looked malevolently from the floor to Miss Verity, without paying the least heed to

Miss Buckler. He did not, she noticed, urge either of them to take the untouched drink, nor did he give Laura away. She hadn't touched the sherry and they both knew it. Suddenly Laura saw the lift open, and with an incoherent mutter she darted into it like a rabbit into its burrow, leaving Miss Buckler like an outsize ferret on the polished floor of the lounge.

"I am quite sure that woman thinks I am mad," reflected Miss Verity. But, after all, it mattered very little what anyone thought. In a few weeks she would have ceased to hold communication with inhabitants of this planet; for none of these recent developments had altered her intention to retire from life before the longest day of the year. As these reflections passed through her mind, it occurred to her with a slight sense of shock that perhaps the precise date would be no longer a matter of personal choice. She firmly believed that one attempt had been made on her life since her arrival at the Royal Crescent Hotel, and she had possibly foiled a second by her refusal to drink her sherry half an hour ago. As she smirked a little at the thought of her discretion a new and (to her) terrible thought flashed into her mind. She had heard that hotel servants frequently finished off drinks left by the clientele; it would be appalling if one of them should suffer on her account. But was it conceivable that Fennel would take such a risk?

"But it isn't a risk, really," she argued. "Suppose something of the kind does happen? It would not be an instantaneous death. Of that I am certain. Very well, then. The glass containing the sherry would be washed before the first symptoms began to betray themselves. The sufferer might die without being able to answer questions, and even if he did give an account of what he had eaten and drunk he would scarcely include a glass of sherry paid for by one of the guests. He would not accuse a guest of such an act." In which Miss Verity greatly exaggerated the chivalry of waiters, and also their innocence. There is nothing waiters in the Royal Crescent would not believe of one of their visitors. Nevertheless, she could not rest. It was possible that Mr. Fennel would contrive to upset the glass; but on the other hand he might retain it in the hope that she would be persuaded to drink it later on.

"If I am to have any basis for my suspicions I must have evidence," Miss Verity declared to the uninterested fittings of her luxurious room. Somehow I must contrive to have that drink sent up here."

Colouring a little, she picked up the room telephone and called the hotel porter.

102

"This is Miss Verity speaking from Room 478. I was having a drink in the lounge just now and I suddenly had to return to my room. Would you have the drink sent up to me?"

"Certainly, madam. What drink was it?"

"Er—sherry."

Was it her imagination or had there really been a horrified pause before the porter spoke? In any case, Laura realized now how she would stand with the personnel of the Royal Crescent. Worse still, was the thought that the drink might already have been disposed of, while the one brought to her room might have been poured out fresh from the bottle. She could not, however, voice her suspicions and felt she could only hope for the best.

The drink arrived a moment later and hard on the heels of the drink the ubiquitous Miss Buckler.

"Thought I'd come and make sure you weren't foxing again," she boomed. "What's been the matter, really?"

"My doctor considered a little rest—all this fuss and anxiety . . ."

"Don't see what you've got to be anxious about. Bet you haven't enjoyed yourself so much for years. This is a bit of a change from Earl's Court, what?"

"I was very happy in Earl's Court," returned Miss Verity, with dignified mendacity.

"You would be! All the same, y'know, it doesn't do to lose your head."

"I don't understand you."

"Always speak my mind," announced Miss Buckler, quite unnecessarily her companion thought. "And I tell you I can't stand seeing a woman of your age making a fool of yourself over a boy young enough to be your son. If you heard some of the things they say about you when you're not there, you'd open your eyes."

"You surely haven't come up here to repeat them to me," said Laura in despair.

"Not likely. No, but I think you're not half a bad sort and I just wanted to warn you. It isn't as if you knew that young man well. He's just told me he never set eyes on you till a few days ago, and you're dogging his footsteps and getting him to have drinks with you and never leaving him alone. It's a mistake, take my word for it. That's not the way to attract a man."

"I haven't the slightest desire to attract Mr. Fennel." said Laura furiously, opening the door of her built-in wardrobe and affecting to hunt for a non-existent wrap in order to hide her burning cheeks. What impertinence, she thought. What's it to do with her? Or—is it possible she's jealous? But she's as old as I am or very nearly.

"I don't say he isn't attractive," Miss Buckler continued. "But it's sheer cradle-snatching. After all—well, I'm forty-nine and you must be all of that."

"You don't understand . . ."

"I dare say I understand more than you think. You're like a lot of women—disappointed in youth, don't see why you should have been done out of your share of fun. But that young fellow's got a girl of his own. What's wrong with that fat chappie you show up with sometimes? Now there's much more sense in that—if he isn't a married man, that is . . ."

Miss Verity came out of the wardrobe, her face flaming, her voice trembling with rage. She was now very angry indeed.

"I consider this is quite unpardonable," she exclaimed, but she might as well have hurled her defiance against a young tank.

"Do you want to drive that poor wretch out of the hotel?" Miss Buckler demanded.

Laura stopped dead. She hadn't thought of that. Of course there was nothing to prevent Harry Fennel walking out and vanishing into thin air; and until she had formulated a definite case she didn't want anything like that to happen. At present the various scraps of information and the unrelated hints she had collated were like the odd pieces of a jigsaw puzzle, and as yet she could not fit them together into any coherent pattern. Until that happened she wanted all the players under her own eye.

"Suppose you think this is none of my business," snapped Miss Buckler.

Miss Verity did.

"Well, just thought I'd speak. Don't like to see you make a laughing-stock of yourself. Lots of things in the world besides men. That's all." She turned and stamped out of the room, leaving Laura still shaking and amazed. She lay down carefully on her bed. If she were not careful she might even faint.

"I must be cautious," she decided. "Nor must I take the risk of either of them waylaying me again."

She resolved not to be visible until she had completed certain inquiries; she therefore telephoned to the porter, asking to have her dinner sent up to her room. Crook might be back this evening, and she didn't want him to blow her new theory to smithereens with his loud vulgar laughter before it had so much as been put to the test.

"You keep right on, honey . . ." She could hear his voice in the silent room so clearly that she looked round in a hurry in case he had somehow slipped in. But he wasn't there. . . .

There remained, however, the little glass of sherry that she had steadfastly refused to touch. She might be crazy in supposing that it had been doctored, but she intended to take no further risks. Rising, she discovered a small bottle among her toilet articles and, emptying and washing this she carefully poured in the contents of the glass. Some of it was inevitably spilt, and this she mopped up with a piece of sponge she subsequently rinsed under the tap. She rolled up the little bottle in a piece of thick brown paper and attached a label: "Arthur Crook, Esq. For examination. Very urgent and private." This she put at the back of her dressing-table. To-morrow when she returned from her investigations she would hand it to him. By that time she would know more clearly where she stood and whether her suspicions were firmly grounded upon fact.

Down in the lounge Harry Fennel was turning the pages of the "Sporting and Dramatic" without any appreciation of the fine photography or witty and instructive letterpress. His thoughts were full of the odd little woman to whom he had been talking.

At last he stood up, casting the paper from him.

"I wonder what the hell she knows," he muttered to himself. "She can't have guessed anything—and that woman would never have told her. Why should she? All the same, there's something damned queer, and I don't like it, don't like it at all."

He looked out for Miss Verity, resolved to press the point after dinner, but she did not appear. Miss Buckler, however, was in evidence, and after a little hesitation he went over and spoke to her.

"Do you happen to know if Miss Verity is dining in her room?" he inquired.

"My stable-companion? I shouldn't be surprised. What d'ye make of her?"

"I think myself she's a little . . ." he hesitated, then tapped his forehead.

"I'm not so sure. I thought so at first, but now—well, I wouldn't be surprised if she hadn't been leading both of us up the garden."

"What on earth does that mean?"

"Well, you admitted yourself before dinner that she'd made a dead set at you. I thought at first she might be one of these women that can't leave a good-looking young man alone. But now I'm not so sure."

"I wish I had the faintest idea what you were talking about," exclaimed the bewildered young man.

Miss Buckler leaned a little closer. "You rich?" she asked meaningly.

Poor Harry Fennel nearly jumped out of his skin. "Rich?" he repeated. "I haven't a bean. I shall have to pop my cuff links to get out of this place. What on earth's all this got to do with Miss Verity, though?"

The woman drummed her big knuckles on the tablecloth. "Tell you something else," she volunteered. "What's a woman of that type doing in a luxury hotel? I bet she usually goes to Channel View or The Limes when she stays away. And who's that big. blustering chap she goes round with? I tell you, I don't like it when that sort of man is on easy terms with the staff. Looks a bit odd to me."

"I suppose all this means something, Miss Buckler?"

"Tell you another thing. Caught her trying to get into your room the other day. Didn't know I was there, of course. If you take my tip, if you want any cuff links left to pop, you'll hand 'em over to the manager till you want to take 'em round to Uncle. That's what I've done, anyway. Deposited all my valuables and spare cash with the management. They don't take any responsibility here, y'know. for anything you lose if you haven't had it locked up in their safe. Well, just thought I'd pass you the word. It's either you or your belongings she's after, and—well, I don't think it's you."

CHAPTER ELEVEN

It was past midnight when Mr. Crook returned. He asked the night porter if there were any letters for him or any messages. The porter, having handed over several bulky envelopes, told him that Miss Verity had asked for him earlier in the day. Mr. Crook grinned good-humouredly.

"Any sign of the body yet?" he inquired. "No? I must give the police a hint, Everything as usual." By which he meant that he wanted a large bottle of beer sent to his room; he said it was the best nightcap there was.

The next morning he was down early, eating an enormous breakfast. While he was stuffing ham and eggs down his throat he heard that he was wanted on the telephone. The message came from his colleague and employee, Bill Parsons, who gave him information carefully veiled, but of the utmost importance. Crook was a balanced person in all the ways that matter. He was letting himself become involved in the Missing Manicurist Mystery—the alliteration that would have irritated most people delighted him—in the same way as a man gives himself an evening's pleasure at a night club or a casino. It wasn't important, and he didn't care two pins who had killed the girl; but Miss Verity amused him, and as his work was also his pleasure it made an agreeable change from the job regarding which Bill had telephoned. Still, that was urgent enough; it looked uncommonly likely that Mr. Crook's client was going to get fifteen years for uttering counterfeit notes, and that prospect was unthinkable. The fact that Crook was convinced the fellow was guilty made the position all the more delicate.

So, "I'm coming," he told Bill promptly. "Hold everything. Shan't be long."

All the same, he found time to stop at the police station en route, where he found Inspector Relph and his subordinate, Carson, discussing the Missing Manicurist—only they called it The Nook Murder. Both were coming to the conclusion that Benton had reached at the outset—namely, that there wasn't really a body and that Miss Verity was either crazy or else one of those female detective novelists, who (as everyone knows) have no conscience, and don't a bit mind who they make a fool of, so long as their royalties came rolling in. Probably when her book was published she'd spill the beans to her readers, and put her sales into five figures.

Relph had just made this sour observation to his companion when he became aware of Crook's presence. The sight of this plump, cheerful red-faced Londoner, grinning brightly from ear to ear, put the final touch to Relph's exasperation.

"Well?" he said sharply.

"Precisely," returned Crook in bland tones.

"What do you mean by precisely?" snapped the inspector.

"Figure it out for yourself. You said, 'Well,' which actually was what I'd come to say to you—give you a tip, as it were. But I see you don't need it. I dare say you'll have some news for me when I come down this evening—that is, if I haven't seen it all over the placards before then."

He nodded with aggressive goodwill, tipped his atrocious bowler hat more arrogantly over one eye with its stiff sandy bristle of eyebrow, and jumped into his ramshackle car. He had his own methods of obtaining extra petrol and seldom travelled by train.

"When the police force can prevent murders as well as solve 'em I'll take out a season ticket," he used to

107

say cheerfully. "Nobody likes a good crime better than I do, but I don't want to be the principal feature. Besides, what 'ud the force do without me to lend the murderer a hand?"

Whether his enemies were really so numerous or so dangerous as he affected to believe no one was sure; but when Crook pointed out that they couldn't build railways without tunnels and that tunnel murders were uncommonly successful, no one had a good answer for him. Anyhow, whatever the reason, Crook went most of his journeys by road.

After the car had disappeared, with as much noise as a Messerschmitt 110, Carson observed, the two policemen stared at one another.

"Off his chump," suggested the younger disrespectfully. "If you ask me, sir, it's like an epidemic. First Miss Verity, then this chap . . ."

But Relph shook his head. "I'd sign an incarceration order for the old girl any minute it was put in front of me," he remarked. "But Crook's a different matter. That chap's not often caught napping, and he doesn't waste his time. If he came round here just to say 'Well' to us, that means something."

The next instant he was on his feet, snapping his fingers with exasperated excitement.

"Of course. My oath, what fools we are. Well."

"Yes, sir," murmured Carson, bewildered.

"Well, you fathead. Where does the water at The Nook come from? Not from the main. The house is too isolated and stands too high. It 'ud cost a fortune to take water up there, even if it could be done. No. Of course, it come from a well. That's what Crook meant."

"You mean, the body . . ."

"Of course. Have they come upon a well, by the way?"

"Not so far as I know, sir, and they've been searching pretty close."

"For something half of them are persuaded doesn't exist. But the well's another matter. Wells are concrete things. They don't appear and disappear in the course of an hour, as bodies apparently do. I'll come up and see about this myself. We'd better take ropes and some extra men on chance."

He was more worked up than he had been since the case opened. To tell the truth, he didn't much care for the flood of letters, many of them unsigned and some quite incredibly abusive, that had come pouring through the letter box since the affair gained publicity. Cummings had managed his side of it well. Although the police had learned nothing, he kept his public's curiosity whetted by meaningless hints that they assumed had some foundation. A number of readers, who always liked an opportunity for shying bad eggs, said portentously that it was scandalous the country should maintain a well-paid force that could prove itself so incompetent in a crisis. The best of these letters Cummings kept to himself for his private enjoyment. Relph had seen quite a number of similar efforts, but in his case the enjoyment was lacking.

Digging was going on with undiminished fervour in the woods. Relph, however, made straight for the cottage, still closely guarded by the police.

"Found anything?" he demanded of the man on duty.

"Not yet, sir."

"Found out where the well is? Yes, I said the well. Where the water comes from. It isn't likely to be in the garden. We'd have found it already if it had been. Besides, people who build cottages like these make things difficult on purpose. Now, then, how about that shrubbery? Done any digging there?"

"No, sir. It's pretty dense."

"It's not alone in that," snapped Relph. "We'll take a look round."

"All the same," he confided to Carson, "that chap's right. The bushes seem to grow in a solid formation. Besides, it doesn't make sense. A well's got to be more or less available, and I'd say this was definitely less." Carson was examining the position with a countryman's eye.

"There's something queer there," he said slowly.

"Just discovering that?"

Carson took no notice of his superior's irritation. "Of course, they've argued that if a man broke through a thick mass of shrubs he'd be bound to leave traces. Even if you were a fairy you couldn't get through that, specially if you were lugging a body in your arms, or dragging it after you, without smashing down some of the plants."

"Carry on," said Relph.

"And there aren't any busted bushes."

"Well?" said Relph. And swore.

"What I think's queer is that all the bushes aren't alike, which you'd expect in a place like this. I mean, if there were six of one and half a dozen of another, that wouldn't be queer, but when there's about forty of one and just one of another . . ."

"If you'd stop talking like the Red Queen we might get somewhere," Relph suggested with dangerous politeness.

"This is what I mean, sir. If you stand just where I am you'll see that near the middle there the bushes don't seem so close together, and yet there's no entry. But there's a bush here which is quite different from all the others. Well, why's it there?"

"The answer is a lemon. Come on."

"It's there because whoever planted it didn't want you to see there was a path leading into the shrubbery. Look at this, sir." He caught the branches of the scrub in question and gave them a good tug. "It's loose in the earth, and if it weren't for all the snow it 'ud be a whole lot looser. If you ask me, that bush is a plant. No, no, that wasn't meant to be funny. But I wouldn't be surprised, if you took that bush up, to find it had been uprooted from somewhere else not so long ago."

Relph stared. "You mean, you think it was deliberately put there to block the entrance?"

"It wouldn't surprise me," said Carson modestly.

"Fellow must have been a lunatic to take that chance. He must have known he hadn't much time. Presumably he saw Miss Verity go down the path and he'd guess she was going for the police . . ."

"There's one other solution, and that is he didn't know Miss Verity existed. He might think he had all the time there was. Nobody ever comes this way; it's much too high to be seen from the road. He wasn't likely to be disturbed. He thought he might as well finish off the job. Assuming that no one had seen the girl dead, no one would guess she came up here. It's the last place anyone would expect to find a stranger."

Relph, however, was still frowning. "But could he do it in the time? It was snowing that morning, remember. That 'ud hold him up."

"It would hold everybody else up, too, though. And though the snow was heavy it didn't last long, not on the Wednesday. Afterwards it came down all right and went on coming down. It could be done, sir."

"In the time? When did this woman say she left the cottage?"

"About half-past nine. She'd have to walk down to the high road, and she doesn't seem to have known about the private footpath, so she'd go down the drive. When she got to the road she'd have to wait for a bus. They don't run very often. The first comes out about nine o'clock, and there's another about 10.05 from Brighton. That would be the one she'd catch. Say it got here at

10.15 or 10.20. The snow might delay it a little. They are pretty old-fashioned, those buses. She couldn't be in Periford—the town, I mean—before twenty to eleven. Then she had to tell her story and get the police to come up here. It would be eleven to half-past before they arrived. The chap would have a good hour and ·more, even if he didn't come right away. It could be done, sir."

Relph nodded. "It could, Carson, though it all sounds a bit too much like something on the stage to please me. You'd better get a spade; or is there one at the house?"

They sent a man to make inquiries, and he came back shortly afterwards accompanied by the sergeant in charge of the digging operations.

"There wasn't a spade on the premises, only a fork and a trowel," this man explained. "We thought it queer."

"Perhaps we'll find the spade where we find the body," said Relph, his eyelashes flickering a little. "Look here, we want this bush grubbed up. Oh, just a theory of ours, that's all.

It was quickly obvious that a bush that has grown in the same place for five and twenty years does not allow itself to be pulled out of the earth with the speed with which this particular shrub was uprooted. In a very short time it had been removed from its place, and all the men could see the white and mutilated roots.

"Someone else dug them up not long ago," said the sergeant triumphantly.

"You don't say," returned Relph. "By jove, Carson, you're right. There is a path here. Pity about that snow. It's covered everything."

"Look at this, sir." Carson's voice was low with excitement. He put out his hand and detached a limp fragment from one of the nearby twigs. "That's a bit of material, silk of a sort. And didn't Miss Verity say the girl was wearing a silk scarf on her head? This might be a bit of that."

"It might," Carson agreed. "She said it was dark blue and this is green to my way of thinking, but that doesn't make any odds. She very likely didn't know the difference. Lots of people don't. Ah, we look as though we're on the right trail at last."

The denseness of the shrubbery had protected the earth from the heaviest falls of snow, and it was soon easy to discern the lid of a well set in a semi-circle of dark green bushes. Relph bent double to the earth.

"See this?" he demanded of his companions. "Some of these ground plants have been trodden and kicked aside quite recently. And some of the twigs are snapped.

By heck! I believe we're there. Later on, when the snow's melted a bit, we may be able to find the place where that bush originally grew. He must have been a hefty chap to drag it out."

"He's chopped the roots all to bits," said the sergeant dourly, and Carson contributed, "Before the snow there'd been quite a lot of rain. The ground wouldn't be too hard, you know."

There was a great iron ring in the lid of the well, which came up without much difficulty. This argued to Relph that it had been raised not so long ago. The men stood round the black hole and peered hopefully in.

"Don't stand like a row of dummies," said Relph. "D'you think the body's going to put its head over the top and say 'Good morning'?"

Carson took up a pebble and dropped it over the side. They all listened, and after an instant they heard a faint splash.

"There's water there all right," said Carson a little foolishly. "I'll bet it's cold."

"You shouldn't be a policeman if you value your life," Relph told him. "Come on, no sense wasting time."

It was a grisly job, but it was soon over. The youngest and lightest of the men went down the shaft; the rest paid out the rope. They heard a splashing noise as the body touched the water, waited with their hearts in their mouths, the sullenness of the atmosphere and the solitude of their surroundings adding to the macabre effect of the scene; then they got the signal to pull and slowly, slowly, they brought up their burden, reinforced by another burden, at the sight of which a cry broke from all four men. For now they realised for the first time why the murderer hadn't worried much about the time factor and the peril of discovery.

CHAPTER TWELVE

Miss Verity was, she firmly believed, taking no further chances. She had arrived at the stage where she thought everyone was doing his or her utmost to prevent her following her suspicions. Crook, Fennel, Miss Buckler—she wished to avoid them all until this evening. By that time she would know whether she was on a wild-goose chase or the right track. She therefore remained in bed for breakfast, and ascertained from the chambermaid that both Crook and Fennel had departed before she dared descend. Miss Buckler was less a danger than a nuisance, but fate favoured her there also, and when she reached the lounge she found it empty.

· At the desk she left a message that she would be back to dinner, though possibly not to lunch. In return she was told that Mr. Crook also expected to be back that evening. The clerk had no real notion what was going on, but he treated Laura with far more respect than formerly. Laura had just reached the street when she saw a police car coming down the road. She moved on hastily, and from her cover of a shop entrance she saw it stop at the hotel.

"It is what I might have expected," she assured herself. "They have come for me." They want to ask more questions. Or it may even be that they have discovered the body and wish me to attend the inquest."

Since such a course would seriously impede her own plans and might even compel her to voice her own (somewhat fantastic) suspicions, she darted into the nearest shop, which chanced to be a draper's and general outfitter's. She had forgotten her handkerchief, she explained mendaciously. Then, while she waited for a farthing change, she caught sight of the hat department and that gave her a fresh idea. If the police did not find her at the hotel they would certainly learn that she had only just left the premises, and would probably follow her. The clerk, she supposed, could give them a description of what she wore.

"Then I must disguise myself," she told herself firmly; she was finding life more enthralling each day, particularly now that she had established such a faith in her own abilities that she discounted any possible plot that might be formulated against her. Crossing to another counter she asked for some veiling. The assistant brought some stiff narrow net of the kind used for decorating inexpensive hats. Miss Verity shook her head.

"I want something thicker, with a close mesh," she explained.

"You mean, for use as a bandeau?" suggested a supercilious young lady, pronouncing the last word bond-o, which confused her customer for a moment. It proved, however, that this was precisely what she did want, and she bought a generous length. A man would need to be a magician to recognize any face hidden under that heavy covering. Next she asked for coloured scarves and chose a georgette one in a blurred floral pattern This accomplished, she went to the hats and chose a large garden hat in bright yellow straw. Carrying all her purchases, she made her way to a teashop where she instantly disappeared into the ladies' cloakroom. When she returned she was wearing the straw hat with the scarf twisted round it and floating out in long artistic ends behind, and had draped the veil over her small and insignificant face. It must now be obvious to everyone who she was—or rather, what she was—a woman who had no desire to be recognised, but who, at the same time, was ensuring that nobody who chanced to see her would forget her. She ordered a cup of coffee that was brought to her after a short delay; she had taken a table in a dark corner by the wall, and when she rose to leave the shop she left also the bag containing her own simple black felt hat, certain that it would be some hours before it would be found.

"And even then it is improbable that they will trace it to me," she assured herself. "Whereas, if the police are looking for me in a round felt basin, they will certainly not know me in my present headgear."

A good many people turned round to watch her solemn procession down the street. It was in any case early in the year for straw hats, and such a hat, so bright, so broad, so reminiscent of the Riviera or Blackpool, that is not easily distinguishable from it, attracted all eyes. Impervious to these curious and amused glances, Laura made her way on foot to the offices of Messrs. Hunter and Dickon, the solicitors to whom Miss French had referred her should any technical hitch occur during her tenancy of The Nook. Here she proposed to make a few discreet inquiries that might confirm her suspicions. Moving like an alert little sparrow she hopped across the roads and round corners until, about twenty minutes later, she was face to face with a trim young woman who looked at her in undisguised scorn. Miss Merriman knew all about women who went about to Brighton in hats of that description in March. Loopy. Not a doubt about it. Clean off her nut. They had quite a number of them at Hunter and Dickon at one time or another, all eager to start law-suits against non-existent foes, or to draw up wills leaving money they didn't possess to relatives who could never be traced. Or possibly she belonged to the class that is perpetually complaining to policemen that they are being followed by strange men for sinister motives.

Miss Verity, however, by no means discountenanced by the frigidity of her reception, proceeded to take the matter in hand.

"Will you kindly tell Mr. Hunter or Mr. Dickon that Miss Verity has called in connection with their client,

Miss French, the owner of The Nook. The matter is very urgent."

Like everyone else in Brighton, except a few old pedants whose boast it was that they never read the crime sheet, Miss Merriman knew all the developments of the alleged Nook murder, and her interest in this peculiar visitor increased.

"Have you an appointment?"

"You know perfectly well that I have no appointment. Had I had one I should have mentioned the fact."

The young woman, by no means deflated, went into the partners' office. Mr. Hunter had been dead for many years. Mr. Dickon was an old gentleman who only attended the office three days a week, of which this was not one, so Miss Verity saw the man who now organised the business and whose name was Wilkes. He was a solid, black-haired, black-browed, black-visaged individual with a ponderous legal manner.

"Ah, Miss Verity. Kindly take a seat."

Miss Verity did so.

"Miss French told me to come to you should any difficulties arise in connection with my tenancy of The Nook," she announced, coming to the point with commendable brevity. "As you are aware, difficulties arose from the very first, and I have come to discuss the position with you."

"Naturally we are at your service," began Mr. Wilkes heavily, "though it is hard to see how we can be of assistance."

"It is part of every agreement, as you are naturally aware, that a property shall be habitable. If not, rent is not due to the owners. It is my claim, in which my own lawyer will be prepared to support me, that The Nook is not habitable for reasons you know as well as I do."

Mr. Wilkes thoughtfully stroked his blue chin. He didn't for a moment believe she had a lawyer; if that had been the case, he would have been approached through that channel. But he seldom believed anything his female clients told him, and in Miss Verity he saw a woman cunningly endeavouring to wriggle out of her agreement.

"A nice point of law, Miss Verity," he remarked. "Of course, if you had found that the water supply was deficient or if the roof had fallen in or a wall crashed, then naturally you would have a case. But I can't recollect any precedent in such circumstances as the present. A court of law might well hold that the fact that a person had died in unfortunate circumstances on your premises, for technically they became yours from the morning of the twelfth, is no responsibility of the house's owner. Nor, since the body had been removed—the legality of such removal scarcely enters into it—within a few hours might they hold that the house was uninhabitable."

"You mean, you seriously think they would expect me to go on paying rent for a house in which a murder had taken place before my arrival?"

"I think you might find it difficult to sustain your claim in court."

"Then perhaps you will give me Miss French's address, so that I can get in touch with her."

"I'm afraid that's out of the question, Miss Verity. We are managing Miss French's affairs in her absence . . ."

"I don't call it managing affairs to wash your hands of them. If I bring a case, am I to understand that you will fight it?"

"My client might meet you on compassionate grounds, but as to that I should, naturally, have to consult her."

"Then will you kindly do so? And if I write her a letter, will it be forwarded?"

"She will, of course, receive all correspondence in due course."

Laura looked at him suspiciously. "That sounds very peculiar. She isn't in a madhouse or anything?"

Mr. Wilkes stiffened as though someone had suddenly thrust a poker down his throat.

"Certainly not."

"Then has she gone for a trip round the world? But she can't with a war on."

"I have assured you that correspondence will be forwarded, but you will realise that I am not in a position to say anything definite about her circumstances. As a matter of fact, I understand that Miss French left The Nook early on Tuesday morning, so that at the time that the young woman met her unfortunate death under that roof, you were legally the tenant. Miss—er—Green did not leave her place of employment until midday, by which time Miss French's liability for the premises had ceased. I am afraid you have no legal case against your landlady; but I will, if you wish, put forward a claim on compassionate grounds. Though I am bound to add that, if my opinion is asked, I shall feel compelled to advise my client against making any reduction."

Laura looked at him casually. "I don't propose to argue that point with you. I have my own lawyer, who will no doubt meet your legal objections. I take it you will not tell me where Miss French is at this moment?"

"I have already informed you that that is impossible."

"You'll have to tell the police, won't you?"

"The police?" Mr. Wilkes looked startled.

"They'll probably want her. After all, it is her house. They might even suggest she left the body there. Oh, I don't say I believe that, and I'm sure she'll have all the right alibis, but I'm equally certain she'll be expected to answer questions like all the rest of us."

Mr. Wilkes resolved to try the effect of a little sarcasm. "I take it, madam, you do not represent the police?"

"Do I look like a policeman—or a plain-clothes detective?"

Mr. Wilkes said nothing. This interview was not turning out at all as he had anticipated.

"I suppose if Miss French were implicated in this affair I should be able to reclaim my rent?" she suggested.

Mr. Wilkes made a pompous and horrified gesture. "Now, my dear lady, we are dealing with improbabilities utterly unacceptable to the legal mind."

"I should think women lawyers would be highly successful," observed Miss Verity with unexpected sharpness. "Nothing is inconceivable to them."

Mr. Wilkes judged it best to leave that comment unanswered. Miss Verity mused on, "There is no doubt that Miss French is a most extraordinary woman. Her manner of living—that love of solitude, coupled apparently with a dislike of humanity, shows that. She appears to have lived at The Nook without visitors or correspondence for a great many years. She has nothing to do with her relatives and inevitably a good deal of gossip is bound to circulate."

Mr. Wilkes pricked up his prominent ears. "It is not always wise to listen to gossip, Miss Verity," he observed severely.

"And yet how much one misses if one does not. For instance, it is common knowledge that, although she lived so frugally, she was actually a rich woman."

Mr. Wilkes froze . . . "Miss French's affairs were her own concern."

"And she saw to it that they shouldn't be anyone else's."

"You may not be aware, madam, that Miss French's only sister died some years ago. There was no reason why interest should be taken in her private affairs."

"Then she should have lived normally. If you bury yourself in a forest you must expect people to talk a lot. After all, she isn't the only person who's had an unhappy love affair."

"That," said Mr. Wilkes coldly, "I cannot discuss with you."

"I'm not asking you to. I'm only saying what other people must have said twenty-five years ago, that it is odd to cut yourself off from life because something goes a bit wrong. But perhaps there was something in the family?" She looked at him inquiringly. Mr. Wilkes understood at once what she meant, and hastened to vindicate his client's sanity.

"On the contrary, there has never been a hint of such a thing. I may say that this firm managed not only Miss French's affairs, but those of her father, Mr. Philip French, a most distinguished and respected resident. Why, he was Vicar's warden of St. Jude's for nearly twenty years."

"I don't wish to cast aspersions on the dead," Laura assured him quickly. "Only it's well known that some people do take a disappointment like that very much to heart. And I dare say she wasn't very young when it happened."

Hurriedly she subtracted twenty-five from forty, and made the answer fifteen. That, she thought, explained a good deal. The war had been responsible for a lot of peculiar engagements, and nothing short of war, she thought, could have encouraged the most courageous hero who ever faced the Boche to propose to such a dragon of a woman.

Mr. Wilkes suddenly let down some of his defences. "It was during the war," he agreed. "Naturally it was a great blow to her. She had been nursing at a local hospital and Mr. Fielding was one of the patients. The gentleman was a little younger than herself, and—after all, such things do happen."

"It is a pity she could not console herself with the reflection that it is better to find out a mistake before it becomes irreparable," suggested Laura softly.

"Quite so, quite so." Again Mr. Wilkes attended to his chin. "I dare say if the gentleman had jilted her for anyone but her own sister, and if he had not actually allowed the banns to be called, she would have felt less bitter about it. As it was . . .", he shrugged, and even smiled at Miss Verity as though acknowledging, for the first time since the interview opened, their common humanity.

"That, of course, would account for a great deal," admitted Miss Verity, generously meeting him half-way. "At least, it could not be urged that his motive was a financial one, since Miss French had means of her own."

Mr. Wilkes seemed suddenly to realise that he was being indiscreet. "Quite, quite," he said hastily. "Well, Miss Verity, I'll put your point to my client, and if you

118

care to write to her, I will see that the letter is read-dressed." He stood up to indicate that the conversation was at an end.

"Of course, nothing we've been able to discover so far explains why this girl should have gone to Miss French's cottage," Miss Verity mused. "However, as she was a very dark horse—Miss French, I mean—there may have been some connection."

"Nothing of the sort," spluttered Mr. Wilkes.

"Well, you aren't suggesting that Miss Green went up in a professional capacity, are you? I mean, I don't suppose Miss French ever had her nails manicured during the last twenty-five years of her life. She wasn't much of an advertisement for a beauty parlour, was she?"

Before Mr. Wilkes had recovered from the shock of that she had reached the door.

"I fail to understand your interest in my client's private life," gasped Mr. Wilkes, following her.

"Just natural curiosity," Laura assured him: "But of course you're right. Mr. Crook would be the first to agree that it's absurd to go about doing other people's work for them. We employ an extremely well-paid and adequate police force to deal with criminals," and on these words she swept out.

St. Jude's Church, they told her at the baker's on the corner, was in Apostle Street, about ten minutes' walk. Miss Verity, as keen on the chase as a bloodhound, made her way there immediately on foot. From her interview with Mr. Wilkes she had learned all and more than she had hoped. It was reasonable to suppose that the Vicar's warden's daughter (it sounded like a musical comedy hit) would have her banns called in her father's church. As she scurried along she thought of the story Mr. Wilkes had told her. Poor Harriet French. She must have been thirty at the time, and the younger sister might have been a good deal younger and she could certainly have been a great deal prettier without causing people to turn round in the street and look after her. Miss Harriet had doubtless taken her fiancé home to meet her family, and the damage had been done. Still, he might have broken it off before it came to calling the banns.

"However, Miss French may have hurried things rather," she reminded herself. "She seems a forceful kind of woman."

She switched her thoughts away from the human side of the affair to wonder whether records of banns were kept for five and twenty years. But I'm sure they must be, she consoled herself. I know I've sat thousands of times at the back of the church and listened to a string of meaningless names. Oh, yes, the record is practically certain to exist.

She said as much to the Vicar of St. Jude's, a tall dyspeptic man, not at all disposed to be helpful. He saw much, too much of women in church to welcome them at his vicarage. Besides, there was nothing noticeable about this one except her appalling hat.

"I am afraid you are inquiring for records a long way back," he said testily. "I have only been here since 1931; I know nothing of my predecessor's affairs."

"The records will have been preserved," insisted Miss Verity, standing her ground.

"If it is the baptismal register you require, that can be produced," he admitted grudgingly. "We expect strangers to contribute something to the upkeep of the church if they consult our documents," he added suspiciously.

"It is not the baptismal register."

Mr. Fenton instantly became more cheerful. "The Town Clerk's office would give you information about marriages and deaths."

"This is neither. It is the record of banns that must have been read in this church some time in 1915."

"Banns? I can't say that book will have been kept."

"But perhaps you could make certain."

He advanced other arguments with the intention of discouraging her, but he might as well have tried to budge a young tank. So at last, with an ill grace, he had the search made, and after some time he did find among papers that would otherwise lie undisturbed until his death or his relinquishment of the living, his predecessor's records of banns for the year in question.

"The month?" he inquired sulkily, but Miss Verity could not enlighten him. Patiently she insisted on turning the pages until at length she discovered what she sought. In November, 1915, the banns had twice been called of a forthcoming marriage between Henry Fielding of St. Martin's Church, London, and Harriet Ethel French of the parish of St. Jude, Brighton.

"Only twice," reflected Laura, aloud.

"Presumably the marriage did not take place. In fact, I see that there was a record of a third calling, but it is scratched out, so clearly something occurred to prevent the marriage." His manner suggested that it was, on the whole, a pity this did not happen more often.

."Thank you," said Miss Verity in her politest manner. "You have told me what I want to know."

She put half a crown into the box marked Church Expenses, and returned to the street. Her wrist-watch told her that it was now two o'clock.

"No wonder he was irritated. Probably his lunch will be ruined, and he suffers from indigestion in any case."

She decided not to return to the hotel until she had made a written precis of her impressions. She lunched at a little restaurant all arty blue check cloths and mob caps and the odds and ends of yesterday's food dished up with weird sauces, and labelled Three-Course-Lunch one-and-nine. Now, she thought, lingering over her cup of synthetic coffee, I really have something definite to put before Mr. Crook. Remembering that gentleman's vigorous conduct of conversations, however, it seemed to her that it might be wise for her to note down her points in writing and have the document sent to his room, so that he might read and digest it before they met face to face. These, coupled with the little bottle containing last night's unsampled drink, might give him a new respect for her intelligence and flair. Having left the Blue Dog, therefore, she turned into the free reading-room of a sect calling itself the Brighton Ethical Union. Here books on the Union's theory of existence, here and hereafter, were available at a central desk and, more important still, notepaper and pen and ink were provided. Equipping herself with a large volume, Miss Verity settled down to her task. The librarian took her for one of those earnest ladies who enjoy a middle-age of Doubts; there were not many other people in the place. A second elderly lady, equally uninspiring, sat at an adjoining table; a man read the daily paper on the left. This reading-room was a godsend to the respectable unemployed; they would spend half their day here, and it was impossible to turn them out without a most unpleasant scene. Miss Verity began making notes on a pad. She was a creature of method and disliked being hurried. Presently she took a fresh sheet and set out a heading.

Points for Consideration in the Brighton Mystery.

She evidently had a number of points to make, and she set them out with energy and precision. They covered two sheets and part of a third. When they were complete, she folded the pages and put them into an envelope, also provided by the Union and inscribed on the flap with its name and address; the envelope she addressed to Mr. Crook, Royal Crescent Hotel, and marked it Personal and Urgent. Then she rose and returned her book to the librarian.

"I hope you found all you required, madam," said he.

"Most interesting," said Miss Verity clearly, "and most

instructive. I shall probably be coming back. I wonder if you could tell me the time."

"Half-past four, madam."

"Thank you. I shall just manage to get a cup of tea at my hotel."

The clerk saw her go down the stairs and emerge into the street. He also saw her enter a sweet-shop where she remained for two or three minutes. After that, he lost sight of her. Later, it seemed as though she must have changed her mind about returning to the Royal Crescent for tea, because as late as seven o'clock there was no sign of her; nor was she in her accustomed place at dinner.

CHAPTER THIRTEEN

Mr. Crook, having completed a busy and prosperous day in town, jumped into his fantastic little car and ran her down to Brighton. On the posters he saw everywhere, "Brighton Mystery, Body Found," and grinned to himself.

"So Relph took my hint. I thought he would. Well, this is where the fun begins."

He didn't buy a copy of the paper; there would be plenty when he reached the hotel. Besides, he was of a suspicious mind and claimed to know newspapermen.

"I don't blame the poor devils," he would explain. "They have to earn their beer like the rest of us; but between you and me I wouldn't be surprised if the body was the corpse of a rabbit. Naturally, they have to use all their wiles to sell the paper, and if the public complains it can realize it's only getting what it's asked for. It wants sensations; it grouses if it don't get them."

On the seat beside him were the latest works of two of the acknowledged masters of detective fiction. This, besides the crime sheets of the press, was his only form of literature.

"I always like to learn," he would say modestly, "and the things some of these amateurs get away with beat my methods all to blazes. F'r instance, it wouldn't occur to me, if I was escapin' from the police, to hop up on a pedestal and pretend to be a statue of Abraham Lincoln, but that's what Jeremy Blood does in "The Blood at Wapping Stairs," and gets away with it, what's more."

This evening he had put all thought of The Nook murder from his mind and was occupied in an earnest endeavour to put a fast one over the police on behalf of a gentleman known as The Dude, and so enthralling was this consideration that he had reached Brighton before a satisfactory solution had struck him. Jeremy Blood, he knew, would have solved the problem by the time he'd left the suburbs behind. There were times when Crook envied Blood and all his brothers-in-law.

At Royal Crescent he stopped at the desk for his key.

"Any messages?"

"Miss Verity asked for you. She said she'd see you at dinner."

"Wonder what she's after now. Got an evening paper?" The man handed one across.

"I see the police have found their corpse," observed Crook chattily.

"Yes, sir. That was a surprise."

"Not to me. I knew it was there."

"I meant a surprise for the police," said the man with a discreet smile Crook didn't quite understand.

"They must be used to that."

"Quite so, sir."

There was still something Crook couldn't quite fathom, but he was never the man to allow psychological details to distress him. It was his uneducated opinion that nine-tenths of psychology is poppycock. Intelligent poppycock, because it made a handsome living for all sorts of chaps who would otherwise be lining up for the dole, but poppycock just the same. When he reached his room and flung himself on the bed to read about the police sensation—one of the headlines had called it that—Police Sensation at Brighton—he realised the meaning of Welch's expression. For what the police had found in the well in Butler's Wood had been the body of Harriet French.

"It 'ud take the Archangel Gabriel to pull a fast one on me," Crook liked to boast, but on this particular evening he gave the Angel Gabriel game and rubber. This was something that had never entered into his calculations. He read the account thoughtfully, then stretched out his arm and picked up his telephone. But though he called Miss Verity's number confidently enough, there was no reply.

For once he omitted his usual custom of spending some time in the bar before dinner; instead he dined early, looking round the while for Miss Verity. As the minutes passed and she did not appear, his uneasiness grew.

"Three corpses lay on the shining sand," he hummed mournfully. "It could be, y'know, it could be. And you can't say she doesn't ask for it, boarding strangers' cars and going off on her own the way she does. Damn it all, it's ten minutes to eight, and you can set your watch by her as a rule." He looked across the room and saw Miss Buckler sitting alone at her table. Although his spirit shrank within him, for she was the type of woman he most detested, he forced himself to go over and speak to her.

"What's happened to my young woman?" he demanded.

She looked back at him with eyes that shone furiously under dark brows.

"I was going to ask you. I asked at the desk and they just said she was out, but was expected back for dinner."

"I expected her back," said Crook mildly.

"Did you indeed? I wonder."

"I wonder, too."

"What do you mean?"

"What that last thing was meant to imply."

Miss Buckler turned more fully towards him, straightening her impossible tweed coat over her flat bust. He found himself wondering if she ever took off that frightful hat, even in her bath.

"Do you mean to tell me you didn't know she was going to London?"

"I didn't, though it don't surprise me much."

"It doesn't, eh?"

Crook shook his large head. "That woman's got enterprise. She's deceptive—in her appearance, that is. Looks as if she couldn't say Boo to a goose, but you take it from me she's got more spunk and pep than lots of women twice her size. She gets hunches and she follows 'em up. I don't say she don't have to be yanked out of some of the jams she gets herself into, but it takes a bit of grit to get into a jam."

"That's very convincing," said Miss Buckler, not looking convinced in the least. "I suppose you've known her for years?"

"A comparatively short time," said Crook airily.

"How much do you know about her?"

"I'm always ready to learn."

"Well, I'd like to know a lot more than I do. Why should she suddenly go up to London—for I saw her at the station waiting for the five o'clock train—and she was carrying a brown bag, a big brown bag. Now I'd like to know what was in it."

"I can guess," said Crook promptly. "Gas mask—for Miss Verity's one of your loyal citizens that wouldn't go to the bathroom without it—purse, registration card, pen and pencil, no powder or lipstick I think, handkerchief, no, two handkerchiefs in case of emergencies. . ."

124

Miss Buckler made an impatient movement. "Oh, don't waste time," she exclaimed. "She didn't want a bag that size for clap-trap of that description. I've had my doubts about her from the beginning. As you say, she's very deceptive."

"Well, she don't confide in me," said Mr. Crook with a sigh.

"I suppose you don't happen to know where she is now?"

"I've just been asking you," said Mr. Crook, rather indignantly.

"It might be worth getting into touch with the police," remarked Miss Buckler with meaning.

"Gott in Himmel! I'm never out of touch with them." He came away from the table feeling more apprehensive than ever. Miss Verity was capable of the most incredible follies; he wished he had some idea of how she had spent the day. Having gobbled down some Southdown mutton of quite unusual quality he went down to the Police Station, having impressed on every official in the hotel that if Miss Verity returned she was in no circumstances to be allowed to go out again. Relph was still on duty when he arrived.

"Glad to see you took my hint," he observed jauntily.

"It's no use your trying to fool me that you knew what we were going to find," returned Relph in sour tones. "You'd no more idea than we had."

"Makes it a bit more interestin', don't you agree?" inquired Crook with unimpaired spirits. "By the way, any sign of the other body?"

"We'll find it—if it exists. Or perhaps you can give us a line on that one, too."

Crook shook his head. "Fair do's," he reproached his companion. "Matter of fact, I may very likely hand you a third body to find in the course of the next day or two. Thought I'd just give you a yellow warning, so to speak. By the way, what did Miss French die of?"

"She was strangled by a silk scarf tied tightly round her neck."

"You know," said Crook after a moment of pregnant silence, "I feel uncommonly like taking off my tie before I go back. All these throttlings give me a queer feeling. And I would," he added ruminatively, "if it weren't that it's a made-up bow and doesn't unfasten."

"You're all right," Relph assured him.

"Who says so? You? But how can you tell? Your man's done away with two women for certain, and a problematic third. My idea of a police force is one that prevents murders, not merely solves 'em."

"You must give us a little time," observed Relph stiffly.

"Don't mind me," said Mr. Crook. "Found out anything about the old lady, beyond the fact that she's a goner?"

In point of fact, during the few hours that had elapsed since the gruesome discovery of the morning, the police had unearthed a fair amount of information. A certain Dr. Wrayford came forward with the statement that he had been consulted by Miss French as to certain acute and persistent pains that had been racking her for a considerable time. He had had no hesitation in diagnosing cancer, and had warned her that her only hope was an operation.

"And it wasn't too strong a hope at that," he told Relph. "A fifty-fifty chance at best. Like so many women, she'd left it much too late. I thought at first it was indigestion, she said. They all think it's indigestion or tell me they do. Why people can't realize that Providence gave them nerves in order that they could register pain and deal with the injury to the body causing that pain no doctor will ever understand. They seem to think pain is an end in itself, and if they can find anything—a drug or any substitute—that deadens the pain, they forget it's only a symptom of something essentially wrong with the machine." He paused abruptly; evidently this was his King Charles' Head.

"Did she agree to the operation?" asked Relph.

"Not right away. She made all the usual objections. She'd have to settle up her affairs before she entered a nursing home. She must have a little time to think it over. Nine times out of ten that means they're going to fade out. I did the little I could, gave her a pretty strong sleeping-draught because she said the pain kept her awake, and urged her strongly to agree to an operation. Mind you, I think it quite probable she wouldn't survive the shock, but it was my duty to urge her to have everything possible done. Nothing happened for a bit, and then I got a letter saying she was prepared to enter the home as soon as I could get her a vacancy. Luckily there was no need to wait long, and it was arranged that she should come in on Tuesday, the 12th March."

"And when she didn't turn up, what did you think?"

"I was beyond thinking anything just then; in fact, I didn't even know she'd cried it off. I went down with a bad bout of 'flu on the Monday evening. Apparently the matron received a telegram about midday on Tuesday cancelling her room and promising to write. She passed the news on to me but, as I told you, I was hors de combat. I only heard about Miss French this afternoon, and I've come posting round to tell you all I know."

"When matron didn't get a letter of explanation from Miss French, didn't she start feeling anxious?"

Wrayford looked at him with an air of incredulous contempt. "She didn't expect to hear. It's always happening, and you may as well cut your losses. No, no, matron's a busy woman, and there are always people waiting to come into that home. She simply passed the vacancy on and thought no more about it."

"And you—would you have moved in the matter?"

"Yes, I think I'd have written."

"And when you got no reply?"

"How am I to say? I wouldn't have been surprised to hear she'd taken an overdose of veronal; that often happens, when the chance is as thin as this one. But naturally I shouldn't have dreamed of murder. After all—correct me if I'm wrong—the proportion's only seven to the million. There didn't seem any reason why she should be one of the seven."

The case presented certain perplexing anomalies. To begin with, there was mystery connected with the luggage the dead woman had been presumed to have taken with her. No trace of any packed bag could be discovered; railway stations and parcels offices were examined without result. The quantity of clothing in the locked press that had already been opened by the police was very small; while Miss French's toilet articles, brush and comb, etc., had completely disappeared. The general police view was that the murderer, having disposed of the body, had then pitched the suitcase, that was not likely to be a large one, into one of the many hollows or ravines in the woods, trusting that the weather conditions would prevent its being discovered for some considerable time.

"She must have taken most of her underclothes," observed Relph, "her slippers, sponge bag and brush and comb, in fact everything you would take if you were going to a nursing home. Not many shoes, no umbrella— well, she wouldn't be going out for a long time, if ever. Then there's her handbag; that must be somewhere. Probably with the suitcase wherever that may be."

"How about the diamond ring?" drawled Crook when Relph had finished making these points clear.

"The ring?"

"Yes. Miss Verity says she wore one on her finger, a handsome diamond ring, she said. That seems to be missing."

"That makes it look like murder for gain."

"What else could it be? She didn't know anyone well enough to have any enemies. Wonder how much money she had on the premises?"

"We've seen her banker. She drew a hundred pounds two or three days before she was supposed to be entering the home."

"That sounds a deuce of a lot."

"She seems to have had a passion for paying in cash, and there'd be the nursing home fees and incidentals, in addition to the surgeon's fee, that presumably she would settle by cheque."

"Any trace of any of the cash?"

"She had seventy pounds stitched into her stays. The other thirty has disappeared. We've got the numbers of the notes, and we've already circulated them. But it's sheer luck if any of them turns up. It's days since she was killed, and the notes may have been changed the same night. Ten of them were single pounds, anyhow, and naturally the bank didn't note the numbers of those; but there was a tenner and two fivers. I suppose they were in her handbag."

It seemed reasonable to assume that Miss French had been murdered some time after 12.30 p.m. on Tuesday, the 12th March. Had it been the previous day, it must have been late in the evening, since she had called at Mrs. Home's farm shortly before five o'clock and taken away a chicken and some eggs. Besides, there was the question of the telegram. It seemed likely that this was genuine; no tramp would know of her plans or take the trouble to telegraph, even if he did. The first thing to be done was to trace the original telegram. It had been handed in at the Churchill Street Post Office. This office handled a good deal of telegraphic business, and Relph hardly expected anyone to remember a particular wire. But it might be possible to prove whether the message was in the dead woman's handwriting.

"Actually there was no need for her to go into Brighton," commented Relph. "There's a call-box not a quarter of a mile along the road; but I dare say the dial system was a complete mystery to her. On the face of it, it looks as though she did go to Brighton and came back later to her cottage and intercepted the murderer near the gate. She had a hat tightly pinned on her head, and she'd hardly be wearing that unless she was either going or coming."

"I wouldn't say that," remarked Crook gloomily. "I believe some of 'em sleep in their hats."

"Of course, we've no means of knowing what she meant to do if she wasn't going into the home. She'd let her cottage for three months, and a sick woman

128

doesn't have much fun staying in private rooms. I wouldn't be surprised if she didn't have a good supply of aspirin tablets in her bag. I've known that happen quite often."

"She wouldn't need those," said Crook, who had already been treated to a condensed story of the doctor's evidence. "Didn't that chappie say he'd prescribed a sleeping draught? Veronal or chloral or something of the sort. That 'ud do the trick."

"By gum, yes. I wonder now, did they find that bottle at The Nook?"

"Be your age," suggested his companion. "She'd not be likely to leave it for Miss Verity. No little farewell notes discovered anywhere, I suppose?"

Relph shook his head. "We've searched pretty near everywhere, in the sort of places where notes are found, I mean."

"Looks as though she took the count comin' back from Brighton. She might have meant to send a letter to her lawyer explainin' what she was doing, but didn't get the chance. It didn't go to him, that's certain, or he'd have been on the warpath long ago. Oh, this is murder all right. When you're planning to put yourself out you don't hide your suit-case and handbag, and then strangle yourself with your own scarf and pop neatly into a well, and then pop out again to block the entry with a bush from another part of the garden, just to put the police off the scent. I can believe a lot—a man like me has to —but that's just a trifle too much even for me."

The police considered the possibility of the woman having hanged herself in the woods and been found there by some tramp, who dumped her into the well for fear of being accused of murder; but the medical evidence speedily negatived that suggestion. For one thing, the police surgeon said, the ends of the scarf wouldn't have held; for a second, they clearly hadn't been knotted round a branch or anything else. No, it was murder; and it was reasonable to suppose that whoever murdered one woman was responsible for the death of the other.

After that the routine inquiry went on at full swing. First of all, questions were asked at the Post Office in Churchill Street, where the original of the telegram was produced for their inspection. This proved disappointing from an official point of view, since the message—"Regret unexpected change of plans, writing. French."—had been neatly printed in pencil. The name and address on the back were similarly inscribed. French, The Nook, Butler's Wood.

"The odds are she did send the wire herself," Relph decided. "Not many people knew of her plans. A stranger certainly wouldn't. Her lawyer may have done, but he'd no motive for the murder, or if he had we've yet to learn it. She didn't seem to have any relations. I wonder who benefits from her death. There was the doctor and the matron, but it's pretty safe to rule them out. It was to their advantage that she should enter the home for the operation. No, the chances are she made up her mind she couldn't face it, and either meant to go ahead and take her chance, which I don't think very likely, or else to take the law into her own hands. And she didn't even have to do that. Some obliging fellow did it for her."

Churchill Street Post Office is a large building, and it seemed improbable that anyone would remember this particular telegram being sent. It was, therefore, the more surprising that one clerk did vaguely remember a wire being handed over the counter by an elderly woman "who gave a sort of brown effect," she explained. "I remember her because my mother had just been in a home for an operation and it didn't do her a bit of good; I thought this one was sensible to change her mind. I wouldn't know her again because she looked like hundreds of other people, but I just remember there was such a woman."

"She must have made a snap decision," remarked Relph. "Otherwise she'd have written. It's a moot point whether cancellation at a couple of hours' notice doesn't imply financial liability, but in the circumstances she probably wouldn't be worrying about that. As to whether she really intended to write to the matron, we'll never know; we'll need to learn a bit more about a lady before we can start advancing theories, but so far it looks to me as though this is one of the Tramp Crimes. She sounds a fierce bit of goods, and if she threatened a fellow with the police he might try to stop her mouth. If he didn't know the place very well he mightn't realize you could yell your head off without anyone hearing you."

A description of Miss French in the clothes in which she was found was circulated throughout Brighton, and any possible clue was asked for by the police; but nothing was forthcoming. No one in the town itself remembered seeing her, and as she only went into the place for her shopping and appeared to buy wherever goods took her fancy it was unlikely that she would be recognized. Of personal friends and acquaintances she had none.

The next step of the authorities was to call on Mr. Wilkes. He had already heard the news from local rumour and expressed himself as profoundly shocked and even unbelieving concerning the whole affair. He had known, he admitted, about the nursing home and the operation, and had urged her to take the doctor's advice. In the event of her death he had instructions to put her will into instant effect.

"Who was her legatee?" Relph wanted to know.

"All the money was entailed to her nephew, her sister's only child."

"Entailed, eh?"

"Yes. Miss French had a very comfortable income of between eight and nine hundred a year left to her by her godmother, with the proviso that if she did not herself marry and have children, it was to go to her next-of-kin at her death."

"Could she touch the capital?"

"That was tied up."

"And this nephew—where is he?"

"That, unfortunately, we do not know. For some years after Miss Alice married her sister's fiancé, we heard nothing of them; then one day Mrs. French, Miss Harriet's mother, admitted that the marriage was not a happy one, but vouchsafed no details. About nine years ago Mrs. Henry Fielding died, and her husband did not long survive her."

"And the boy?"

"He disappeared after his mother's death. When his father died there was so little except debts to inherit that he presumably preferred not to come forward. Now, of course, we should wish to get in touch with him, if we knew where he was to be found."

"Does he know he's his aunt's heir?"

"I could not say for certain, but presumably his mother knew the nature of her sister's inheritance."

"Then he may come forward."

"That is what we must hope for."

"On the other hand he may be dead."

Mr. Wilkes bowed his head, as who should say, We must submit ourselves to Providence. In spite of his appearance, for the moment he reminded the onlooker of Uriah Heep.

Crook, who had accompanied Relph (for it had proved impossible to establish contact with the lawyer the previous afternoon), here remarked, "How about the army? He'd be the age."

"We shall make all the necessary inquiries," snapped Relph. "He may not be using his own name."

"I don't know how the police suggest I should discover a young man who has been missing for nine years," observed Mr. Wilkes in offended tones. He disliked this intrusion of the police into what he regarded as his personal department.

Crook, however, was equal to the occasion. "Ask my friend, Jeremy Blood," he advised Mr. Wilkes. "J.B. would find that chap in the twitch of a cat's whisker. Well, we're up a gum tree all right—at least you are. It doesn't matter to us."

"Unless you are suggesting that Mr. Fielding, Jr., is connected with the crime."

"Have a heart, Wilkes," Crook protested. "The police have some logical sense. If he did do it, then you can be sure they'll drop on him soon enough. Eh, Relph?" He winked cheerfully. "I suppose there's no one else Miss French was likely to talk to about her operation?"

"She assured me that she was speaking of it to no one. Indeed, she said, there was no one who would be interested. A very sad case, very sad indeed."

When he lost his job for inefficiency or because people couldn't stand his damned patronizing manners any longer, reflected Crook with interest, Wilkes could adopt the profession of funeral mute. He'd lend a cachet to the meanest entourage.

"Well, if no one else knew her address—no one's asked for it, I suppose?"

"Only that rather peculiar tenant to whom she had let the cottage. I must admit that she pressed very hard for the address. I assured her, naturally, that letters would be forwarded, but she hardly seemed satisfied. She . . . I beg your pardon?" This was to Crook, who was staring at him in a most peculiar manner.

"Are you telling us that Miss Verity has been here?"

"I believe that was her name."

"A little shrimp of a woman in black?"

"Small certainly, and yes—I believe she was in black. What I particularly noticed was the ridiculous hat she wore, a yellow hat with a flowered scarf round it."

"A scarf?" Crook's voice sounded dangerous.

"Certainly." What on earth was the matter with the fellow?

Crook paid no further heed to him, but turned instead to Relph. "There's one thing about this case. It ought to put scarves off the market for the next six months. If you're going to have three women strangled with their own scarves . . ."

Mr. Wilkes looked horrified, but obscurely pleased. "Three? You don't mean . . . ?"

"Well, the police haven't found her yet. However, that don't signify. What time did she come?"

"She had no appointment. I should say about eleven to eleven-thirty."

"Did she happen to mention where she was going?"

"She said nothing to give me a clue."

"Did she tell you why she'd come?" Crook snapped out his questions like bullets leaping from a machine gun. Crack, crack, crack.

"She wished to ascertain whether, in the circumstances, she would be liable for the rent of the cottage. Her contention was that it could not be described as a habitable dwelling."

"Well, no more it could, not with a policeman doing Peeping Tom at every window. It ain't a pleasant idea, you must admit, not for a lady of refinement. Miss Verity isn't—one of those."

Mr. Wilkes changed colour. He detested ribaldry.

"What did you tell her?" Crook continued inexorably.

"That I would report her complaint to my client, but that I doubted whether she had a case."

"Like hell she has," returned Crook vigorously. "I hope she referred you to me."

"She said something about her own lawyer."

"I'm the boy. What happened then?"

Mr. Wilkes looked annoyed. "I don't understand you. Miss Verity did not remain long."

"Did she tell you where she was going?"

"Certainly not. May I ask why you say that?"

"She's the third missin' lady in the case, that's all. And mark this, my boy." Wilkes drew down the corners of his mouth and tilted his head. "That's your responsibility. Oh, yes, it is. Something you told Miss Verity yesterday afternoon sent her off on a wild-goose chase from which she's not yet returned, from which she may never return." He leaned closer, his wicked little green eyes staring into the lawyer's fearful face.

"I—I told her nothing that could possibly account for her disappearance. Why, I'd never seen the lady before, and I must say that if my client had consulted me in advance I should most strongly have recommended her not to accept her as a tenant."

"Cheque been dishonoured?" asked Crook lazily.

"Certainly not. Or at least, not so far as I know."

"That's all the interest you take in her, isn't it?"

"I should have said myself she was not—er—quite compos mentis."

"You should know," agreed Crook heartily. "Heaven sees to it that we run across plenty of that sort in our profession. But tell me something else, Wilkes. Have you got any sane clients who aren't bad hats?"

Wilkes looked, if possible, more outraged than before. He began to wonder at Crook's mental make-up.

"I beg your pardon?"

"It always seems to me Heaven works on a law of compensation. If you have virtue you have precious

133

little else, as a rule not even common sense. But if you have common sense you don't have virtue. Perhaps the truth is the two don't go together. Now Miss Verity hasn't any common sense, but she has something you might call flair. And she don't mind putting her theories to the test. The fact that she's added to our problems by providin' us with a new mystery doesn't alter my opinion of her. She's an enterprising woman and I admire her for it. What did she say to give you the impression she'd got bats?"

"Her appearance, in the first place. It was most peculiar. That outrageous yellow straw hat with the thick veil, as though she were trying to elude the police."

"P'raps she was," suggested Crook. "Go on. What else?"

"Her manner—and the questions she asked. After all, what difference could it make to her what happened to Miss French a quarter of a century ago?"

"A natural romantic, perhaps. What did you tell her?"

"Obviously, I could not discuss my client's affairs."

"You didn't see which way she went when she left your office?"

"Certainly not."

Crook stood up. "Not very helpful, are you? Well, Wilkes, my boy," again the lawyer winced at the familiarity, "I only hope on the Last Day you may not have a murder on your conscience, because, whether you realise it or not, something you said is responsible for Miss Verity's next move."

"I tell you I told her nothing," cried Wilkes, black in the face with rage and the knowledge of that rage's futility.

"You don't know that woman. She's the complete amateur. No clue too improbable, no clue too small. She'd find something sinister about the colour of that tie you're wearing—and so, for a matter of that, do I. I suppose you're sure you didn't tell her anything that might guide us on our way?"

Wilkes seemed goaded almost beyond control. "I simply told her that I was unable to furnish her with Miss French's address, but that letters would be forwarded."

"No getting any forrader here," said Crook decisively. "Come on." He tilted his bowler at Wilkes and rolled out of the office.

Relph didn't seem too happy as they left the premises, but Crook was in his usual fettle.

"Next thing we've got to do," he observed, "is decide which of the corpses is the horse and which the cart."

Relph, nettled by that bland "'we," said dryly, "I suppose you couldn't be a bit more explicit?"

"Which death occurred first. Was little Ivy slain because she knew too much about Miss French, or did the old lady come back at an inconvenient moment and so have to be put out of the way to save the murderer's neck? Or is it our old friend, John Coincidence? He has a way of turning up at the most unlikely moments."

"Nothing so far gives us any motive for the murder of either woman," said Relph, looking harassed.

"I thought we agreed that Miss French was murdered for her diamond ring and any money she had about her. As for the girl, when your dilatory police force find her body, I might be able to suggest half a dozen motives."

"One'll be sufficient," said Relph dryly.

CHAPTER FOURTEEN

Crook, returning unaccompanied to the Royal Crescent, found Harry Fennel standing about aimlessly in the lounge.

"Seen anything of my young woman?" Crook asked him.

Young Fennel was looking troubled. "No. Matter of fact, I wanted another five minutes with her. I wanted to ask her what she's got in the back of her mind."

Crook looked at him pityingly. "You'll grow out of that."

"Grow . . . ?"

"Expecting women to tell you what they've got at the back of their minds. Why should she have anything, so far as you're concerned?"

"She said some damned odd things to me. I suppose you don't know where she is?"

"I'd be a lot easier in my mind if I did. She went off like Hawkeye the Detective without a word to anyone. I've confirmed Miss Buckler's story. She was at the station at that time; a porter remembered her asking him some questions about the five o'clock train to town. After that she just seems to have vanished. It wouldn't surprise me to learn she was at the bottom of the sea."

Fennel stared. "Why on earth should she be?"

"It's the kind of thing that does happen to people who want to know too much. Y'see, she's like these chaps that won't vote Capital or Labour, but want to start a party of their own. She don't think much of the ways of the police, and she even thinks she knows

more than I do. A lot of people have done that in
their time, and it ain't healthy, my boy, take it from
me. Most of 'em have ended in jug, and a whole lot
of them under prison flags. She's up to a bit of no
good or she'd have let me into the secret, but she's like
a lot of women, thinks feminine intuition better than
the official trinity of Motive, Opportunity and the one I
can never remember. I'd awfully like to know, though,
what that lawyer did tell her."

"Lawyer?" Fennel sounded startled.

"Yes. She went round to see Miss French's lawyer,
dressed up like a sunflower. I don't suppose he had
any reason for putting her out. Hallo, what's up?"

"Did he tell you what he'd told her?"

"Swore he hadn't told her anything, but that's a lawyer
all over. I ought to know."

Harry Fennel was looking past him, his face twisted
into grim lines.

"Well, what could he have told her?" Crook persisted. "You may as well tell me. It'll come out in the
end. Something about Miss French? Or you?" Suddenly he smote his thigh. "Jumping Moses, I've got it.
You're the missing heir."

"And how much further does that get you? Don't
go jumping at wild conclusions, as I've no doubt Miss
Verity has already done."

Crook's eyebrows rose like two woolly bear caterpillars.
"Does Wilkes know about you, though?"

"I don't doubt Miss French told him."

"He's a better liar than I gave him credit for, if
that's so. But what the heck are you doing calling yourself Fennel. Isn't your own name good enough for you?"

"Would you have stuck to it in the circumstances?"
The young man's eyes were blazing.

Crook gentled him, like a bucking horse. "Easy now,
easy. You don't want to get all worked up about this.
Remember, I don't know your personal history."

"I suppose everyone will know, now this has happened.
As soon as I heard they'd found Miss French's body, I
realised I'd have to come into the open sooner or later.
I wonder if that's what Miss Verity was driving at. I
wonder if she knew."

"Hadn't you better open up?" suggested Crook. "Come
into the bar. It ought to be open by now."

When they were seated at a table with long drinks at
their elbows, Fennel said, "It was never what you might
call a happy marriage; even as a kid I never remember
anything but rows and nagging. I once heard it said that
it was cursed from the beginning because of the circumstances. You probably know that my father jilted Miss

136

French, practically at the altar steps, in order to marry her younger sister. Actually he wasn't a man to make any woman happy. Aunt Harriet was luckier than she knew. Then, when I was almost seventeen, my mother died suddenly of an overdose of a sleeping-draught, and a lot of people, including the police, weren't at all sure she'd taken it herself."

Crook nodded sympathetically. "It could be, Fennel, it could be."

"I haven't any idea which theory is the truth, because I was away at school most of the time; in a sense, neither of my parents ever seemed quite real to me, but when I was at home I could see it was a cat-and-dog life. My mother was too much awed by my father. I don't believe Aunt Harriet would have been so tame. Anyhow, I loathed being at home. I felt—embarrassed. All the same, I've never felt that my father would have gone to the lengths of murder. It would have been so much simpler for him to walk out."

"Quite a lot of chaps haven't thought of that," Crook reminded him.

"Of course, it was natural that everyone should talk. Was she murdered, directly or indirectly, meaning did my father drive her to take an overdose; or was she an hysterical kind of woman anyway, who might be expected to cut out when things got too hard? The police asked a hell of a lot of questions, though it never actually got as far as a trial. My father was detained by the police for a time, and he didn't make things any better by behaving in a ridiculously high-handed way. You couldn't expect the police to know he was always like that, even in his own home."

"What happened to him?"

"He packed his things and left, said he couldn't stay in the place after that."

"And you went with him?"

"No. I couldn't. I wasn't certain, you see. It seemed to me my chance. Naturally, I had to leave school. There was a good deal of scandal, and I couldn't have faced it, even if the authorities hadn't drawn the line at a boy whose father was quite likely a murderer. I was lucky enough to find a man who took me abroad and gave me a job, a New Zealander. I liked the country and out there no one had ever heard of the case, but I changed my name, because you never know when English people won't come over, and I wanted to leave the wretched story behind me. I've been Fennel for nine years, and when I go into the army it'll be as Fennel and not as Fielding that I'll be enrolled."

"Did you change your name by deed poll?"

"Not much. Too damned expensive. Besides, there'd been too much of a stink as it was."

"Did Auntie know you were in Brighton?"

"When I found out who she was I thought I ought to go and see her, as she was my only relative. I'd always felt rather bad about her, seeing the way she was treated by my father. I had a sort of idea I might be able to do something for her—not financially, I'm broke to the wide—but . . ."

"A cosy little home life," suggested Crook. "How did Auntie cotton to the idea?"

"She took an instantaneous dislike to me, which was a bit dashing, assumed I'd only come to stake out a claim, and then asked me if I'd brought my birth certificate along."

"And had you?"

"Actually I had, but I didn't expect to be asked for it on the nail like that. After all, why should I pretend to be her nephew if I wasn't?"

"People have done more desperate things in the hope of making a touch. You didn't, I suppose?"

"Try to borrow money? Certainly not."

"Did she take any interest in you when she knew who you were?"

"I wouldn't put it as high as that. She almost stared me out of countenance, and then told me I wasn't much like either of my parents. But the impression she gave me was of someone who's been dead for years. Honestly, she doesn't seem any more dead to me now than she did then."

"You pop down to the mortuary and have a look at the body after it's been in the water a few days, and see if you don't change your mind," Crook suggested grimly.

"She told me she lived absolutely alone, and when I asked her if she wasn't afraid of tramps she looked at me in that cold, inhuman way of hers, and said, 'It's never the people who don't value their lives who lose them.' I thought her a bit touched from living alone so long."

"Chap I know in Harley Street says we all are," confided Crook chattily. "I don't know that it's any more lunatic to shut yourself up in a wood than to spend your life shut up in a club playin' bridge for stakes you can't afford. That the only time you saw her?"

"Yes. She wasn't exactly pressing in her invitation to come again. Besides, I didn't much like her notion that I'd only come for what I could get."

"She didn't make a sporting offer, I take it?"

For a moment his companion looked bewildered. Then he said, "A tip, you mean? Not much. But she did tell me that one day, if the government hadn't spent all her substance on A.R.P., I'd have a nice little income and wouldn't need to court a girl for her cash."

"That's what's called a give-away. Still, your father jilted her for a girl with nothing but what Burns calls her wee coatie."

"He came into money suddenly, and spent it just as soon." He moved restlessly. "I suppose all this will be featured in the gutter-press. I ought to go along to the police."

"And the lawyer. You won't get your inheritance if you don't. Oh, and don't forget to take your birth certificate there."

Fennel flushed at this characteristic lack of breeding on his companion's part. "I meant, if I laid low, which is what I'd like to do, they might think it a bit queer."

"I'm damned sure they would. By the way, they'll ask you what you were doing that day."

"They've asked me that already in connection with Ivy Green. I was up at the Golf Club, doing a round on my own. I wanted to get some practice with a niblick, and there's a hole there that gives you all the chances you can want. I mucked about there till it was too dark to see. I was expecting to play a round the next morning, but the snow put an end to that. They'll have checked all that up already, though. What I can't understand is what put Miss Verity on to me in the first place. Unless she knew I was Miss French's nephew; and even so, nobody at that time knew Miss French was dead."

"It was feminine intuition same as I told you," Crook assured him. "Unless you think Miss French confided her sad life-story the only time they met. I wouldn't chance sixpence on it myself."

"Nor would I. All the same I hope no harm's come to her."

"Why should it?" murmured Crook.

"If she's got in the way of someone who's already got two bodies to his credit, he mightn't make too much difficulty about putting out a third."

A large figure came thumping into the bar, carrying the latest edition of the evening paper. It was Miss Buckler and she stamped over to Crook's table.

"More publicity," she snapped. "I suppose you're pleased."

Crook took the paper from her with scant ceremony. "Woman Witness Vanishes," he read. "Mystery surrounds the whereabouts of Miss Laura Verity, whose name is known all over the country in connection with the double murder at The Nook, near Brighton. Local opinion believes that Miss Verity had obtained a clue to the

ANTHONY GILBERT

murderer's identity, and fear that she may have paid for
her subtlety with her life."

"I don't see how anybody can be expected to pay a
handsome subscription to a lending library when you
can get such gilt-edged fiction for a penny a night," was
Crook's comment as he handed the paper back.

"Does that mean you know where she is?"

Crook didn't reply, and she turned to Harry, catching
him by the arm and shaking it fiercely. Both men had
risen by this time, and other people in the bar watched the
trio with interest.

"What was it she was saying to you that night? You
wrote something down for her, didn't you? I saw you. I
suppose you didn't know I was there, but I was sitting
in a corner. I tell you, there's something queer about
that woman. What was she up to? Was she trying to
get money out of you?"

"She'd be damned clever if she did," said Fennel.

"You needn't pretend you're penniless, because I know
better. I saw you sitting in the lounge the second night I
was here with a great roll of notes in your hand. That
was the night she came, and if she saw it, too, that might
account for a lot."

It was time something accounted for the various developments, thought Crook, as the woman left them. That
story about Fennel and the roll of notes was interesting.
He'd talked of pawning his cuff links, but suppose he'd
got the money by pawning something else? Suppose,
thought Crook, he'd pawned a diamond ring? You
never knew about luck; it was like a chameleon perpetually changing colour. He went out of the hotel and
into the jewellers from whose doors Miss Verity had
first seen Harry Fennel emerge.

When he came out a little later there was a furrow
between his stiff sandy eyebrows. It hadn't been difficult
to learn what he wanted to know. He had only had to
murmur "Police" to get an answer to any question he
chose to put. And it was what he had surmised. Fennel
had gone into the shop to sell a diamond ring; all that
remained now was to find someone who could tell them
whether it was the ring Miss French used to wear. If
it was, then the case was virtually at an end.

The difficulty would be to find a witness who could
give them that information. The only person who might
have helped them was Miss Verity, and of her there
was still no sign.

By this time Crook knew that something was seriously
wrong. He thought her quite capable of following a
hunch up to London, but he didn't think she'd stay there
without getting into touch with himself. It even occurred

140

to him that she had left a note in her room explaining the possible course of action, and he insisted on conducting the search himself. But the only thing he found was a little bottle full of yellow liquid, wrapped in brown paper and labelled: Arthur Crook, Esq. Urgent and Personal. To Be Examined.

"Curiouser and curiouser," he reflected. "Pity she doesn't tell me where the stuff came from. But then she's one of these people who believe in making things difficult. Probably thinks that adds to the fun."

And going downstairs he rang up Relph and said he'd like to meet him at his convenience in the bar of the Hoop and Toy. Then he carried his little bottle round to the police surgeon's private residence, and asked him to have the contents analysed as soon as possible.

CHAPTER FIFTEEN

"What you want in this case is Maskelyne and Devant," said Relph gloomily, putting away his second tankard. "First of all you have a disappearing corpse, then you have a different corpse turning up where it's least expected, then a disappearing female and in her place the long-lost heir putting his spoke in the wheel just to make things a bit more difficult. I ask you, what d'you expect the police to make of that?"

"You might make out quite a nice case against our Mr. Fennel," Crook rejoined seriously. "Point 1. Who's interested in Miss French's death? Answer: Mr. Fennel. Point 2. Who knew the layout of the house (because she took him round the premises that day. Sorry, I forgot to mention that)? Answer: Mr. Fennel. Point 3 Who knew Miss Ivy Green? Answer: Mr. Fennel. Point 4. Who's hard up at the moment? Answer: Mr. Fennel. Point 5. Who had motive and opportunity? Answer: Same again. I will, too, thanks very much."

"You seem to have worked everything out very nicely," said Relph in not very friendly tones.

Mr. Crook threw out his chest and declaimed, "I get my man. Sometimes, of course, the police see him nearly as soon as I do, and as there are more of them they get an unfair share of the picture, but all the same, it's a nice motto. Inspires confidence, and that's always a good thing."

"One of these days, Mr. Crook, you ought to go on the pictures," repoined Relph sarcastically. "Much more paying than being a lawyer."

Crook's hands did not move, but he gave the impression of laying one thick finger against the side of his large aggressive nose.

"Sez you! Oh, Relph, you don't know the disadvantages that dog you, havin' to be an honest man. One thing I will say, anything the police get they deserve. Besides, all they ask on the pictures is sex-appeal. I'd call it degrading to a man of my intelligence."

"I didn't know there was anything you couldn't supply," said Relph pleasantly.

"And they don't even allow you to be subtle about it. And subtlety is my middle name. No, no, I occupy a unique position, and I wouldn't like to see my pedestal empty. To come back to our Mr. Fennel. How does he strike you, cast as the criminal?"

"He has a motive of a kind, I dare say," acknowledged Relph grudgingly. "I don't say he had no money, but I dare say he hadn't got enough."

"No man ever has enough, and he'd got to the pitch of selling all that he had, not to give to the poor but to pay his own hotel bills. Fact. He admitted as much. So," he wound up cosily, "I put two and two together with the usual result, and went along to see a chap nearby and put a certain question to him."

"Do you imagine you're in charge of this case?" demanded Relph wrathfully. "Why couldn't you give your information to the police direct and leave them to get on with it?"

"Because hustle's another of my middle names. Besides, the police are a government department; they have to behave like gentlemen as well as honest men, whereas I, bein' a freelance and just a yellow dog of a lawyer with his own bread and scrape to find somehow, don't labour under all those limitations. What's red tape to me but a music-hall joke, whereas to you it's your swaddling clothes. And some of your chaps never seem to get out of the cradle. Matter of fact, it occurred to me that my young lady—Miss Verity to you—first saw young Fennel dashin' out of a jeweller's. She's like all amateurs, tells you everythin' in detail, mostly twice over, to be sure you haven't missed it. There's a lot to be said for amateurs, Relph."

"You must have said most of it," retorted the goaded inspector.

"Anyhow, I went round and represented myself as an official, and the fellow opened up to me as easy as a tin of toffee when you insert a copper coin under the lid. What Fennel was doing in there was getting a price for a remarkably fine diamond ring." He paused a moment, waiting for his effect. "Might be worth your while going down to take a peep at it when you've got a minute to spare," he added casually.

"Do you expect me to recognise it?"

"I doubt it, Relph, I doubt it. I don't suppose you've ever seen it before, not unless you were on calling terms at The Nook, and I don't think you were. But it wouldn't surprise me to hear that that ring belonged, not more than two or three days ago, to Miss Harriet French."

"If that's true, it looks as though the end's in sight."

"I wouldn't be so sure. Who's going to identify it for you? There's Mrs. Home, of course, but I doubt whether she'd take the responsibility. There are the clerks at the bank, but it's putting a lot of responsibility on them, unless at any time she parked the ring there, and even then, as you know, the bank don't want to examine what you put in its care. And there's Mr. Wilkes He might be able to help, but, of course, the one person who could give you a definite Yes or No is our missing witness. She particularly noticed the ring; the odds are she'd know it again. The only difficulty is we don't know where to find her at this moment."

"She'll have to turn up for the inquest."

"If she's able to."

"We shall issue a subpoena."

"Provided she isn't somewhere where even subpoenas don't mean a thing."

"We might put out a message through the B.B.C."

"All right, if she's listening to the B.B.C."

"Look here, Crook, do you really think she's really another case of foul play?"

"Well, put yourself in the killer's place. Would you allow an insignificant little rabbit like that to stand between you and whatever you'd killed the other ladies for? And though she's as keen as mustard she's got the usual amateur's fault, forgetting that other people have brains, too. She may be hot on a trail, but no hotter, I'll take my davy, than the chap who did in Miss French and little Ivy Green."

Relph signalled to the barman to come over and collect their tankards.

"Same again. You expecting the force to dig this body up, too?"

"Well, it's what they're paid for, isn't it?"

"But look here, could Fennel conceivably be responsible in this case? Has he been to London recently?"

Crook considered. "Miss Verity was seen at the station at about 5 p.m. Just before five, because the London train hadn't left. Fennel was in the hotel at six. No body's been found in a railway carriage or chucked out on the line, and you can't just sling a corpse in the rack and trust to luck nobody will notice it. No, he didn't go to town that evening. Only you have to remember this. We're up against a tough guy. He's hidden little Ivy Green where the whole local force can't find her, probably hiding a cock-sparrow like Miss Verity is child's play to him."

"What do you suggest we do now?" asked Relph politely.

"I think a stroll round the golf course is indicated. There's something I want to find out."

They climbed into Crook disreputable car, known affectionately as the Scarlet Woman, and set off.

"We've checked up on Fennel's statement that he was up here on the Tuesday." Relph explained as they took a corner rather more sharply than the inspector cared about.

"Didn't go round the links, did you?"

"No. But you have to remember it was snowing on Tuesday morning."

"Didn't amount to shucks. No, I'll lay that Fennel was on the links that day. What I want to find out is whether he was on the links all the time."

At the clubhouse they saw the secretary, a thin colourless man in rimless glasses, who rubbed his hands all the time he spoke.

"Practice - with a niblick?" he said in response to a question from Crook. "I suggest the fifteenth hole. In fact, our fifteenth hole is famous.' If you can do that hole in bogey you can call yourself a pretty fine golfer."

What Crook called the hole was untranslatable; Relph said more mildly, "Bit of a stinker" and was content to leave it at that. It seemed mainly pits and depressions, sand-pits under overhanging brows of rank grass; and on the farther side was a hedge where an industrious caddie could probably reap a fortune. Below the hedge was a ditch of long grass and beyond the hedge the trees grew thickly. "Just what I thought," said Crook. "Know where we are? That's Butler's Wood or I'm a Dutchman. Now d'you see what I'm driving at?"

He approached the hedge and began to examine it along its entire length. When he was at work he seemed to have no notion of the ridiculous sight he presented; for nature had not built him for dignity. His sincerity, however, was so tremendous that he achieved a certain effect in spite of his appalling figure, his appalling clothes and his unpardonable hat. Relph silently joined him and they worked their way along the hedge inch by inch. It was Crook who found what they were seeking, a shred of brown material caught on a sharp spine of the hedge.

"The coat that came out of will have a nice little triangular hole in it," observed Crook happily. "Come on. Let's find out if Mr. Fennel has a nice brown suit."

There are times when it appears that the stars in their courses are fighting against justice and truth. When Relph arrived at the hotel he found Fennel had just come in and was having a short drink in the bar. When he saw the inspector he said, "Hallo. This one's on me. What'll you have?"

Before Crook could reply Relph said quickly, "Not allowed to drink on duty. Look here, I want a word or two with you. I ought to warn you that any answers you may like to give me may be used as evidence against you."

The hand in which Fennel was holding his glass shook a little.

"You're riding a bit in front of the hounds, aren't you?" he suggested. "What am I supposed to have done?"

"Use your wits, laddie," Crook advised him dryly.

"You mean, in connection with Aunt Harriet's death? Oh, but that's ridiculous."

"The easiest way of proving that is by helping us all you can," Relph assured him. "Now, you admit you were on the golf course, practising by the fifteenth hole on Tuesday, the twelfth. What time did you come in to lunch?"

"I didn't come in. I didn't get to the links till nearly twelve, so it didn't seem worth while. I had some beer and a sandwich before I left, and that carried me through."

"Can you remember what clothes you were wearing that day?"

Fennel stared. "Just flannel bags and a pullover and a Norfolk jacket."

"What coloured jacket?" •

"The usual thing. Sort of oatmeal."

"Have you got it here?"

"Yes. It's in my room. Do you want to see it?"

"If you don't mind."

"Of course I don't mind. I'll get it."

"I'll come with you, if you've no objection."

Fennel shrugged. "We must be providing the hotel with a lot of free entertainment. Everybody knows who you are, of course . . ."

"Don't flatter him," said Crook tranquilly.

The three of them went up in the lift to Fennel's room. He opened the built-in wardrobe and took down a pale coloured jacket with a half-belt.

"That the only one you've got?"

"Yes. It's a new one."

"I saw that. When did you buy it?"

"Just after I came over. The one I had was all right on the boat but it wasn't classy enough for a place like this."

"Where's the old one?"

"I gave it away. There was an appeal pinned up in the lounge—it's there still—Clothes for Finnish refugees—so I shoved it in."

"What colour was that?"

"Oh, a kind of brown."

"The same shade as this?"

"Darker than that. A sort of ginger."

"Can you tell me the actual date you bought this one?"

"I'm afraid I can't."

"You probably paid for it by cheque."

"In a place where I'm not known? Be your age. No, I paid for it ready cash, twenty-one shillings, and damn good value for the money."

"Where did you get it?"

"Bush Brothers. My God, you want to know a lot, don't you?"

Relph paid no attention to that. "Did you buy it before or after the day you were practising on the links?"

"Before. I told you I was wearing it that day."

"You're quite sure you weren't wearing the old one?"

"Absolutely."

"Do you remember the day you gave that away?"

"How the hell should I? There was a great chest standing in the hall and all sorts of clothes were being bunged into it. There was a chap standing there, reading the notice one evening, and saying to his wife, 'Well, I may not have many clothes, but I've more than those poor devils,' and he went up and got something or other and shied it in and I put mine in the same day."

"Is he staying in the hotel now?"

"I don't think so. In fact, I know he isn't."

"How long have you been staying here?"

"Between seven and eight weeks."

"Do you remember his name?"

"I never heard it."

"What did he look like?"

"Oh, Lord, like everybody else."

"But you'd know him again?"

"I shouldn't think so. I never saw him properly."

"Not exactly helpful, are you?" snapped Relph.

"Well, what do you expect me to say? That he had red hair and green eyes and spoke of living in Dublin? How would that help?"

"We could have the records examined."

"Anyhow, he didn't say that. Or if he did I didn't hear him."

"I see, Mr. Fennel." There was a dangerous finality in Relph's voice. "One more thing. I believe this was your ring." As he spoke he laid something that glittered on the table.

Fennel picked it up. "You don't mind snooping, do you?" he exclaimed. "How did you run that to earth?" Then, as Relph said nothing, he cried angrily, "There's no law in this country, is there, to prevent my selling a ring if I need the money?"

"Of course not. Do you mind telling me where you got this ring?"

"I brought it over with me."

"It belonged to your mother, perhaps?"

"No. It was given to me."

"Perhaps you could open up a little."

"Why the hell should I?"

"Actually, the position's a bit awkward. A diamond ring was taken from Miss French's house, and . . ."

"And you think this may be it? I can assure you it isn't. How does that help me?"

"Not very much. Could you produce anyone who saw this ring before the thirteenth?"

"It isn't the kind of thing one goes flashing around."

"It isn't the kind of thing a man has as a rule."

"Well, I did have it. If you must know, there was a chap out in Sydney. He got in a bit of a mess and I happened to be on hand and got him out of it. His mother gave me the ring, in case, she said, I was ever in a hole. If I was, I wasn't to be sentimental. I was to use it."

"She's in Sydney still?"

"She died last year."

"And the son?"

"I haven't the faintest idea."

"And you needed money so much you sold the ring?"

"I needed the money and I didn't need the ring. I—the girl I'd like to marry can't stand diamonds, so when I discovered that, I didn't think there was any point keeping it."

"What's the lady's name?"

"You're not going to drag her into this."

"She might be able to help you."

"How?"

"Perhaps she'd seen the ring before the thirteenth."

"She's never seen it. I didn't show it to her. Why should I? As a matter of fact, I never even told her I had it. She happened to say that emeralds were her stone, so I thought I'd trade this in for an emerald ring.

Only, as a matter of fact, they hadn't got one I fancied, so I took the cash."

"I see." Relph was acutely impersonal.

"That's nice of you. I'm damned if I know where I stand."

"At present I'd be glad if you didn't leave Brighton."

"Not going to clap the gyves on me right away?"

"You promise us that?" Relph sounded stern, paying no heed to the young man's bitter tone.

"Of course, I promise. You'd lay me by the heels in a couple of hours, anyhow. Besides, where the hell could I go? I don't know anyone. I wouldn't be staying in a bloody great hotel like this if I did."

"Just an inch short every time," observed Crook judicially, as the two men left the hotel. "Fennel had a brown coat, but you can't swear it was the one that got torn in the hedge by the fifteenth hole. He sold a diamond ring, but there's no proving—yet—that it was Miss French's. He was on the golf links that morning, but so were a lot of other people."

"I suppose only members can get onto the links?"

"Actually, No. There's a public footpath running right through them. They're not a very expensive course. As I see it, almost anyone could have done the old girl in. This time you'll have to rely on motive, and the only person with any motive, so far as we can tell, is young Fennel. He seems to have been pretty hard up . . . ."

"All the same, you don't generally strangle a woman and then chuck her down a well and elaborately block the entrance just because you're in need of cash."

"It's been known," returned Crook dryly. "Don't forget, too, that he's the only person we've so far discovered who knew both the dead women. He says he didn't see little Ivy that afternoon, but suppose he arranged to meet her in the wood? You never can tell."

"What would help us most now," ruminated the inspector, "would be to get our hands on the missing notes. The B.B.C. is going to send out a police message this evening, reminding people of the numbers on the chance that something develops. I've tried Turtle, of course, but he swears they haven't turned up at the hotel. He seems a very methodical sort of chap, dots down the number of every note over a pound. I quite realize," he added hastily, as though to forestall his companion's obvious comment, "that in a sense it's playing into the criminal's hands. Once he knows we have the numbers of the notes he can destroy them, but we shall have to hope he's changed one at least. After all, it's time a bit of the luck came our way."

"Well, that's your job," agreed Crook heartily. "I've got to get ahead with mine."

"Yours being?"

"I've got to find Miss Verity. It's what novelists call of paramount importance."

"You think she'll be able to help us?"

"I wasn't thinking of that. I feel, as you might say, responsible for the woman. My clients don't go round getting themselves murdered. I'm feeling very touchy and professional about this, Relph, and I don't mind admittin' it."

As he returned through the hall the clerk handed him a letter that had just been brought by hand. Crook ripped the envelope open. The note was from the police surgeon and said:

"It's as well your friend didn't sample the sherry you sent me. There's enough veronal in it to send him or her to sleep for the duration."

With a sudden gesture Crook crumpled the sheet in his hand, then carefully smoothed it out again.

"Damn Miss Verity," he said heartily. "She's holding everything up by not being on the spot. Just like a woman. They can never realize that a man may have other fish to fry."

And for luck he had one more pint before dinner.

CHAPTER SIXTEEN

That evening, after the six o'clock news, the radio broadcast a police message.

"Brighton police are anxious to trace three bank-notes in connection with the Missing Manicurist Case. The notes in question are one for ten pounds and two for five. The numbers are (here followed the numbers, repeated at dictation speed). Any information available should be passed immediately to the Police Headquarters, Brighton, or any police station."

The result of this appeal was unexpectedly rapid. Within half an hour of it being uttered, a man in civilian clothes walked in the main Brighton station. As soon as he began to speak it was clear that he was of foreign extraction, for though his English was good enough he had an unmistakable Parisian accent. He gave his name as Marcel Duval, and explained that he had travelled from France the previous week on official business. He had landed at Dover and travelled thence to Brighton.

where he was the guest of a man whose name was well known to the British public. This man was engaged in war work of a very important kind, in connection with which Duval was making this visit to England.

"You must understand, messieurs," he said, "I was very much engaged in my mission. It was important that I should lose no time, and therefore—I paid little, if any, attention to local happenings." Here he bowed rather apologetically to Relph, as though his lack of interest in a local murder smacked of discourtesy. "My host was in the same position. In any case, he is not a man who would be greatly interested in the death of an old woman, no matter how unusual the circumstances. So—it was only when I heard the police message on the radio that I had the curiosity to examine my English notes."

"And found you had one or more of them? The notes for which the police are inquiring, I mean?"

"One, monsieur, the note for ten pounds. Owing to certain events in my country I left rather hurriedly, bringing with me a good deal of French money and not very much English. I arrived on Tuesday, the 12th, in the late afternoon, and proceeded straight to my friend's house. On Wednesday he counselled me to change my money at the office of Hackett's, a travel agency who, he said, would give me the best possible exchange. I went there on his recommendation, and in return for my money they gave me certain notes, of which this is one." He opened his pigskin wallet and produced a ten-pound note that he laid on the table.

"Jee-roosalem!" said Crook gently. He had a good head for figures and there was no need for him to compare the number with the list of three that were jotted down in his pocket book. Here, then, was the note to which they looked for aid in solving this extraordinary double crime.

Relph glanced at the watch on his wrist. "We'll go round at once," he said. "Let's hope the place isn't shut. Hopkins," he called a subordinate, "get Hackett's on the phone and if there's anyone there, say I want the whole staff to remain on duty till we arrive. Monsieur, you'll be able to accompany us, I hope. You might be able to recognise the clerk who gave you the note."

"I think I should," said Duval slowly. "I remember saying to myself that in France a man of that age would not be behind a counter but in the front line."

Hopkins, having made his connection, came up to say that the office normally closed at seven, but that all employees would be kept on the premises until the arrival of the police. The three men, therefore, Relph, Crook and the foreigner, went down in the indefatigable Scarlet Woman. Duval was as good as his word, and instantly pointed out a weedy-looking youth who was lighting a cigarette, in defiance of the notice pasted on the walls that smoking was not permitted during working hours.

"Working hours stop at seven," said the young man to no one in particular.

The manager, a middle-aged man, with a trim black moustache, came forward to meet them.

"I hope nothing is wrong," he said, with some foreboding.

"On the contrary, a great deal is wrong, and we hope you may be able to help us," Relph told him. "Will you tell all your staff to remain for the moment, and then perhaps you and that young man with the cigarette in his mouth could go into your private office. I want to ask him one or two questions."

Still in the dark, the manager agreed, and the four men went through a glass door into an inner room.

"Now," said Relph, coming to the point at once, "this is going to be a good memory test for you. What's your name?"

The young gentleman, who wore a veneer of sophistication over an insolent manner, said, "Meaning me? Matthews, if you must know."

"I want you to look at this gentleman," indicating Duval, "and tell me if you remember seeing him before."

The manager broke in. "I don't think, Inspector, you quite realise the numbers of people we have coming in and out to change money or arrange journeys. We do English as well as foreign travel; and though, naturally, we're not so busy as we were some months ago, still it's asking rather a lot of my clerk to expect him to recognise one particular person."

"I don't suppose you have as many foreigners as you used," suggested Relph.

"That's true," drawled Matthews. "And thank God for it. The government's taken its time coming to its senses about the alien menace. Yes, I do remember this man. He speaks with a foreign accent, and I remember wondering whether it wasn't my duty as a citizen to do something about it."

Crook put a restraining hand on the Frenchman's arm. "Don't worry about him," he said. "He's what we call an oaf. It's a special breed."

ANTHONY GILBERT

The young man flushed an unbecoming plum colour.
"All damn' fine the country asking us to lend a hand in
this spy menace," he said loudly, "but when we do begin
to keep our eyes and ears open we get insulted, that's
all. Not much encouragement . . ."

Relph answered him. "I take it, in this case, your
duty as a citizen wasn't quite up to stratch. I don't seem
to remember seeing you at the station."

Matthews looked sulky. "It was a French voice, and
after all, they're our Allies. If he was a foreign agent,
I wasn't to know. But I remember passing the remark
that if I were the P.M. I'd intern the lot."

"I'm sure you've written to tell him so. Now then, are
you certain you do recognise this gentleman? Because,
I warn you, you'll probably have to swear to him in a
court of law."

Some of Matthews' langour fell from him. So I was
right, was I? Yes, I do recognize him. It's a long time
since I'd had a foreigner, and then he had a good deal
of French money about him, about thirty pounds worth,
so I had to ask the manager if it was all right. We have
a limit, you see. But he said, when he heard the address,
it was all right."

"D'you remember the address?"

"Clarendon Lodge. You know, it's the big white
house . . ."

"Quite so. Well, that's quite smart of you, Matthews.
So you changed it?"

"Yes. He asked for pound notes chiefly, but said he'd
take one ten-pound note. Of course, I took the number
of that. We always do. Just a part of the Hackett
Service."

"So you can identify the note you gave him?"

"It'll be in the books."

"Could you verify it for us?"

"Of course."

"That's the first step," observed Relph to the manager
as Matthews went off on his errand. "Now comes something harder. I want to know who brought that ten-
pound note in. Any chance of your being able to tell
us that?"

"Shouldn't be difficult," said the manager. "We're like
most of these money-changing businesses always up against
the chance of bad notes. So nowadays we keep a record
of the numbers. I can't tell you who changed that note,
but we ought to be able to find out who brought it here."

Matthews returned with the information that the number of the ten-pound note talled with his record of it.
He said he might have changed the note in the first

152

place, but if so he didn't remember it. However, that was easy to discover. The records showed that the note had been brought in on Wednesday, the 13th March, by a Miss French, of The Nook, Periford, Sussex.

"Call it a day," murmured Crook when he heard that. "Oh, boy, do the police have fun or do they? What's the next move?"

"I'd like to get in touch with the clerk who cashed that note," said Relph with surface composure that did him credit. "What time did you come along to the office, M. Duval?"

"It would be about half-past nine, I think."

"So Miss French was along earlier still. What time do you open?" He turned to the manager.

"Half-past eight."

"Hold on a minute," said Matthews. "I remember when this gentleman came in and said he'd like one note for ten pounds I turned to the man alongside me—I didn't happen to have a tenner at the moment, and asked him to pass me one. That would be Chetwynd. He's out there still. I could fetch him, if you like." Eagerness had now replaced his former boredom.

"Send him along," agreed Relph. "And don't go yourself for a few minutes, in case we want to ask you something else."

Matthews' face fell. Clearly he had hoped to remain for the rest of the interview. A moment later Chetwynd came in, a small thin man with fair hair going thin on the scalp.

"As a matter of fact, I remember the lady," he said, speaking with a clipped precision that was a great contrast to Matthews' casual manner. "She was one of these elderly people who seem to imagine that anything they do is bound to be interesting to other people. When she gave me the note she said it would be very kind if I would change it, small shops made so much fuss about taking a note that size; it had just been sent to her from London, and she wasn't often in Brighton. She hadn't gone to her bank because the bank wasn't open . . . I didn't pay much attention. We hear a lot of that kind of thing, and as a rule it's quite unimportant."

"Do you remember what she looked like?" Relph was taking no chances.

"Oh, she was one of these middle-aged women dressed in brown. There wasn't anything particular about her. Tweed suit, felt hat, no face powder—you know the type."

"I know. Well, thank you very much. I'll want both these men to come along to the station and make a statement for our records, and later they'll be wanted at the inquest. But I needn't keep anyone any longer to-night."

Outside, the Frenchman asked tentatively, "And I myself, monsieur? You understand I may have to return without warning—I am not my own master."

Relph said he quite understood. "If you'd make a statement that can be read in court, if it proves impossible for you to attend the inquest, I think in the circumstances that will meet the case. And we shall want the note for evidence."

There wasn't much likelihood of finding fingerprints on it after it had been through so many hands, but Relph doubted whether that mattered. He took Duval back to the Station and when he had made his statement Crook took him off to the Hoop and Toy and bought him beer.

"My story, I hope it is of some use," said his guest courteously, gazing with admiration at a man who could apparently swallow a pint at a gulp and then call for more.

"I'll say it is. You know, I've always had an open mind about ghosts. Now I know they do exist, and I take off my hat to them."

It was difficult to disconcert Mr. Crook.

"Come, come," he said in disapproving tones to Relph, when the Frenchman had returned to his host and Crook had made his way back to the station, "look on the bright side, my boy. Be thankful for your blessings or one of these days you may find you ain't got any left."

"One of these days," said Relph ominously, "the police will be called in to investigate your murder."

"And you hope it'll be one of those that the police boggle from start to finish. No. don't tell me. It's as plain as the nose on my face and nothing could be much clearer than that." He grinned thoughtfully, "How you'll miss me if that day should ever break."

"Perhaps you'll tell me what it is we've got to be grateful for this time," Relph continued viciously.

"You know one thing, at least. Ivy Green wasn't killed to cover the murder of Miss French, because Miss French didn't die till the next morning. In fact, if you ask me it's as clear as daylight. X came back to get the body out of The Nook—no, don't ask me why he came back, because that's one of the ones I can't answer, but perhaps he'd left some important clue behind—and Miss French sailed over the horizon just in time to meet the gentleman, complete with corpse, on her front doorstep. Use your imagination, man. What would you do in his place? Put out her light, too, of course. And that's what he did."

"We're as far as ever from knowing why Ivy Green was murdered," Relph reminded him.

"Not for her money, because she hadn't got any. Not because she was dangerous on Miss French's account, because Miss French wasn't dead then. No, she must have known her murderer and I dare say known him a bit too well for her own safety. They arrange to meet in the woods—his doing, I dare say, because no one bar a lunatic would go walking up there in that kind of weather."

"You're supposing premeditated murder?"

"It could be, Relph, it could be. Well, anyhow, it seems safe to believe he didn't want anyone to know he was meeting the girl, or what was wrong with the ice-cream parlour on the parade? They met, perhaps the girl was unreasonable, perhaps she was obviously going to be a nuisance and he was a married man . . ."

"You're giving us a lot of perhapses," interjected Relph.

"If your incompetent bobbies would find the corpse we could wash out some of 'em. As it is, even I don't work miracles. Well, it was very cold and the wind was blowing like blazes, and presently they saw a little cottage in the woods . . ."

"That's Grimm's Fairy Tales," Relph interrupted again.

"So it is," agreed Crook, unabashed. "Well, anyway, there was a row. Perhaps he wanted more than she was prepared to give, and she started to yell her head off; and he had to stop her somehow; or perhaps it was just that he didn't want a maintenance order out against him. The upshot was he finished her, and left her body in the cottage. They must have had a whale of a conversation and what not, because he was only just through when Miss Verity arrived. She swears she saw the glow of his cigarette, and she don't smoke and nor did Miss French, but there was ash scattered around on the floor when we got there the next day and some crushed stubs lying about. I don't know what he intended to do with the body at first; I don't suppose he expected Miss Verity to arrive like a bird out of the night. And I don't know either why he felt he'd got to go back and fetch her the next day. Perhaps he hoped to get her away before she'd been identified. We'll learn that in due course. But the fact remains he did come back. What bothers me is—why the hell didn't he dump the pair of them in the well? I suppose you're sure he didn't?"

"Dead sure," said Relph briefly.

Round and round the problem they tramped. The essential facts were incontrovertible. Miss French was alive just before nine on the morning of the thirteenth. The girl had been killed on the evening of the twelfth.

The murderer had contrived to conceal both bodies in record time. One, indeed, had still to be discovered. As for the other two banknotes, there was always the chance that they might turn up, but the odds were that they were in the dead woman's handbag, wherever that might be. Or they might have been destroyed. Any murderer with the smallest knowledge of police routine would realise that the numbers would be known at the bank, and it wasn't likely he would try to change them until all the thunder had died down. And for makeweight, just for luck, Miss Verity herself had disappeared. As Crook remarked, no Crime Club reader could demand more for his money.

"That's where you're wrong," Relph told him smartly. "They demand a lot more. They want a solution, with every tangle smoothed out and every end neatly tied up. We may have to work miracles to provide it, but what's that to them?"

As soon as Crook re-entered the Royal Crescent he received a message that the manager, Mr. Turtle, would like to see him.

"It's about Mr. Fennel," Turtle explained, offering Crook a drink that he accepted, and a cigarette that, as always, he refused.

"Don't tell me he's been murdered, too," Crook implored him.

"No, no. Or at least, not so far as I'm aware. But something has occurred. . . . The chambermaid was emptying the waste-paper basket in his room, and as usual she collected all the clean paper to put in the Borough sack. We're strong against waste in this hotel, as you may have noticed."

"I had," agreed Crook, and this time the twinkle was in his eye. "Especially on the menu. Even the cauliflower stalks come in the next night, served up as an entree."

"I see you like your joke." But there wasn't the ghost of a twinkle in Mr. Turtle's glance. "However, this may prove serious. I glanced through the papers myself, a mere routine measure; our clients sometimes are careless and throw away something of value, and afterwards they write to have it returned. And so I happened to find this." He produced a piece of crumpled paper and laid it on the table. It was a square white envelope addressed: A. Crook, Esq., Royal Crescent Hotel, Brighton. Personal and Urgent.

Crook took it up carefully and turned it over. "It's been opened," he pointed out. "There's nothing in it."

"I know, Mr. Crook. But it was addressed to you and it was found among Mr. Fennel's papers. Of course, if you had given it to him for any reason . . ."

"I hadn't," interrupted Crook flatly. "I've never even seen it before." He brooded over it for a while. "As you say, damned odd." Then his head came up with a jerk. "Something has just occurred to me," he announced. "That handwriting. Know whose it is?"

"I can't say . . ."

"Then don't. I'll tell you. It's Miss Verity's, and, seeing the envelope never came through the post, how the devil did it get into Fennell's possession?"

"That was why I kept it to show you. It seemed to me strange, to say the least of it."

Crook threw back his shoulders and dealt the manager a resounding slap on the back.

"You did right, my boy," he announced, in the tones of a film detective. "On this small affair the whole of the Butler's Wood mystery may turn."

Up in his room he examined the envelope yet more carefully. It was of thin pale gray paper of cheap quality; on the back was printed in black letters: Brighton Ethical Union, 9 Settles Street, Brighton.

"So that's where she went when she left the lawyer. I wonder how far that takes us. It's obvious she had something she wanted me to know. I'd left a message that I wouldn't be back till dinner-time, and she couldn't wait to get on with her investigations as long as that. She meant to go to London—Heaven only knows why, though I might have shared Heaven's knowledge if this letter had reached its proper destination. Instead of that, it was intercepted and opened, and the information it contained absorbed by someone else. And it looks uncommonly as though the fellow who absorbed it was our young friend." He lighted a pipe and considered the matter further. "It was about eleven-thirty when Miss Verity left Wilkes's office; she caught the five o'clock train to town. Between those times she discovered something she thought it urgent for me to know, and decided she must go to London at once to follow up a clue of whose nature I haven't the remotest idea. She must have gone into the Union's writing-room to scribble me a note. Either she intended to leave it at the hotel or to put it in a pillar-box. Presumably what actually happened it is that she ran across young Fennel and he offered to deliver it. Or she asked him to. Most likely the latter.

"That gives us another point. She'd been working on the supposition that he was mixed up in the crime; she didn't make any secret of her point of view, and she'd had a long chat with him the night before. Something must have happened at that interview that took her like a homing pigeon to the lawyer's office; and something Wilkes told her turned her suspicions in a fresh direction. Otherwise, she wouldn't have given the letter to Fennel. Also, she made up her mind to go to London; no doubt the letter told me why. It may also have told me where she could be got at and how long she'd be away. The obvious thing for her to do was to call up her old lodgings, but she didn't do that, because Parsons made inquiries, and they'd heard nothing of her. Question is, did she ever reach London? So far as we know she hadn't got any luggage. What did she mean to do about that?"

The answer seemed clear. The five o'clock was a quick non-stop train, reaching London at about six; presumably Miss Verity supposed that her business could be transacted in time for her to return the same night. But, explore every avenue though he might, Crook could find no reason for this mysterious journey. It was true that it had been impossible to check up on her arrival, but it would be almost out of the question to identify one individual traveller in that press; and no body had been found, or any evidence of a struggle. Besides, Fennel had been in the hotel at six o'clock, so clearly he hadn't boarded the train. It seemed, therefore, as though she must have reached her destination. The letter, however, might have given details as to her proposed movements, and anyone who had read it would have advance knowledge and might be able to head her off. After all, Crook reminded himself, he didn't know what Fennel had done after dinner. Suppose he had gone to the station and met her on arrival and contrived to put her away on the walk back to the hotel?

"All the same," he groaned in desperation, "it don't make sense. If she was sure he wasn't guilty and was writing to tell me so, what motive had he got for the murder? And if she still thought he'd done it, why give him the letter? They swear the note was never handed in at the desk, so she must have handed it over of her own accord. Unless . . . Gosh Maggie." He was tramping up and down the room all this time; the unfortunate woman who had the room beneath him promised herself that she'd leave the place in the morning. Up and down, up and down he marched, his heavy tread shaking the electric standard in the room below. Now he stopped in front of the long mirror, shaking his fist at his own reflection.

"You miserable, pot-bellied, flannel-footed, slob-eyed son of a gun," he adjured it fiercely. "You've got all the facts; there's nothing to do but arrange them in a nice picture, and you haven't so much as got the frame. You beetle-necked fool—the truth staring you in the face all this time, and you couldn't see it. Where the heck's that Buckler woman? I've got to find her and ask her which platform it was. Everything now depends on that."

CHAPTER SEVENTEEN

Relph was deeply occupied with a matter not remotely concerned with Miss Verity when Crook burst in unannounced and unceremoniously seized him by the arm.

"What the hell!" exclaimed Relph, with justifiable annoyance.

"Hell it is. And with the lid off. I've just waked up."

"Your rest seems to have given you a lot of energy," commented Relph, but his sarcasm made as much impression on his companion as a pebble on a buffalo's hide.

"I want some men," declared Crook abruptly. "As many as your can spare."

"What for?"

"To help me find Miss Verity."

"You've got half the force out digging for another protegee of yours. Do you imagine we've nothing to do but unearth your careless lady friends?"

"Unearth might be appropriate," said Crook more slowly. "Anyhow, it's a chance in a million, and I've got to take it. I've come down on the police first, which shows you how much faith I have in 'em. Only—there's no time to be lost."

"Have you any idea where you're going to look for her?"

For answer Crook produced a handful of keys, each with a label or wooden tag attached.

"I wouldn't be surprised if she was on one of the premises belonging to one of these," he replied ungrammatically. "Anyway, it's worth trying."

Relph looked hopelessly puzzled. "What on earth are those?"

"Keys of unoccupied houses in the neighbourhood of Brighton Station."

"Why in the name of Pete should you think she'd be there?"

"It stands to reason she's somewhere, and I'd say she's not her own mistress, because if she had been she'd have got in touch with me before this. If she were a free agent she'd have seen about Miss French's death and known she'd be wanted for the inquest."

"Certainly she wouldn't have vanished the way she has. Miss Verity's a lady; she has consideration."

"Thanks a lot," said Relph glumly. "I thought you said she'd gone to London."

"What I said was she was seen on the platform about the time the five o'clock train leaves for town, and like the jays we are we assumed that meant she'd boarded the train. But—mark this! No one saw her get in. I've tackled Miss Buckler, and though she was as sick as a cat because she thinks her pet bit of evidence is being spat on, she's had to acknowledge that she put two and two together and made them the sum total of Miss Verity's journey to town."

"It's not altogether unreasonable," said Relph gently. "If you see someone waiting for a train, you might quite well think she meant to board it."

"Whereas actually there are lots of other reasons. D'you ever hear of friends coming from London? It might have been that. No, no, don't say it. I know no one's asked for her, so it isn't likely to be that; but she might have a passion for trains, what's called a train fixation; or perhaps she'd come to collect something that was being sent from London, a parcel of some kind."

At this last flight of fancy Relph looked pretty sceptical. "No need for that. It could have been delivered to her door."

"You don't understand that woman. She's got all the pep and drive the public likes to think are the prerogative of the police force. Never leave to the morning what you could do to-night."

"What was it likely to be?"

"P'raps she'll tell us that when we find her."

"And where are you going to look?"

"I've already told you. Think for a minute, man. Put yourself in the murderer's place. You've done away with two women, and a third has strong suspicions as to who you are; and she's proposin' to spill the beans to me. Oh, yes, she wrote all right, but the letter got intercepted. The envelope's been found, but that's all. She wrote the letter at the public reading-room of the Brighton Ethical Union, and I've seen the bird behind the desk there on my way. He remembers a female in a yellow hat—we get all sorts, he told me—asking for some book on Christian ethics, and then she sat down and made shoals of notes. He rather hoped they'd copped her for a convert. Actually, of course, that was a blind. She wasn't making notes; she was writing to me. It seems pretty safe to assume that the letter was actually taken from her by the murderer. What we've got to discover is where he deposited her. Because, you see, he couldn't possibly let her live. He could destroy the letter, but as long as she remained she could write it again or give her report verbatim. Well, there you are, what would you do?"

"You ought to have joined the force," said Relph heavily.

"Don't make me laugh," implored Crook. "I'm not the man I was. I tell you, we're dealing with a desperate character. He had to get rid of Miss Verity and he had to get rid of her quick. After all, if you're going to swing for two murders, you may as well chuck in a third for luck. Now, how many places are there in a busy town like Brighton, at about 5 p.m., where you can commit a murder safely, let alone conceal the corpse? You could knock the lady on the head on the platform, of course, but you couldn't hope to get away with it. The same disadvantage applies to the street, and to any sort of conveyance, public or private. There are churches, of course, but quite apart from murder in a church bein' sacrilege, which very likely wouldn't trouble our bird, the body would be found too soon."

"There was that belfry murder in America," began Relph.

"Half a century ago. More. And in America. No, no, we shan't find my client under a pew or strung up to a bell-rope. And I don't believe she was pushed off the pier, because for one thing she must have been seen in that monstrosity of a hat she was wearing, and for another I believe that, wherever she is there is the hat also. Anyway, bodies shoved into the sea have a distressin' way of copying the bread that was cast upon the waters. She can't be in a cinema, so there's really only one place left, and that's a private house."

"There are still several thousand private houses in Brighton. Are you proposing to examine them all?"

"Not necessary," said Crook contemptuously, and again he swung his link of keys. "She won't be in an occupied house, unless you think this is a gang murder, and I don't believe it is. What we've got to do and do damn' quick is ransack all the empty houses anywhere near the station. Houses with gardens specially. Houses with shrubberies where you could hide a body and it wouldn't be found for weeks. Houses with side doors; houses with tool-sheds and coal cellars opening from the back garden. Houses in quiet places. Specially houses that could be entered without a key. It 'ud amaze you how many people leave a broken pane of glass or something, and then are surprised that tramps sleep uninvited on

the premises. Y'know, I'm the world's champion boy
scout letting you in on this."

"You wouldn't have come near us if you didn't want
something out of us," was Relph's ungracious retort.

"Right first time," agreed Crook. "I don't want to be
told I put the lady there for purposes of me own. And
I'm going to take one of your chaps with me, so no one
can suggest that I hooked her out of my vest pocket
and hung her on the hall chandelier, just to put a fast
one over on the police. As if I'd need to take all this
trouble. I can do that in me sleep, with one hand
tied behind my back, my boy, and well you know it."

All the time he was pouring out this farrago of nonsense, he was rapidly sorting through the various orders-
to-view he had obtained from a number of house agents,
setting several of them aside as practically impossible,
marking one or two as the most promising.

"You do realise we're looking for a little dried-up chip
of a spinster, don't you?" Relph reminded him. "Not the
sort that breaks into empty houses with a boy friend
for a roll on the bare boards. If it was Ivy Green you
were looking for I'd be more inclined to back your
fancy, but a woman like Miss Verity—she was respectable."

"They're always the ones that give you the greatest
surprises," Crook assured him. "Now, then, if you send
your men out in pairs . . . I've put this lot of houses on
one side; they're semi-detached villas or avenue houses.
It isn't likely the crime was committed in any of these.
Too many eyes at neighbouring windows. Our bird don't
appreciate publicity. I'll take three—it's a long job
going over a big house, tryin' all the cupboards and
outhouses, going through the garden. . ."

"Are you proposing to dig up all the gardens?" demanded Relph, really horrified now.

"Not necessary. She won't be under the ground, though
she might be in a cellar somewhere. You'll be here so as
to take reports? Right. We better be going. I haven't
many hopes after all this time, but she was a tough
little soul and you never know your luck."

Relph, not really impressed by a single word that Crook
had spoken, knew that if he refused this help, Crook
and his yellow journalist friend, Cummings, would plaster
him in the press. There was also the unfortunate fact
that the woman's first story had resulted in the discovery
of one body, and if they hadn't found Ivy Green dead,
at least no one so far had found her alive. The inquiries
about Harriet French were still in progress. No one
remembered an elderly woman booking a room for a

night at any local hotel or boarding house, she had no friends to whom she could have gone, and in such weather it was inconceivable that she had spent the night out of doors. In any case, in any affair involving Mr. Crook, too much energy was better than too little. So he gave the necessary instructions, and the men went off.

Crook's first destination was a large corner house with wooden fences round it, a deep basement descending into the shadows and a dark garden stretching behind. He pushed the key into the lock and he and his companion entered a great echoing hall, with a cracked marble bowl hanging crookedly from dingy chains.

"Not been lived in for some time," said the constable, with a shiver.

"That's what we're here to discover. Take the basement, will you, and I'll go upstairs. The place is honeycombed with cupboards, and it won't be safe to disregard lofts or cisterns."

He stood still for a moment, listening to the heavy feet clumping down the uncarpeted kitchen stairs. Then he heard a brief exclamation.

"Not found anything already?"

"No, sir. But—there's a range here and a copper that 'ud take a couple of bodies apiece."

"One's all I'm looking for." But even his hardy spirit shrank from the thought of what either copper or range might conceal. It appeared, however, that neither contained more than the usual stale and burnt-out rubbish that seems to accumulate in empty houses. Crook went upstairs. There were three floors above the ground, and by the time he had reached the top the man down in the basement seemed as far off as though he were in another building. Dark blinds hung askew at many of the windows; the house was in a shocking state of repair; floorboards were worm-eaten, windows cracked and filthy. Crook was not imaginative, but he experienced an extraordinary sensation as he opened door after door, prepared each time for something inert to fall out at his feet. Once he lifted up his voice and called to Samson, his companion in the bowels of the house, but the great shadowy stairs caught his voice and made nothing of it. Wherever he moved, his feet seemed to arouse echoes; looking over the banisters he was certain that he saw a white face looking slyly up, but when he came down, cursing himself for a nervous fool, he saw it was only a trick of the light striking at a tattered drapery the last tenants had left behind. The whole place seemed impregnated with ghosts. Crook could see that little

163

woman, like a defiant cock-sparrow, suddenly finding herself in the power of her enemy, struggling desperately for her life. He choked down an exclamation, and then stopped dead. From a room on the right he heard a strangle struggling sound.

"Surely I went in there," he muttered. "Could I have missed anything?" He remembered his own warning delivered to so many clients. When you follow a man, be sure he is not really following you. Suppose someone had come into the house, had crept into this room?

"I'm losing my nerve," he exclaimed aloud in simple amazement. And flung open the door. A big black cat jumped off the window-sill, and came to rub itself against his legs. From the hall the voice of Samson hailed him.

"Nothing down there, sir. You couldn't hide a kitten where I shouldn't have found it."

"Tried the garden?"

"Two bushes and an overgrown grass plot, and a couple of gravel paths. She can't have been dug in there. No spade's touched this garden for months."

"All right," said Crook. "I've drawn a blank, too. Let's get on to the next place."

It was not Crook but a party of the police who eventually found Miss Verity. Arrived back at the station during the early afternoon Crook found the place agog with excitement. The sergeant, who had made the actual discovery, was waiting to repeat the story to the bustling little Cockney lawyer. He behaved, thought Crook, disgustedly, as though it was his initiative, his energy, that had saved Laura at the eleventh hour.

"It was that house in Braythwaite Avenue," he explained, "the second one we tried. I had my suspicions, because I thought any fool could have opened the French windows from outside. They hadn't been bolted, you see. A penknife would have turned back the catch, and I'd say that's how it was done. There are new scratches on the woodwork."

Crook said in a sort of desperate rage, "Is she dead? Your fancy details can wait."

"She's in hospital. A private nursing home, that is. There was one at the end of the road and we took her there right away. Mind you, she's pretty far gone . . ."

"You'd probably have gone all the way, if you'd been locked in an empty house for three days. Where did you find her?"

"In a kind of cupboard boxroom under the roof. It's the size of a small room, only it hasn't any window; the roof slopes right down to the floor in front. But you could pack a dozen bodies in there easily. She had a scarf tied round her throat, but I'd say the murderer got interrupted at his job and shoved her in there, and locked the door. Anyhow, she must have come round after a bit, but she couldn't get out or attract any attention. The thing I noticed as we came up the stairs was a bit of dark stuff trailing along the floor. It turned out to be a bit of the blue veil over her face that she'd pushed through the crack, in the hope that someone would see it."

"I told you she was tough," said Crook.

"There were a number of chocolate wrappings, quite fresh ones, on the floor. And in her pocket was a bag of lemon drops."

"The perfect murderee," commented Crook with approval. "Never caught napping. What did she do about air?"

"I must say she showed good sense," admitted the sergeant, a little grudgingly, Crook thought. "The door of the boxroom wasn't much of a fit, a good inch and a half from the ground, and she lay down and put her mouth there. She got a constant supply of fresh air in that way, though come to that it wouldn't be so fresh with all the house shut up and no windows open. And, of course, it wasn't easy for the foul air to escape. If we hadn't got there when we did, she'd have meant another little job for the undertaker. But as it is, the doctor seems to think she'll pull round."

"She'll pull round," agreed Crook heartily. "She's not the sort to let a fellow down. Was she knocked about in any way?"

"There's some nasty marks on the neck and throat," replied the sergeant reprovingly. "Someone had it in for her all right. But I suppose something happened . . ."

"Someone else came to look over the house, I expect, and X didn't dare stop. Of course, she shoved the veiling through the crack to arouse curiosity."

"Perhaps whoever came in didn't go all over the house. If he did, it's funny he didn't spot it."

"Not a bit," contradicted Crook. "I don't suppose it was there then. You wait till you've been knocked and strangled as near as a touch, and see how long it takes you to come round. She was probably completely in the dark for some time. Then she realised that, barring a miracle, she was done for. It's lucky she had that chocolate. It probably just kept her going, but three days in a dark room is no fun. God, what she must have felt like when she realised her letter was never going to reach me, and she might be a skeleton before she was found. People ain't so keen on houses that size

nowadays, and not keen on anything along the coast
come to that. Y'know, there's one thing I simply cannot
understand."

"What's that?" Relph sounded a bit sarcastic. It was
infuriating the way Crook's most fatuous notions contrived to ring the bell.

"Why it took me so long to realise she hadn't gone to
town. Of course, she didn't give that letter up. It was
taken from her. This chap took it, and then tried to do
her in. No thanks to him he didn't succeed. I suppose
he didn't dare go back afterwards. Or perhaps he thought
he'd done the job. I say, we'll have to see he don't make
a bolt for it. We'll want Miss Verity's story."

"As soon as he knows she's been found, he most likely
will."

"He'll wait to see if she's going to pull through. There's
always the chance she might snuff out. She was pretty
low." That was the sergeant speaking.

"You can't see her to-night," Relph added warningly to
Crook. "They won't allow it, and anyway it wouldn't
do any good. She's still unconscious."

"Might see someone in charge, though." Flinging
himself into his car he drove in a way that would help
Hitler exterminate every living Englishman, which apparently was his intention, said Relph sourly.

"Trust Crook to put one over on us every time," he
wound up. "All the same, if this woman does collapse,
we're not much forrarder. I don't see how we're going
to prove a case, and Fennel's only got to swear the
chambermaid made a mistake to cosh our story about
the envelope."

"Still, someone in the hotel chucked it into the basket,"
Carson pointed out, and Relph brightened up a little
and said, Yes, that was so. But he didn't propose to
question Fennel just yet, not till they had further bulletins
about Miss Verity.

At the nursing home an agitated and overbearing
nurse led Crook to the matron. Miss Snell was one of
those puritanical women who can't bear to think other
people enjoy an obviously sinful world.

"It will be quite impossible for you to see Miss Verity
to-night," she told him. "She is still unconscious and the
doctor can give no great hope that she will recover."

Crook shook his great bull head. "The doctor don't
know our Miss Verity. A woman who could keep herself
alive all that time on sixpenn'orth of chocolate and a
breath of fresh air won't be knocked out by a mere
nursing home."

"The patient is having all possible treatment," returned the matron in outraged tones.

"When can I see her?"

"When the doctor gives you permission."

"Where's the doctor?"

"He is not here."

"Will he be coming back to-night?"

"Not unless he is sent for."

"You don't think of sending for him in connection with Miss Verity? She can't be as bad as you make out, or he'd be sitting by the bedside with his watch in his hand."

"Dr. Atkinson is not a defeatist," observed the matron icily. "Nevertheless, he makes no secret of the fact—of which you may not be aware—that this is a matter of life and death, Mr.—er—er——"

"Crook—Arthur Crook. The Criminals' Hope, is my other name." She stared at him, haughty, more outraged than ever. "And I know all about life and death. I'll be round in the morning, Miss—er—er. If she should come round before then—all right, all right, I only said if—even doctors can make mistakes, here's my telephone number." He stood up. "This is a murder case, you know. Or perhaps you hadn't realised."

He marched out without giving her a chance to ask questions. From the nearest telephone booth he abstracted a telephone directory and began to look for Dr. Atkinson. There were two, he found, but one of them was an oldish man who didn't go out much. Dr. Francis Atkinson was Crook's man. The Criminals' Hope slammed the book shut and went to call. Atkinson was a tall thin fellow with an amusing Irish face and the usual Irish charm.

"I thought it was an odd affair," he acknowledged. "Someone tried to choke her, didn't they? And it didn't look like sex run wild."

"How bad is she?" asked Crook.

"She's got a devil of a lot of resistance. That's obvious, or she wouldn't have come through as much as she has. If they've got the will to live, that helps more than you can get the layman to believe."

"She's got that all right."

"She's low, of course, but it's not a hopeless case. I'm going in again in the morning. Nothing else to be done to-night. I'll ring you, if you like, after I've seen her. No, I'm not asking any questions. I've got eyes in my head, and I can see there's been some monkey business here."

CHAPTER EIGHTEEN

The next morning Crook's telephone extension whirred at about 11 a.m. He was waiting to attend the inquest of Miss French, though he doubted whether it would get them far even when they heard the verdict. Still, it couldn't be held over any longer.

Atkinson's voice spoke. "Mr. Crook? I've seen your client. No change. There's still a fighting chance. Ring me some time after five, in case there's fresh news."

Crook hung up the receiver. They couldn't do anything now till they had her story. At twelve o'clock he went down to the inquest. As he had anticipated, nothing very much transpired. All the usual people gave evidence. Mr. Wilkes identified the body; Mrs. Home agreed that she was the last person (bar the murderer) to see the dead woman, in a human capacity, that is. There was a girl at the Post Office and the supercilious young clerk from Hackett's, but they hadn't known her as anything but an elderly woman coming into their respective offices on business. Wilkes wasn't easy in his mind. He looked like a cat about to be plunged into a cold tub. The doctor gave professional evidence about the disease from which the dead woman had suffered; the matron produced the telegram. The coroner was impatient; the foreman of the jury kept asking questions. The only lady member kept saying it wasn't right, she wasn't right, she meant poor Miss French, not right in the head, no one living like that could hope to be.

The small crowd that had assembled had hoped for fireworks when Harry Fennel gave his evidence, but they were disappointed. True, he admitted his relationship to the deceased, but that wasn't evidence of murder. He had been hard up, he said, but who wasn't these days? He had only seen the old lady to speak to once, when he called at The Nook to tell her who he was.

"What was her attitude?" asked the coroner. "Did she seem glad to see you?"

"I wouldn't say that. You couldn't really expect it. Neither of my parents had treated her well, and it wasn't by any wish of hers that her money would eventually come to me."

"Did you ask her for a loan?" the coroner demanded unexpectedly.

Crook moved his stiff eyebrows. There were things coroners weren't supposed to say, but you could never get them to believe it.

Harry said No, it hadn't occurred to him. As a matter of fact, he had felt a bit delicate about going to see her at all. But since he was her relative he had felt he hadn't much choice. When he went up to the bungalow he had the haziest notion of her finances; it was only when she told him that one day he'd have a very pleasant income through her that he realised she had more than a mere pittance.

"No one seeing her could have imagined she had more than a couple of hundred a year," he explained. "I don't suppose she spent more than that. She had a pretty thin time."

Pressed by the coroner, he acknowledged that her attitude had been, on the whole, a hostile one.

"I don't know why you came, if it wasn't for the money," she had said. "Your father over again."

"Did she show you round the place?"

"There wasn't much to see."

"Did you know there was a well there?"

"She pointed it out to me as we walked down to the gate."

"I see. And that's the last time you saw her?"

"Yes."

"What were you doing on the Wednesday morning, the thirteenth?"

"I went up to the Golf Club about nine-fifteen. I was supposed to be playing golf that day."

"It was snowing, wasn't it?"

"Yes."

"Pretty hard?"

"It stopped later in the morning."

"But when you got up there?"

"Yes."

"So you couldn't play?"

"I found a message when I arrived postponing the game."

"What did you do then?"

"Hung about for a bit in case the snow stopped and I could find anyone to give me a game. Then, when I saw there wasn't going to be any golf that morning, I got back into my car and drove into Brighton."

"Can you remember what time this was?"

"Ah, about ten or ten-fifteen."

"What did you do then?"

"Went to a cinema."

"Can you remember the picture you saw?"

"It was that girl who always wears a sarong. In this picture she'd adopted a tiger. I don't remember what it was called."

"Did you happen to mention it to anyone else?"

"I don't suppose so. I didn't really know anyone. Anyway, I shouldn't have thought it important."

"I see. Thank you, Mr. Fennel."

The jury didn't take long over their verdict. They plumped for Murder by Some Person or Persons Unknown, as indeed on the evidence they could do little else. Crook and some others were a little surprised they had done more than formal identification, seeing how keen the police were to rope in Harry Fennel as the murderer, but he supposed they'd realised they hadn't enough evidence to hang a white rat. Anyway, they were holding their hand until they could get Miss Verity's story. The coroner, accepting the verdict, added a rider that the case might be reopened later, by which everyone understood that he was referring to a possible inquest on the body of Ivy Green, if this ever came to light. On the whole, it was a disappointing morning for everyone but Harry Fennel.

For more hours than she could count, hours that seemed if they must stretch into days, if not weeks, Laura had been trying to combat wave after wave of blackness that poured down on her like clouds of soot, blinding and choking her. Behind the blackness was something of terrific importance, something to be accomplished, something no one but she could achieve. She fought with all the puny strength of her body and the enormous strength of her mind to clear a path and escape. Quite what it was that so filled her consciousness she could not always be sure, but of its tremendous significance she had no doubt at all.

This darkness had gone on for a long time. It was mingled with footsteps on uncarpeted stairs, and hard boards, and voices she couldn't recognise. There was something she knew and had to say, but it must be said to the right person. It was still impossible to recognise faces; she was like someone in prison. But if she could hear one voice among the general turmoil and churning of voices, she would know it, and it might establish the contact she so desperately sought. When the nurse came in in the bright efficient way nurses do, she turned to her earnestly. It seemed to her that she made a definite and very firm gesture, and that she asked a very definite and important question. But the nurse only said, "Not dead yet. That's one thing. Trying to move. That's a good sign. Still, you never can tell."

The colourless lips parted; queer sounds came from the toothless gums, for of course they had taken out her teeth and when she got them back would depend on when they thought it the right moment. That's one of the humiliations of illness; all decisions are taken out of your hands.

"What's all that, dear?" asked the nurse, but not, of course, trying to listen. Poor old thing, she looked for all the world like one of those young half-fledged birds that fall out of the nest and then, when you try to pick them up and put them back, open their gaping yellow beaks at you and gasp.

"Man," said Miss Verity weakly. "Big—big—man."

"Poor thing, she has had a doing," thought nurse kindly. "Still, she asked for it by all accounts." And to the haggard patient she said briskly. "Don't go on worrying about him, dear. You're quite safe with us. We'll look after you."

With an enormous effort Miss Verity moved a little in the bed. Her eyes, sunk in the bony whiteness of her face, moved incuriously round the room, seeing nothing about her, nothing but the pictures in her own mind. Outside the window stood a big walnut tree; the home was proud of that tree. No one quite knew why, since it never yielded any fruit and was admittedly a source of danger. The heavy falls of snow had tried the ancient branches to the uttermost; one of the doctors had said emphatically that the sooner it came down the better. In any case, it was likely to come down of its own accord any time. Miss Verity's eyes wandered on to the tree and the pale sky beyond it, and still she saw nothing. "Snow," she whispered.

"Pretty snow," agreed the nurse, who was remembering the last patient who had been in this room. A nice appendix he'd been, a bit hasty in his manner, but—well, nice just the same. Too bad she had this old freak now, while a fresh case that had just come in last night had gone along the passage to that scheming little cat, White. Ah, well. She approached the bed. When she saw that pink sensible meaningless face, something happened to Miss Verity. It was as though hope died in her. She closed her eyes and sagged back on the pillows.

"Nothing yet, I'm afraid," said Dr. Atkinson to an eager Mr. Crook an hour or so later. "But these are early days for developments. She's holding her own and that's

171

something; more, in fact, than we had any right to expect in the circumstances."

"I consider that a fool remark," said Crook inelegantly. "I expect the earth and I dare say by the time I've finished hoeing my row I'll have all of it that I care about."

"She's certainly stronger," Atkinson conceded. "She tried to talk a bit to-day. Of course, she only wandered; her mind's like a pond choked with leaves . . ."

"You take my tip," said Crook rudely, "and leave people's minds alone. Bodies are your job, aren't they? Well, then, you stick to 'em. I'll answer for her mind. What did she say?"

"Oh, just what you'd expect. Something about a man, a big man. But she was wandering. She saw the snow and said Snow and then she seemed to lose all interest. It's better really. She's not in a state where she can afford to have any strain put on her. No, I'm afraid it's quite impossible for you to see her. You're the very last person to see her just yet, because it's obvious you're going to make demands on her. You might drag her down the little bit of hill we've pulled her up."

Crook heartily damned the eyes of all doctors and replaced the receiver. To a man of his active temperament this suspense was intolerable. A big man——Fennel wasn't exactly big, but probably he seemed big enough by comparison with herself. Then another thought struck him. A big man might refer to himself. She was trying to make them realise how important it was that she should see him.

Poor little thing. She was struggling hard. A big man and snow. Nothing about the house and how she got there. Had she had her suspicions, did she deliberately risk her life? But why on earth not tell him? Or had it been a matter of hours? He raged up and down his room. It was a pity since, she'd had her moment of consciousness, that she couldn't have told them something useful. And as he thought that, for the second time in twenty-four hours his brain flashed like lightning, almost dizzying him by what it revealed. And he saw the terrific, the incredible thing that she had told them before she slipped back into the dark.

"If you want more men to-day you'll have to provide 'em," said Relph bitterly, the instant Crook appeared on the threshold.

"All right by me if it's jake by you." At moments of intense excitement Crook fell into these lamentable vulgarities. "Only, seeing I've saved your priceless police force more than once for appearin' in the county in their true colours, I thought you might like to be in at the death."

"The death? Mr. Crook, you're not trying to tell us there's another body?"

"Well, in a sense."

"And you know the criminal?"

"I wouldn't go as far as that. Who am I to poach on the police's preserves? Come on. We've lost enough time as it is."

The exhausted police were still digging in the woods round The Nook, though there was a fierce scepticism in the bearing of most of them that boded ill for any chance trespasser.

"If you ask me, luckier chaps than us will be marching into Berlin before we find this blasted body," one of them remarked forcibly.

"Hitler ought to send a few of his Gestapo down here. They wouldn't stand an earthly with that band of desperadoes," was Crook's heartless comment. "Come on. You can leave that for a bit. Ivy Green isn't there."

"Perhaps you know where she is."

"I've a thundering good notion. One of you better go ahead and warn that woman at the farm to keep her kids inside. It isn't going to be a pretty sight."

His manner was so urgent that a young constable instantly hurried up the slope. The remainder of the party followed at a more leisurely pace. Their heavy tramp brought down some of the snow from the trees; the ground was so frozen that they were walking on the hard surface of the snow. They went up and up; presently they turned the corner where the snowman still stood with his hat over one eye.

"There you are," said Crook laconically. "Now—then— Dig for Victory."

And lifting his stick he smacked the disreputable bowler off the solid lump of snow that was the creature's head.

"Didn't Miss French keep a hat hanging in the front hall to discourage visitors?" he observed. "And we none of us gave it a thought."

"So that's what Miss Verity was trying to tell us," observed Relph some time later, when Crook's (apparently) preposterous suggestion had turned into the truth. "Pretty shrewd of you to recognise that."

Crook made what he believed to be a Gallic gesture. "My clients' minds are like an open book to me," he boasted. "A thing they call telepathy, I'm told."

"I know all about telepathy," Relph assured him.

"A hell of a lot more than I do, I expect. My parents never gave me any of the higher education. They just said, 'See, sonny, there's the world, millions and millions of crawling ants, and what you've got to do is get a living out of 'em, and what they all want to do is get a living out of you. So now you know.' "

He seemed almost beside himself with pleasure at this latest development. Relph by this time knew him well enough to realise how very much he had doubted the success of this bizarre experiment. Now that his intuition had proved him right, once again he was at the top of his form. It was part of his birthright that the gruesome and dreadful side of his work never seemed to touch him at all. Now, before his companion could speak, he was off again.

"Never knew I was a poet under my rugged exterior, did you, Relph? What do you think of this?

> "You may talk of your Wimseys and Frenches.
>   Your Priestleys and Poirots and such,
> But an ornery yellow low dog of a fellow
>   Called Crook has 'em beaten at touch.

Oh, my sam, Relph, to think that poor girl's been watching your wooden-headed bobbies dig out the wood all these days and couldn't give 'em a lead, like the princess in the glass tower—words fail me."

"Just as well," snapped Relph, who for all his experience of crime, found something peculiarly sickening about this one. . . . "Well, now p'raps you can tell us who walled her up there."

"I can tell you who didn't, and that is Harry Fennel. He hadn't the time. Come to that, no one had the time to account for both women in the way we know they were accounted for in roughly an hour and a half. We've slipped somewhere, Relph. Say X arrived the instant Miss Verity disappeared; even so he had to get to the house, remove the girl, strangle the old woman, dump her in the well, transplant the bush and make the snowman all in the space of an hour and a half."

"He had longer than that," Relph pointed out. "Fennel hasn't got a watertight alibi for Wednesday morning."

"He got to the club about nine-fifteen. The telephone call came through at nine-thirty—yes, I've checked up on that. He says he hung about for a bit in case the snow stopped. He couldn't have been down here before nine forty-five at the earliest. He got into the cottage—how did he get in, Relph, when Miss Verity had locked the front door?"

"That's another thing we're waiting for you to tell us."

"Besides, diggin' up a thunderin' great bush like that and replantin' it in a snowstorm—oh, it don't make sense and that's a fact. Because that bush was transplanted, no doubt about it. And then lugging the girl all up that hill . . ."

"It was a mad thing to do," muttered Relph.

"It seems to have worked. Gosh Maggie, why can't that poor little lady come round and tell us the truth. Because she's the one living person that knows it—beside the murderer. X must have been pretty sure of his onions before he told her what's he'd done with the girl. He couldn't have thought she was ever going to have the chance of repeatin' what he'd told her. And no thanks to you that she did."

"There's the envelope in Harry Fennel's pocket," Relph added.

"Strewth, yes. We've got to fit that in somewhere. Let's get away from here. I need a drink and I need it quick."

He plunged down the slope towards the road where the Scarlet Woman awaited him. Seated in a corner of his favourite bar he began methodically to put away more pints of beer than it seemed possible for any man to hold. And as he drank he reflected. There were so many points to be cleared up; Miss Verity might be able to help with some of them, but it was unlikely that even she knew everything.

1—Why did Fennel keep that envelope?

2—What was the motive for killing the girl? and, having killed her, why go back to the cottage?

3—How did he get into the cottage? The door was locked and the windows bolted.

4—Why did he do it in the time?

5—Why weren't both bodies dumped in the well?

6—Where did Miss French spend the last evening of her life?

7—Where was her gear now?

Over these problems he brooded interminably. All the questions were, he was convinced, interlocked. Let him once find the master-key and he could open all those closed doors. The most urgent was No. 4. The time factor held the clue to the whole. If he could solve that, he would put his finger on the truth. But after a while he let it go and passed on to Question 5. There could only be one answer to that. The bodies weren't both put in the well because they hadn't been simultaneously disposed of. Yet there was evidence to show that Ivy Green had died on the Tuesday afternoon, while Miss French had been seen in Brighton on Wednesday morning. If Ivy had been buried first—but he discarded that theory. There was no point in killing her unless she could talk, and in such circumstances she could be no danger. Besides, once the murderer had climbed so high, what sense was there in coming down to the road again, when it was both quicker and simpler to mount to the quite passable motoring road above the woods?

He came back to Question 1. Why had Harry Fennel kept the envelope? A man whose life is in jeopardy would surely be more careful. Crook knew that it's trifles that hang men, but even so he remained inconvinced. Well, then, say it wasn't Harry Fennel; say the envelope was planted. How did that help? It didn't, naturally, help in the least with Question 2. Nobody, not even the omniscient police, had been able to suggest a reason for killing Ivy Green—unless she was put out of the way because she knew too much. But, since Harriet French hadn't been killed till the Wednesday morning, there was no sense in that. As for Question 3, who could conceivably have got hold of the key to the cottage? Only two people had keys, Miss French herself and her new tenant. Unless, of course, she'd given one to Wilkes. That was possible, though the fellow hadn't mentioned it. Crook called for his fourth pint.

Then—Question 6, and its corollary. Why had Miss French gone back to The Nook on Wednesday morning? She could hardly have expected Miss Verity to turn out for her, and certainly they couldn't have shared the place. If she'd intended to commit suicide, why go back to the woods? And what methods would she employ? The answer to that was simple. She had been supplied with veronal—and veronal had been put into the drink Laura Verity had had too much sense to taste. And Harry Fennel had bought the drinks and Harry Fennel had been at The Nook—and there wasn't any veronal there now, so it seemed probable that Miss Verity's veronal was also Miss French's veronal. So the murderer, as well as getting rid of two women and disposing of Miss French's suitcase, etc., had had time to examine the cottage and find the veronal and take it away. That brought him to Question 7. Where was Miss French's gear? Either in a hollow in the woods where it hadn't yet been found or . . . And as he shouted for yet another pint everything suddenly fell into place, and the bar was treated to the unusual spectacle of an elderly gentleman damning his own eyes and yelling for more beer.

Mr. Turtle, the manager of the Royal Crescent, found himself in a quandary, the most unpleasant kind of quandary at that. He was obliged to refuse a favour to a valuable and important guest.

"I'm very sorry, Mr. Crook," he said, "but it's simply out of the question."

Crook looked at him like a great peering bird. "Police case, Turtle," he said.

"If you were the police, Mr. Crook . . ."

"I haven't sunk that low," said Crook indignantly.

But Mr. Turtle remained adamant. "I'm sorry, sir. Really I can't. Goods deposited with the management by guests can only be returned to the depositor—or, of course, the police."

Crook nodded mournfully. "It's just that I hate to disturb the inspector again," he explained. "He's finding me such a nuisance just now."

Even that didn't move Mr. Turtle, recognising which Crook stepped into a telephone booth and put through his call. It was not very long after that Relph entered the swing-doors of the hotel; he was frowning but there was anxiety behind the scowl. He walked up to the manager, who was standing in the lounge, and put the same request as Crook had proffered not long ago. This time Turtle unwillingly agreed. He led the two men into a private room and unlocked a safe set in the wall. From this he took a small square case, sealed and labelled. Crook glanced at the name it bore.

"Like to make a book on it, Relph?"

But Relph scarcely listened to him now. Turtle was still obviously ill-at-ease. "I don't altogether understand what you gentlemen expect to find in here," he remarked, reluctantly breaking the seal.

"I'll tell you," said Crook. "A fair amount of junk and one very handsome diamond ring. Am I right?"

It was clear that he was; the rest of the contents consisted of some bracelets, a brooch shaped like a double heart and inset with pearls, a heavy amber necklace, a gold cross set with sapphires and a couple of bits of folded paper. When Crook saw the ring he nodded jubilantly.

"Matter of hours now," he announced. "Miss Verity won't fail us, I can tell you that."

But it was Relph who had the last word. "No need to wait for her testimony," he said in sombre tones. "Look here," and he unfolded the two pieces of paper. "The five-pound notes we were looking for," he said. "Well, I think that clinches it."

Crook was very alert and bright-eyed. "Hope you took my tip and brought the warrant," he said.

Relph turned on him with none of that sense of gratitude you might have expected. "That, at least, is a thing you amateurs can't do—thank heaven. The next step you can leave to us."

The news appeared in the Stop Press columns of all the

evening papers. The enterprising proprietors rushed through a special poster for Brighton.

BRIGHTON MURDER SENSATION
Criminal Arrested.

And then a few lines, still smudged from the ink of the presses:

Andrew Stroud, the homicidal lunatic who escaped from a private asylum at C—— at midday on Tuesday, the 12th March, was to-night arrested at the Royal Crescent Hotel, Brighton, for the murder of Miss Harriet French, whose body was recently found in a well on her own premises by the local police force.

CHAPTER NINETEEN

"I blame myself," said Miss Verity, earnestly. "I can't imagine how I can have been so blind. It's what G. K. Chesterton always said—if you see a sideboard you don't expect to find a hamadryad in it. And when I saw a middle-aged woman wearing clothes exactly like Miss French's it never occurred to me that they might be Miss French's. You know, we did wonder if she ever took that hat off. We never saw her without it."

"And now we know why. But don't fret yourself, honey, you did fine. It's not many people who'd have had the sense, just before they were going to be murdered, to stoke up with chocolate and what-nots."

"I never dreamed," repeated Miss Verity, wonderingly. "And there we were sitting cheek to jowl, meal after meal. And I was suspecting that poor young man. Of course, Miss Buckler—I can't think of her as Andrew Stroud—put the veronal into my drink that evening. She had plenty of opportunity; she came into my room to warn me not to—not to cradle-snatch, she said, and while I was getting a dress out of the wardrobe she could easily drop it in, and no one would ever have suspected her. Oh, and I suppose she was the doctor, too," she added in sudden enlightenment.

"It could be, y'know," agreed Crook. "It could be. You've nothing to blame yourself for," he added. "That's twice you stopped her little game, and the third time didn't matter because I was around."

"Oh, yes," admitted Miss Verity faintly. "Perhaps, after all, I needn't be so severe on myself. I couldn't have saved Ivy Green, because she was dead when I arrived, and so was Miss French. I was the only victim or would-be victim after that."

"It was a compliment in a way. If she hadn't thought you dangerous she wouldn't have tried to put you underground."

"I was just beginning to piece things together, though I must admit I was still a long way from the truth. But one thing I had realised, and that was that Miss French was probably dead, too."

"That was cute of you," said Crook in undisguised admiration. "How did you figure that out?"

"It was the letter, the bit of the letter the girl had clutched in her hand. It's true it was signed Harry, but after all, Mr. Fennel wasn't the only Harry in the world. And when I realised that she had been jilted by a man called Harry Fielding, I started putting quite a different construction on the letter. Because, you see, it was twenty-five years old, then the only way it could have been found was if someone had unlocked the press in Miss French's room. That first day I went to The Nook she showed me the cupboard where she was going to leave some clothes and a box of papers. And when the police went over The Nook the day after Ivy Green was strangled, they had to break open the cupboard, because it was still locked. Well, you see where that gets us."

Crook agreed that he did. "It means that someone had opened the cupboard and abstracted the letter."

"It means even more than that. It means that someone opened it with a key, and the only key was on Miss French's ring, and I was sure she wouldn't give it up living, so it seemed to me, appalling though it was, that she must be dead, too. That would explain how the murderer got into the house in the first place. He must have killed her* before he killed Ivy, and let himself in with her key."

"That was where we went wrong," acknowledged Crook grimly. "Talk about white sheets! Relph and I could get through a whole laundry-load. Just because someone in a brown tweed suit offers a tenner and gives the name of Harriet French, we swallow the story, line, hook and sinker. And everybody was warning us all the time that the country's packed with middle-aged women in brown suits, and we had one right under our eyes from the beginning of the case. Of course, it was our Miss Buckler changing that note. And then she took the bus to Butler's Wood and—you must just have missed one another, you goin' down the drive and she comin' up the footpath."

"That was bad luck," agreed Laura.

"Bad luck!" Crook started at her. "Gosh, honey, that's the best piece of luck you had this trip. You'd have been

179

the third corpse, if she'd found you. Don't you realise even now what we're up against?"

"But there was no reason . . . I couldn't have recognised anyone in the dark that night."

"What's reason got to do with a homicidal lunatic? You'd have been alone in an empty place. That was what did for Miss French. Didn't you tell me Miss Buckler said she always liked a crowd, didn't like solitude? Sure sign. There wasn't any attempt to commit a murder at the Royal Crescent, too many people about, too much light, too much noise. But up at The Nook—it was as safe as the Arctic Circle. It doesn't do to think about it too much. I suppose Stroud was looking for a change of clothes. He must have known he'd be recaptured as soon as he showed himself unless he could find some sort of disguise. He must have come across the golf course—lucky no one met him—and squeezed into the wood. And he met Miss French as she came through the gate. He wouldn't stop to reason—she was alone, she was helpless; that 'ud be enough for him. You don't know much about maniacs, do you?"

Miss Verity shook her head.

"She didn't stand a chance. Nothing, nothing could have saved her. It's no wonder he didn't hurry about the funeral. He had all the time there was. He couldn't know you'd be coming . . ."

Miss Verity shuddered. "And I was so angry about missing my connection," she whispered. "And if I'd caught it, I'd have reached The Nook soon after four, and . . ."

"Don't think about it, honey, don't think about it. No need for those poor beggars to go on looking for the handbag and the suitcase. They found them all right, in Miss Buckler's room. Impossible to suggest a better place. That handbag was lying around the hotel for days and we all saw it. The suitcase and Miss French's clothes were in No. 289, just where no one would think of looking for them. No wonder most of the shoes were found up at The Nook. Stroud could wear Miss French's clothes, but her shoes were another matter. He left those."

"And Ivy Green?" whispered Miss Verity.

"They've cleared that up. In the pocket of her coat they found a purse and a letter. The letter was from a young chap who was due to sail for France the next morning. He was out of the country before the police knew anything about the girl. They've got in touch with him since, and he says they met in the woods and stopped as long as they could. He had to be back by six, and he was, too, so he couldn't have been the chap you saw at The Nook when you arrived. The girl said she'd scoot down the drive and reach the highroad that way. He watched her go a bit of the way—and the rest is only conjecture. Perhaps she saw a light through an uncurtained window and there ought not to be uncurtained windows at six o'clock on a March evening; or perhaps he heard her coming and met her and asked her in. You know, what her friends said—that she was always goin' around with men for the fun of the thing. Well, she went with one too many in the end. Whichever way it was, her death-warrant was signed the moment he set eyes on her. There was a bit of a struggle—we know that—because of the torn letter." He shivered unexpectedly. "I wouldn't call myself a sentimentalist, Miss Verity, and I don't think men are just a little lower than the angels, that is, if the angels are all they're cracked up to be, but there's somethin' about loonies that turns me cold. I mean, when you can't argue with a man, when there's no sense in what he does . . ." He stopped, and this time it was Miss Verity who shivered.

"It's horrible. We can only hope it was quick. And he very nearly did it to me. You know, it's very strange. I can tell you this, because you're my lawyer, so of course you have to regard anything I tell you as confidential—but I came down to Butler's Wood with the intention of—of taking my own life in three months' time."

"You came to the right place," said Crook heartily. "Someone's been havin' a jab at you ever since you arrived. What did happen, by the way?"

"It all seemed so reasonable. I try to blame myself for not seeing through it before, but if it happened again I know I should behave precisely as I have done. I'd been to look up the parish register, and that was how I found out Miss French had been engaged to a man called Henry Fielding. Then, by putting two and two together, as I told you, I came to the conclusion that the police weren't really looking for one body but two."

"It didn't occur to you to pass that on to the police?"

"Certainly not," said Miss Verity, emphatically. "I knew they only half-believed in the body of Ivy Green; and if I asked them to search for a body even I hadn't seen I thought they would most likely try to get me certified. And I'm sure," she added thoughtfully, "my sister Mabel would aid and abet them. She thinks I'm mad to have left Earl's Court to hide at an address I wouldn't even give her. No, it seemed to me of paramount importance that I should confide my suspicions to you, at once. You might disagree with me, but you wouldn't ridicule my suggestions. You know how strange life can be. That was why I went into the Ethical Union."

"You didn't think you might find me there?" hazarded Crook, looking puzzled.

For the first time since the beginning of the interview Laura laughed.

"Indeed no. But they have a free reading-room, with paper and envelopes thrown in. As I left the hotel in the morning I saw the police arriving, and I thought they might have come for me. And most likely they wouldn't let me see you—alone—before they took me away for a further cross-examination. So I decided to take no chances—or so I thought—but to write out my suspicions in full. Then, if I had no opportunity of speaking to you, I could leave the letter for you, and you could take whatever steps you thought most advisable."

"There's a golden rule you can't learn too early," Crook warned her solemnly, "and that is—never put anything on paper. You see how nearly fatal it was for you."

"The murderer had done his best to get rid of me before I had written so much as a postcard," Laura pointed out. "In any case, at the time that seemed to me my best course. I worked everything out very carefully. I remember saying that our suspicion, fantastic though it might seem, very likely had some foundation. And at the end I added, These murders seem to me the work of a madman. Then I signed the notes and put them in an envelope and addressed that to you, and came away, meaning to go straight to the hotel and deposit the envelope with the clerk in the hall."

"And what stopped you?"

"I'd just left the library when I saw Miss Buckler crossing the road. She said, 'Lovely day, isn't it? I've got to go up to the station to meet someone who's coming down from London. Like to come with me?' Well, I didn't really want to, because actually I wasn't attracted by the woman, but on the other hand, I didn't want to reach the hotel too early, either. I knew you weren't expected till about dinner-time, and it was only just after half-past four. So I agreed to walk up to the station. On the way up she said, 'What on earth were you doing in that place?' I suppose she'd seen me come out of the reading-room. 'Hope you're not getting converted.' I thought that rather impertinent, but I only said, 'Oh, I went in there to write an urgent letter.' She didn't say anything else—not about that, I mean—and presently we reached the station and waited for the London train. It came in a little before five, but no one got off it whom she knew, and she asked me to ask a porter something about the five o'clock train. He said it should be the other platform, and then someone wanted him, so I went back to Miss Buckler. She said it was all right, it didn't matter, her friend hadn't arrived; probably there'd be a message at the hotel. Then she began to talk about Brighton, how much she liked it and hated the thought of returning to London; she said she might take a house with the friend and settle down in Brighton. It would have to be near the station, because the friend had business in London and would often want to go up. She had seen one she rather liked that morning, and she suggested we should go a little out of our way and look at it. I didn't mind. Nearly all women love going over empty houses."

Crook groaned. "You do like makin' things easy for the wicked, don't you?"

"I didn't know she was wicked. No one did, then. And I kept remembering that the later I got back to the hotel the better. So we went round a corner and passed two or three houses with notice-boards by the gate, and Miss Buckler stopped in front of each one, considering it, and she shook her head and said No, that wouldn't do and we went on again. At last we reached this house in Braythwaite Avenue, and she looked at that for a long time, and said, That would be admirable. It was a corner house with a garden gate; and she opened the gate and said, 'Quite a good garden. Come in and see.' I came in and we stepped up to the French window to look into the ground-floor rooms. Miss Buckler said, 'I believe that window would open with a penknife. I've got one in my bag.' " She broke off for a moment. "To think that was the bag I'd seen in Miss French's hand the only time we met. And I didn't know it again. Only so many women have big shapeless brown bags. Well, she got out the knife and the latch opened easily, and we walked in."

"Didn't occur to you you were housebreaking, I suppose?"

Miss Verity looked astounded. "It was an empty house."

"That doesn't make any difference. You hadn't any right to be there without an agents' order."

"I really thought she meant to take it. And we weren't doing any harm. We walked into the hall and up the stairs, looking into the various rooms, and she kept saying, 'Cupboards, I must have cupboards,' and opening doors here and there. And each time she would shut the door and tell me, That wouldn't do, not big enough. It must be quite a big cupboard, you see.' I didn't think much about that at first; I thought probably she had things she wanted to store. In fact, I was rather enjoying myself. I've always imagined having a house of my own, arranging my own furniture. Then, suddenly, at the top of the last flight of stairs, I had a—a premonition. I can't explain it, but I was suddenly terribly afraid. That's why I don't like to think of those other two women. It's an appalling feeling, Mr. Crook, to be racked with terror and know you're facing the most frightful danger, and there's no hope of escape. What made it worse, much worse, was that she knew I was cramped with fear. I said something about it's being lonely and wanting to go down, but she put her arm across the top of the stairs and said, 'Yes, very lonely, isn't it? I told you big places full of people are best. Not empty houses where no one could hear you, even if you screamed and screamed . . .' "

"Did you?"

"I don't think so. I just thought how strong she was and that I wouldn't have a chance, and I said, 'Why have you brought me here?' She said, 'Why do you suppose?' I said, trying to look as if nothing were wrong, 'I think it's time we went. I have to see Mr. Crook, give him a letter.' And then she smiled and her smile grew wider and wider until it became a laugh, the most dreadful laugh I ever heard, the way, perhaps, people will laugh in hell." She covered her face with her hands as she spoke, as though even the memory of that sound was almost more than sanity could bear.

"Carry on," said Crook unemotionally.

She lifted her ravaged face. "I don't think I can."

"Of course you can. You aren't going to let me down now. I'm counting on you to tie up all the loose ends." There was a moment's silence: Crook sat like some pudgy idol in modern dress. He knew there was no need to say more. After that instant had passed, Laura went on in the same dreadful controlled voice.

"'Oh, no,' Miss Buckler said, 'you needn't worry about Mr. Crook, because you won't be seeing him again. You understand? You won't be seeing anyone again. You're not going out of this house—ever. Never any more.' And then I saw those big hands coming up towards my throat, and though I didn't know who she was, that she was a man I mean, I knew she'd killed Ivy Green. I said something—it was you—something like that, and she began to nod her head. 'You know too much,' she told me. 'It isn't safe to know too much. But there's one thing you don't know, one thing nobody knows. You don't know where she is, do you?'

"I said, 'The police will find her, just as they'll find me,' and she laughed again. 'Perhaps,' she told me, 'but not yet, not for a long time, a very long time. When the snow starts to melt and he begins to crumble, till at last he hasn't any head left, and the hat falls off, then perhaps they'll find her. And perhaps a tramp will pick up the hat and wear it, and never guess who wore it last. She was a pretty girl,' she said, 'but she didn't wear a hat. So I gave her one, an old black bowler. It made a difference, didn't it? You didn't recognise her when you saw her. You brushed quite close to her, but you didn't know. And to-morrow and the day after and the day after that people will be going to and fro in the streets, under the windows, and perhaps they'll be talking about you, wondering where you are, and why you went to London and when you're coming back to claim your possessions at the hotel; and they won't know, as they pass the house and even stop and look up at it, that there's nothing but a wall of brick between you and them.' I tell you, Mr. Crook, I was paralysed with fear. I always hoped I'd be brave at a crisis, but I'm not, I'm not. I kept thinking, 'So that's why she wanted a cupboard. That's why.' Then she went on in a sort of queer drawling voice that hypnotised me in a way, 'Perhaps it'll be months before you're found. Because the snow melting and the sun coming won't make any difference to you. No one's lived in this house for ages; perhaps it'll be ages before anyone comes here again. And when they do—it's funny to think of—they'll believe they're taking an empty house, and they won't know it's been tenanted for weeks and weeks and weeks. And you won't be able to tell them. Think of that. You were so anxious to find the murderer, pushing your nose into affairs that didn't concern you, but at the end you'll lie here and the murderer will be free. Free, Miss Verity. Think of that.' "

"Don't think of it," said Crook quickly. "Or if you must, remember it as somehing that happened a long time ago, and is over, and can soon be forgotten." He spoke with more feeling than she had ever heard from him.

"Let me finish," she pleaded. "I want to get it out of my mind into words. I knew, of course, that I hadn't got a chance. I knew exactly what she was going to do, that I had to die—in just a minute, there in the dark, like a rat, like a fly you crush between your fingers. I'd often thought about death, but never that death. Her hands came up and caught my throat; they snatched at my scarf. She was quite inhuman then. If I hadn't known it before, I'd have guessed she was mad. And then suddenly I knew the truth, knew it just for a second before everything went black, and I supposed I was dead."

"She supposed it, too. As a matter of fact, some other people were looking over the house and she heard them. We've checked that up with the agents. She shoved you into a cupboard and turned the key, and put it in her pocket. Then 'she waited for her opportunity and slipped away while the newcomers were lookin' at one of the other rooms. But she opened your bag and got the letter first."

"Yes. She burnt that, of course."

"I imagine so. But she didn't burn the envelope. These mad people are the worst kind there are from our point of view. You can pretty well rely on an ordinary chap makin' some crashin' howler that'll land him at Tyburn Tree, but lunatics are different. She saw you'd been after young Fennel, and it seemed to her a fine idea; and she played a very pretty game. You have to give her that. D'you realise she must have pushed that letter into young Fennel's pocket right under my nose? That galls me, y'know. It does really."

"What put you on her track?" inquired Miss Verity.

"Whisper it not in Gath, for I wouldn't have him know for the world, but it was Relph. He kept saying this and that were the acts of a madman, and he had to say it half-a-dozen times before I realised he was tellin' the truth. That's the worst of knowin' the police from the inside. You get so that you don't take them seriously. But that time it was serious all right. She'd parked the diamond and the notes with the hotel manager, where we'd never dream of looking for them. And if it hadn't been for you, she'd have got away with it—for a time. Sooner or later, of course, she'd have been flummoxed by the money difficulty, but even lunatics don't think of everything; and the odds are she hadn't got as far as that."

"And now, what?" whispered Miss Verity. "Will they hang her?"

"D'you think this is Nazi Germany? We're a humane race. We wouldn't let the hair of a mad murderer be touched. Only—I don't think our Mr. Stroud will find life in a state asylum quite so luxurious as he's accustomed to." He lifted up his voice and called for beer. "D'you realise, they won't even try the keepers who let him escape on a charge of manslaughter? Really, there are times I wonder I carry on at all, with justice the way it is."

Mrs. Loveday had invited her friend and neighbour to have a cup of tea and some very nice tinned salmon, while they talked over the Brighton affair. The murder was even more tasty than the fare provided, and both ladies enjoyed themselves tremendously.

"And to think she was with you all that time," said Mrs. Bunt soulfully. "I mean, it does sort of seem romantic, doesn't it?"

"Should never have thought a quiet little thing like that was the kind to get mixed up in a newspaper story," admitted Mrs. Loveday.

"Still waters run deep," her friend reminded her, unoriginally.

The postman rat-tatted cheerfully at the door and Mrs. Loveday jumped up to see if he'd brought anything from her daughter. She was disappointed in this, but when she had opened the square blue envelope, she gave a squeal of delight.

"Just guess, Annie, who this is from. Talk of angels. It's her."

"What, Miss Verity?"

"Yes. And what do you think she says? She wants to come back on the same terms; says she was never so comfortable as she was here . . ."

Mrs. Bunt nodded sagely. "I've always heard those luxury places aren't all they're cracked up to be. But not the same terms, Janet. After all, there is a war on."

Mrs. Loveday was absorbed in the blue sheet of notepaper. "And she says that what she really wants is a quiet life, and she feels she gets that 'ere." She put the letter down. "You know, Annie, for a bit I really thought she might be going to marry that Mr. Crook; they were so thick."

(It was as well that Mr. Crook could not hear this supposition; of all the shocks he had received throughout the case this would have been the most shattering.)

"Oh, I don't know," said Annie Bunt vaguely. "Come to think of it, there's not much to marriage, not if you've got a good 'ome." And leaning forward she helped herself to another slab of tinned salmon.

THE END.